I0685092

Philosopher's Stone

by

Joseph Hullett

Answer Publications
San Juan Capistrano, California

Published by Answer Publications
27511 Vantage Circle
San Juan Capistrano, CA 92675, USA
www.answerpub.com

ISBN: 978-0-9844597-7-3

Produced in the United States

Chapter One

The night the madman came, I was alone in the dark, staring out the rain-streaked window of my office. Behind me on the desk lay a crumpled eviction notice and my ledger.

What was the profit?

I had swiveled my chair toward the window because I was weary of the ledger. In dwindling twilight its tiny numbers had coalesced into a tedious bottom line. When private investigation is your sole livelihood and you stop looking for cases, refuse ones that find you, and forfeit those you can't refuse, you wind up broke. Maybe that's a P.I.s fate regardless. I could count *rich* detectives on my thumb and trigger finger. Besides, rich detectives die, too, and dying is dead broke. In the end we *all* file that bankruptcy. I contemplated the mystery of the balance sheet: the final entry is always zero.

Death closes all.

Sitting so long, I'd grown stiff. I stood, walked to the window, and fired a cigarette. Leaning against the window sill, I watched a misty rain blur the squat San Dismas buildings. Orange County seemed to be slipping away in low, dark clouds like a citrus grove vanishing in smudge-pot smoke. The citrus groves and smudge pots were long gone, of course – things of yesteryear. I lifted the sash to feel rain on my skin.

Four floors below crawled a slow procession of cars, headlights staring, windshield wipers blinking back the drizzle. Across Main, in front of a hole where a bank once stood, a line of black umbrellas waited for a bus. When the bus came, a lone figure scurried from the rear door, ducked his head, and darted through traffic toward shelter.

Coiling cigarette smoke watered my eyes. I jerked the cigarette from my mouth and cursed myself for succumbing again to a teenage dependence I had shed completely until the day Ronnie died.

No. Not that day. Until her funeral. Ten years ago today. November 11. A wet day. Like today. A dark day. Lonely. Final.

Anniversaries resurrect memories. I felt mine pounding against their reliquary. I flipped my cigarette out the window and watched it arc downward to die in the rain. Lights winked on and off. Glistening streets reflected meaningless geometric patterns. Wind and traffic groaned in my ears like noise in an empty shell. The weariness I felt had no name.

I retreated into shadows, opened the vanity refrigerator, and withdrew the last Sapporo. I pried off the cap and swallowed two ... three ... four times. I didn't feel it. I hadn't felt the others. I sat the bottle on the counter to light another cigarette.

I flicked the ancient USMC Zippo Jesus had bought on his first PX run in boot camp. I'd lost mine somewhere, probably when I quit smoking. Jesus had treasured his like a Phi Beta Kappa key. I ran my thumb over the once-gold, eagle-globe-and-anchor insignia long since worn smooth and silvery.

I imagined him bellyaching from his wheelchair about me pissing and moaning in the dark. I remembered his voice more distinctly than his face anymore, so the clearer part was the grumbled, "Pull your sorry self together, *cabron!*"

Jesus could say whatever he wanted. When heaven was falling, he stood with me, and suddenly I wished I could tell him the good-bye he never heard, the one I uttered over his body when the gang who murdered Ronnie ran him down.

The thought breached a stony crust confining an ever-molten rage. I needed to kill the killers again. I needed it like water. Like air. I needed to chase them to hell and collect their debt *one last time.*

I closed my eyes and took deep breaths until my hands steadied. I thumbed the lighter and watched a ghostly coil of sooty smoke writhe above the yellow flame. I snapped shut the lighter and dropped it on the desk. The heat inside me subsided.

I turned to a mirror over the vanity, but in the gloom saw only a murky shadow. When I drew on the cigarette, the flaring ember stained my short, more salt-than-pepper hair a clownish orange and etched deep lines in an unfamiliar face. I tried to recall my real face and picked from a long procession of impermanence one I remembered from an old Polaroid – a clear-eyed, dark-haired, boy's face, a good-guy's face, one unmarked by a lifetime of unpaid obligations. The black-and-white

Polaroid face was as unreal as the ugly, orange reflection. The image in the mirror, however, was closer to the truth.

Much is taken.

And what abides?

The name on the door read Pete Pinel, Private Investigator. The words had meant something once. I said them aloud. The syllables evaporated like sputters of steam from the radiator beneath the open window. I hunched over the sink, splashed my face, and listened to water gurgle down the drain. I wiped my face on my shirt sleeve, swallowed the last of the beer, and dropped the bottle in a wastebasket where it clattered against the other dead soldiers. I sat back down and faced the ledger.

So.

I drew the .45 from my shoulder holster. We had a kind of ... not friendship, but certainly a long shared history – a kinship; even a next-of-kinship. Like my face in the mirror, the gun looked unfamiliar in the dark, but its smell, its weight and balance ... its *feel* was unmistakable. Grips of warm wood. A barrel of cold steel. Heavy, wood-handled steel. Like an ax. Like a scythe. I imagined the sound it would make racking a round, the precise, metallic snicker-snack of machined parts moving with purpose. I hefted it in my hand and judged it heavier than the sum of its parts. The excess was a ghost in the machine, a demon that I had summoned many times with IOU's. How heavy that haunted tool must have felt when I pressed it into Ronnie's frail hand her last, hopeless night in the hospital; how hard it must have been to take my hand *instead* of the scythe.

That I now held.

In my *empty* hand.

So.

A bell sounded as someone entered the waiting room. I heard rustling and a gentle rap at the inner door. I sat motionless, soundless, breathless, playing possum, hoping to be left alone, only I couldn't shake a nagging voice in my head.

Okay, enough already, you win!

It wasn't Jesus' voice.

You're the most woebegone son-of-a-bitch who ever was. Now will you, please, get your shit in one bag!

I pondered the door.

Things known; things unknown.

And in between? The doors.

Entrance doors. Exit doors. Doors and choices. Doors and deals.

Make the deal. Chose the door. Free a lady. Loose a tiger.

From a second knock I gathered that it wasn't opportunity calling. I holstered the .45, albeit *ambivalently*, since it was probably a Goddamm collector.

The bill tolls for thee.

It wasn't particularly funny, so maybe something else was funny, because I'm sure I felt a smile. And for the *life* of me, I couldn't recall the last one.

Chapter Two

I flung open the door. A white-haired geezer, older than me, stumbled backwards, raising his arms to protect his head. He was barefoot and wore a bulky, buttonless pea coat over pajamas stenciled Camino by the Sea Hospital. The pajamas were a particularly bad sign.

"Tis the wind and nothing more," I said.

"Are you insane?" he croaked.

Me? Talk about projection! Despite a sunken, dead-carp face, the old guy's electric-blue eyes crackled with energy, the kind whose dynamo is secret knowledge of the one true answer to the only big question.

"They were waiting for me," he said.

"Lucky for you. Often they leave if you're late."

He peered suspiciously into the dark office. Even stoop-shouldered with age, he was taller than me and had probably been beefy once, although now he looked stick-like and collapsed. Abruptly he pushed past and dashed to the window. His strength surprised me.

"They're gone!" he said.

"See what I'm saying?" I following him inside and tugged the desk lamp chain. I plopped into my chair and swiveled to face him. "Who's gone?"

"The men looking for me, you imbecile!"

"Oh, them ... Say, come away from that open window, okay?"

"Three men in black coats." He pointed. "Right down there."

"Guys waiting for the bus?"

"They're gone now!"

"No accounting for that, is there?"

"My God! I imagined you'd have your wits about you."

"C'mon, pal, no offense, but the window makes me nervous. Take a seat, okay? ... Got a name?"

"How would they know? I ... I must have said something."

"Loose lips, sink ships. How about that name."

He bounded to the door, cracked it, and peeked into the waiting room. Slamming the door, he flipped the deadbolt.

"I used a payphone. They *couldn't* know, unless ..." He pawed at his pajamas.

"Maybe the transmitter is in your head. Maybe they can read your thoughts."

He froze as if considering the idea.

"Okay, pal, let's get real. You waltz in here barefoot—"

He looked down at his feet, purple from the cold.

"Wearing a coat that doesn't fit over Camino by the Sea pajamas. Camino is the Ritz-Carleton of ocean-view loony bins. You either ran or wandered away. Trust me. Whatever you *think* is happening has a better explanation."

"Don't condescend you ignorant buffoon! I'm a physician."

"Sorry, Doc, but you're a few pills short of a cure."

He fell silent in an eerie way – just went blank as if the thoughts had been yanked from his head. I waited.

"Forgive him," he whispered.

"I favor justice," I said. I waited some more, and, sure enough, the gleam returned.

"I found it, you know?"

"Congratulations. Found what?"

"The Philosopher's Stone."

Dredging from some college class the medieval notion of a magic catalyst, I said, "So you're an alchemist. You turn lead to gold, do you?"

"And back ... to lead ..." he sighed, sinking into a chair.

He removed a brown vial from his coat pocket, unscrewed the lid, and shook a peanut-sized, rock-candy crystal onto his palm. Setting the vial on my desk, he pinched the crystal between his thumb and forefinger and began to lick it.

"Whoa, Doc!" I lunged across the desk and grabbed the rock. "Are you *serious*?"

Sitting back, I scratched the crystal with a finger. Soft like talc, it left a thick, powdery residue beneath my nail. When I rubbed the finger across my gum, the electric tingle was unmistakable. I dropped the rock back into the vial, replaced the cap, and – waste not, want not – licked my finger clean. My palm, too.

"You found cocaine," I said. "Only they already had it."

"Your ignorance is monumental." His eyes were glowing again, as mutable as mood rings.

"Sure, sure, lead to gold. Ask Freud or Sherlock Holmes. Been there, pal. I wish it worked."

"Oh, it works," he said. "You'll see."

"Yeah? Well, good luck with that."

"Finding the Stone was my dharma. Its loss is my karma. I need your help."

"Sounds to me like you need a monk."

"Can a monk help me with *this*?"

He thrust his arms forward, palms up. His wrists were scraped and bruised. Camino by the Sea might occasionally use restraints, but they would be soft restraints. Gucci or Prada restraints.

Not handcuffs.

"Who cuffed you?"

"The past. Our *shared* past. Samsara from which neither of us is free ... *Mr. Pinel*."

He produced my name as if it were a dove in a magic trick, but since it was lettered on the office door, I held my applause. Nevertheless, if somewhere in time our paths had crossed, a lucid glimmer in his madness might have led him to me. I figured to find out, because sparks were flying in his eyes. He was fully charged now and about to shock me with his one, true answer to the only important question.

He stood and craned forward. Lips touching my ear, he whispered, "They kept you from knowing."

"Oblivion is bliss," I said. "I'll have to write them a check. Know what?"

"What *really* happened to Veronica."

It was a breath-stopping moment when gaping pupils froze the world in razor-sharp focus, when the blast of adrenalin that cleared my vision also tensed my eardrums making crystalline every sound. It was as if I were watching myself in some herky-jerky, fast-forward mode – I'm springing from my chair; I'm collaring the madman; I'm dragging him toward the door. *Someone* had cuffed him; someone who might actually want him back, just *possibly* because of the name he had spoken. However remote that chance, until he told me what he thought I didn't know, he was mine.

Almost as a single sound, I heard the waiting room bell and the splintered crack of my inner-office door exploding open. Shoving the madman aside, I dove for the desk. A gunshot shattered the window behind me. I heard feet clamor into the room and the madman's scream. A giant in a ski-mask rounded the corner of the desk, but skidded when he saw me ripping the Colt from my shoulder holster.

"Gun!" he shouted, as I raised to fire. A snap-kick knocked the automatic from my hand.

I grabbed his unanchored leg and wrenched him off the other foot. Lodging my shoulders in the desk recess, I lurched upward and drove forward like a tank. A gun roared and I felt slugs bite into wood. I collided with something softer than a wall and dumped the desk onto it. I spun to see another masked thug holding the whimpering old man and the giant scrabbling to his feet.

"Not in my Goddamm office!"

Charging bull-headed, I strained to grab anything that I could squeeze, crush, or tear apart. Ten years earlier I might have made it, but older, slower, and definitely dumber, I was dreaming. The giant simply leveled his gun and fired, dead-bang. A hot, yellow blast slammed into my face, spun me around, and pitched me onto the floor. My empty fingers pumped spasmodically as if squeezing a trigger. Nerves and muscles short-circuited, leaving me flopping like a beached grunion until a crashing black wave dragged me toward nothingness.

They say the ears are last to go and they're right. I heard a screeched, "I can't tell you what I don't know! I don't know anymore. I don't—" but the words were choked off.

"Give'm the needle before he swallows that rag. And find the Goddamm rock."

"How about the peeper?"

I felt a kick in my ribs as fade-to-black became oblivion.

"Head shot. He's done."

Chapter Three

Something existed. I mean, it *had* to, right? Although frankly, who knew?

Then came awareness. Awareness *of* something and, afterwards, awareness of *awareness*, of something *being* aware; awareness of life, of *me*. Conjoined, however, was a parasitic twin – a panicky awareness of me *not*. First fruits of the first tree. Knowledge of Good: that Life was good. Knowledge of Evil: that Life was short.

And then, as always in those recurrent waking terrors – that cacophony of choked screams, rising water and closing doors – a lucid-dream voice demanded a fight or flee choice: knowledge or oblivion. But it wasn't the voice I was used to hearing in my head.

It was a woman's voice.

And not Veronica. *Another* woman.

Urging me to wake.

* * * * *

"Wake up. Wake up!"

Darkness receded with a roar, leaving me beached in the light of the overturned desk lamp. Black shadows loomed against the wall. My arm flailed for the .45.

"Stop squirming! Let me help you."

My reeling eyes fixed on a kneeling woman who had propped me sideways against her lap. A bloodstain blossomed on the silk sleeve of her beige business suit. I recoiled, trying to fit the woman into the jumbled picture-puzzle of my thoughts as friend or foe. Settling for no immediate threat, I touched my throbbing temple. The hair was wet and matted. I probed the wound, worried that my finger would stab my brain.

"Lie still. You've been shot," she said.

"I was there, lady," I croaked,

"Leave that alone!"

"I'm bleeding to death, okay?"

I pushed up on one arm. The woman rushed to the sink and grabbed a handful of paper towels.

"It looks worse than it is," she said, kneeling again. "The bullet gouged your scalp, but didn't penetrate."

"What are you? A nurse?"

"I'm a *doctor*," she said, jamming the wadded towels against my head.

"Easy! It wasn't an insult."

"Hold still."

"You're hurting me!"

"Just hold still."

Her hands were sure, her voice confident. I surrendered *temporarily*, taking the moment to complete the picture puzzle.

The woman was a stranger because, quite simply, she was *unforgettable*. Her voice was exotic, musical, not so much an accent as a residual timbre from some native tongue in which sound meant as much as syllable. Her looks were equally mysterious. She was short, petite, even tiny – waifish, almost childlike. She didn't seem old enough to be a doctor. Despite straight, jet-black hair that suggested Asian stock, her skin – unlike any earthly race – was the shade of coffee with just the right amount of cream. And the eyes! Almost but *not quite* almond-shaped with an otherworldly color – sapphire blue in the way sapphires were once said to reflect the sky.

"No doctors lease here," I grunted. My tongue felt thick.

"I see. You eliminate the impossible to deduce why I'm here." She peeled away the toweling paper, inspected, then pressed harder. "Or you could *ask*. I'm Dr. Nguyen."

"Nguyen?" It sounded bitter when I said it. "Mà bên?" She stiffened.

"Whose *side*? ... I was a child at the time. I was on my mother's side. As you might discern from my face, she was on the Americans' side. When they abandoned Saigon, we were on the Communists' side. But the experience was ... how shall I say it? Unpleasant. After my mother died, I was on *my* side. And because you are either constitutionally stupid or bullet-addled, may I point out that I appear to be on *your* side."

"Some of us still have scars," I said.

"*All* of us still have scars."

"You don't make it to sixty without trusting your instincts, Miss Nguyen."

"*Doctor* Nguyen."

My eyes felt heavy. I blinked a few times.

"Find the body, you're suspect ... *Doc*. And I still don't know what you're doing here."

"I'm a *suspect*?"

"Minus the question mark."

"Mr. Pinel – that's you, correct? Pinel Investigations? – a friend asked me to meet him here."

"A Goddamm flyer party! Was he wearing a ski mask?"

"That's unlikely."

"Must've been the one who escaped from Camino by the Sea."

"Well … yes, he did."

"You just missed him. So what did he want? Why me? Why you? Why here?"

"I … I have no idea. He can't care for himself. He left a garbled message on my answering machine. I had to Google your address. I came immediately, saw the broken door and found you on the floor."

"The floor at the Ritz is nicer," I said, struggling to my feet. "I don't recommend this one."

"You can't stand yet."

"Watch me."

She watched me sink to one knee when the floor dropped like a trap door. I shook off her hand to try again, held the vertical, and started poking through upset furniture and scattered files.

"What are you looking for?"

"Clues."

She waited for me to say more. She seemed practiced at waiting. When my woozy consciousness finally noticed the untouched filing cabinets, I realized the rock was gone. I righted a chair and plopped down, almost missing the seat.

"Your friend. Who is he?"

"You shouldn't be talking."

"I get that all the time."

"Your speech is slurred." She leaned over to scrutinize my pupils. "Make a smile. Good. Now raise your arms."

I felt like a cowboy in a western.

"No stroke anyway. Not yet."

"What the …? Wait, wait! Is that even in the mix?"

Nguyen slid a chair beside me and lifted my wrist to count my pulse. Hours seemed to slip by. My eyes drifted shut. Darkness felt good.

"You're tachycardic," she said, dropping my wrist. "Probably a concussion, maybe a skull fracture. You need a hospital. Tests."

I opened my eyes reluctantly. "If I leave here without calling the cops, it better be for the morgue, and I don't think I'm ripe yet." I bent to grab the toppled phone, but the floor began to waver like heat shimmer. Nguyen caught my shoulder and pushed me back down.

"9-1-1?" she said retrieving the phone.

I nodded and regretted it. She punched the number and handed me the receiver.

I rattled off my story, told the operator an ambulance was unnecessary, and assured her I was hanging up voluntarily. I eased myself to my feet and found the .45. Ejecting the chambered round and the magazine, I placed everything on the overturned desk near the door along with my PI and CCW tickets.

"I'd set my purse over here, too, if I were you."

She stood, but clutched the purse as if about to bolt.

"Did … did Walter shoot you?"

"If Walter is the lunatic, no. Three men in ski-masks broke in. One of *them* shot me."

"Why?"

"I was trying to shoot them. They wanted your pal and a rock he was carrying."

"Rock? Like ... a diamond? Where would Walter—"

"Different mineral. He hinted at some past connection between us, something I didn't know about. That's all I got before the fun started. The thugs doped him. Since he's not under the desk, I assume they took him."

I started to wobble.

"Whoa! I have to sit down again. Let's park our chairs by the window though. Cops get skittish about other people's guns."

"I am quite familiar with the proclivities of policemen," she said coldly, dropping her purse on the desk beside the other stuff.

I started to ask why, when a thought hit me. "The shooter is a cop. Or he *was*. Automatically yelled gun when he saw my 45. It's a cop ... proclivity."

She scooted both our chairs and we sat again.

"So who is this loony I'm supposed to know."

"He has a *name*, Mr. Pinel," she said sternly. "Walter Kling."

"Rings no bells with me," I said.

She smiled smugly. "You know but don't know you know. Your subconscious mind is planting a clue. Walter Kling? *No..bel* Prize winner?"

"Oh, Christ! You're not a doctor, you're a *shrink*."

"Are there any prejudices you've *not* embraced? I'm a medical doctor whose specialty is psychiatry."

The clouds shrouding my brain peeled back enough to admit a brief ray of sunshine.

"Wasn't Kling like the dean or something at UC San Dismas?"

"Chairman of the Psychiatry Department. Until last year. He's on medical leave."

"At Camino. Why do you think he was snatched?" I said.

"It ... it makes no sense."

"It did to someone. *Why* leads to *who*."

"Ransom? ... Walter is comfortable. Quite comfortable."

"Follow the money. It's usually somewhere in the picture. But this was more. These guys wanted what he was carrying. And something else, too. Something in his head; something he said he couldn't remember. Any ideas?"

"None."

"Think about it. Famous psychiatrist, powerful patients. Kling probably knows where bodies are buried."

"Walter was a research scientist, not a clinician."

"What was he researching?"

"Facilitated neurotransmission."

"And this facilitated whatsit is lucrative, right?"

"Walter concerned himself with basic science, not applications."

"Downstream from every Einstein is an Oppenheimer who's into applications *big time*."

"Well ... his work may lead to new treatments for mental illness, of course."

"Drugs?"

"Pharmaceuticals, yes."

"Ka-ching!"

"That's insulting."

"Look, Kling may be a saint, but, believe me, if Mother Teresa were parked on a gold mine, someone would move her."

"Grants have funded his research. It's hardly been a gold mine."

"Drug company grants?"

She paused, considering her words. "Yes. That's true."

"Does that mean any *applications* belong to them?"

"Walter would have a share. And the University, of course."

"*Minority* shares."

"That's the way it's done," she said flatly.

"Time out of mind," I said. "So why is he a prisoner at Camino?"

"Please, Mr. Pinel ... He's an involuntary *patient*."

"If I were wearing the pajamas, I'd consider that a subtle distinction."

"I told you. He's completely unable to care for himself. A court appointed me his legal guardian. I committed him for treatment. I see patients there myself."

"You're not his doctor then?"

"That would be inappropriate. He's a ... colleague."

"*More* than a colleague?"

"*Much* more," she said, holding my gaze defiantly.

"How inappropriate. Isn't he too *old* for you?"

"Yes, Mr. Pinel. When I met him he was just about *your* age now."

It hurt to laugh, but I did. "A counterpunching shrink. That has to violate your oath."

"You're not my patient. And you're *annoying*." She took a deep breath and continued. "Walter recruited me to San Dismas from Stanford twelve years ago. I was pursuing a research career then."

"Not now?"

"Research can be ... Let's just say noble and Nobel are sometimes worlds apart. I lost interest. But never in Walter. I'm always there for him."

The words must have registered on my face.

"What did I say?"

I shook my head to clear it and winced, discovering that shaking, nodding, laughing ... *all* of them were bad ideas.

"So what's Kling's problem?" I said.

"It's a mystery."

"Detectives don't like mysteries."

"Neither do doctors. Descriptively he has dementia."

"Like Alzheimer's?"

"*Like* that, yes. But the onset was acute. Similar to a stroke, although, structurally, his brain is intact."

"He suddenly went nuts. It happens, right?"

"It can. But idiopathic psychosis occurs in a functional matrix."

"I was about to point that out," I said.

She smiled. "*Nuts* retain their intellect – memory, vocabulary, skills. Walter's higher cognitive functions disappeared overnight. We considered *encephalitis lethargica* or some similar etiology, but—"

"Hold on, hold on ... *Encephalitis lethargica*. Brain inflammation drowsiness. Am I close?"

"Don't tell me you took Latin."

"High school. Sign of a misspent youth."

"It's the illness in the movie *Awakenings*. The diagnosis offered hope, but ..." She shrugged. "The evidence doesn't fit. I've had to accept the fact that Walter is hopelessly incompetent."

"Incompetent ..." I chewed on it for a moment. "As in retarded?"

"Strictly speaking, retardation is developmental, but, in a broad sense, yes. His intellect – memory, judgment, language, reason – all gone."

"Is that his *real* doctor's opinion?"

She scowled.

"Sorry. I should have said *official* doctor,"

"Yes, you *should* have. Walter's attending *physician,* also a psychiatrist, mind you, deems him irreversibly demented. I've consulted experts and examined the data myself. Every professional is of the same mind."

"You don't need a weatherman to know which way the wind blows."

As foggy as I felt, it seemed especially clever. Nguyen looked puzzled by my smirk.

Good. I was glad.

Chapter Four

Two cautious beat cops hailed me from the hallway.

Equally cautious, I shouted. "Gun's on the desk along with my tickets and a purse. The woman who found me is here, too. We're standing against the wall, hands in sight."

"Sounds like a trap, Pinel," said a cop.

Palms resting on the butts of holstered Berettas, they filed in and fanned left and right. Rain had stained their blue San Dismas uniforms a darker blue.

"Tough night, Jason?" I said to the lanky, white one, a B-ball star at San Dismas high a few years back.

"Just wet," he answered indifferently. He picked up the .45 with a pen and sniffed the barrel. Everyone relaxed a little once he had control of the gun.

"This man needs a hospital," Nguyen demanded.

"Really?" said Jason's rookie partner, a short Latino shaped like a bowling pin. "And who would you be, Miss?"

"*Doctor* Nguyen."

"Testy ain't you?" said Brunswick-boy. He opened a small, spiral notepad and read aloud as he wrote. "The victim is standing comfortably with no continuing exsanguination."

"Bloody but unbowed," I said.

"Think you'll keep, sir?"

"Doc says the bullet missed my brain."

"Lucky day. Oughta buy a lottery ticket."

"Listen to me!" snapped Nguyen. "I insist—"

"Victim is lucid. Denies need of immediate medical attention," the partner scribbled. "Whew! Glad to get that out of the way, Doc," he said, turning his back. "Felt like a sword hanging over me."

Taking turns writing down our answers, they pumped us with questions. I kept the part about Ronnie to myself, but told them about Kling's cocaine and the thug saying *find the rock.*

When they ran out of steam, Jason plopped down on the overturned desk to wait for detectives. His partner gazed out the window.

"Four more hours," sighed the rookie. "Nothing here gonna get us overtime, is it?"

"You know as much as I do," I said.

Jason's foot bobbed.

"Bathroom's down the hall," I offered.

"I'm securing the crime scene," he said.

Police work.

Good-enough guys enduring countless hours of boredom between those inevitable seconds when earth's foundations flee. For some reason I remembered suddenly how much I used to love my work, and how long it had been since I'd felt that way.

A lab crew arrived. Swarming, they peered and pried, bantered with the uniforms, photographed the office from a dozen angles. They dusted for prints and tweezered little bits of matter into tiny, plastic baggies.

The detective duo came last.

"*You* again," grunted Rick Wagner, a rumpled, overweight lieutenant with a walrus mustache. His younger, second-banana, Tim Mulligan, wore spit-shined shoes, creased trousers, and an expensive sport coat. Since making detective sergeant, he'd gained twenty pounds, though, and the pants were too tight.

"Keep getting shot, Pinel, you'll ruin your health," Tim cracked, eyeballing my wound.

The three of us were palsy over a beer now and then, but not friends and certainly not colleagues. My game was *like* theirs, but we hailed from different leagues with strange rules, and if we played together at all it was mostly on opposite sides.

They poked around perfunctorily, conferred with the others, and finally took turns interviewing Nguyen and me. They talked to us separately, covering the same ground from different angles like the photographer who shot the office. Reuniting us for the finale, seniority took the lead.

"Okay, gang, here's how it lays," Rick said. "Pete claims he doesn't know the nutjob."

"I wouldn't call him a nutjob, Rick. No functional matrix."

Nguyen choked back a laugh. Rick nodded with a who-laughs-last expression.

"Yet for some reason, he has you pegged as just the one to scratch his itch. He arranges a little three-way confab, but..." He paused for his punch line. "He forgets to tell you why. *Either* of you."

"Strains credulity, doesn't it?" added Tim.

"Like I said, guys, he was about to spill something when things got busy in here."

Rick turned to Nguyen. "And the Doc says all he gave her was the ol' meet me on the corner routine."

"Barely a name on my answering machine. That much surprised me. He's catatonic most of the time. Mute for months."

"But off you go anyway."

"I'm responsible for him."

"Still pretty big of you. No orderlies. No cops. Just you by your lonesome."

"I should have called the hospital, you're right, but I … I didn't want him frightened."

"Oh, no, wouldn't want that," Rick said. He made a show of putting away his notebook. "Off the record, though, Pinel, tell me … what's your take on all this?"

"Off the record, Rick? You're a cop, not a columnist. You're supposed to tell me whatever I say will be used against me."

"Well, yeah, that's true. Irregardless, detective to detective, blood-brother, pinky swear and all, what do you think?"

"It's a mystery," I said.

"I hate mysteries," said Rick.

"Me, too," said Tim. "*Hate* 'em."

"Sure no one's holding back?" said Rick.

"Not me," I said.

"And this *Philosopher's Stone* – neither of you know what he meant by that?"

"Supposedly changes lead to gold," I offered.

"My boy, Tim, here, he went clean through college. Got *that* part right off," Rick said. "Nothing *else,* Pinel?"

"Another tale was that medicine made from the stone cured unhappiness. His rock was coke. Works for a while ... from what I've *heard.*"

"Current drug war notwithstanding, no one makes a professional snatch over a single rock," Tim scoffed.

"I'm all in, guys," I said.

They didn't believe me, because they knew as well as I did that everyone lies. But cops are used to watching grass grow.

They had time.

Chapter Five

From the office window I saw camera trucks and a throng of reporters. *Crazy Nobel Scientist Snatched!* was eyewitness film at eleven. I asked Rick to let Nguyen and me skip the gauntlet.

"Word is you could use the free advertising, Pinel."

"Losing a client?"

"All publicity is good publicity and you've been out of the limelight since ... well, since there were lime lights."

"My adrenalin rush got up and went, Rick. I'm crashing fast."

A promise to show at headquarters next morning bought me an okay to use the delivery door. While I could still think, however, I stopped at the cleaning crew's pay phone in the service corridor.

"I have a cell," Nguyen offered.

"Me, too," I said, plunking quarters in the slot. I had to lean against the wall. I would have sat, but the cord was too short.

The night editor at the Banner answered on the first ring, probably expecting one of the staffers outside pushing deadline.

"Hi, Bernie. Pete Pinel."

"Pete! Ain't you dead yet?"

Rick was right. My news heyday was so remote, Bernie hadn't connected the location of the snatch or he'd be interviewing me himself.

"One day at a time, man. Listen, can you steer me to Fred Lynch?"

Fred was night editor when Ronnie was murdered. If *anyone* could feed me scraps not fully rendered in the court transcripts and press reports, he was the one.

"You don't know, Pete?"

"Know what? Fred and I lost touch when he retired."

Lost touch was a euphemism. Fred judged my handling of a *Banner* reporter tied to Ronnie's murder a betrayal of the paper, meaning a betrayal of him. A bond between men can weather most any storm save a conscious screwing, and – although I saw it differently – the friendship ended.

"Fred has colon cancer."

"Christ ... how bad?"

"The worst."

"I still read, Bernie. Fred would get ink."

"Of course he will. Docs are betting on the Sunday bulldog or sooner. If you have accounts to settle, Pete, you better jump."

"Where is he?"

"A hospice in Laguna Beach. Some forgotten nephew turned up when Fred's last surgery went south. Kid was bent on doing the right thing, I guess. Spent Fred's money on an ocean view."

"For *Fred*?"

"Oh, it's a real, *real* nice place, Pete. Just the thirty an old city-beat, news-hawk hopes for."

I took the address and hung up.

Nguyen and I slipped out the alley loading dock. We made it across Main with Nguyen half-carrying me. How – on her tiny frame – I'd never know. We might have attracted attention if Rick and Tim weren't working the crush of mike-waving reporters. The scene reminded me of long ago nights in the newsroom. Sometimes I would swing by and wait for Fred to put the paper to bed so we could retire to Blake's. I remembered him fielding deadline rewrite calls from reporters just like those. Phone squeezed between his ear and shoulder, he would crack wise while two hunt-and-peck forefingers rat-a-tat-tatted a reporter's raw notes and quotes into literature in a hurry.

Fred *loved* his work. It showed in his face, particularly at those times. As much as he badgered management for orthopedic chairs and dispensation from no-smoking rules and a raft of symbolic concessions, the suits knew that, if they wanted to call his bluff, they could have him for free.

"You can't drive this way," said Nguyen, shrugging my weight off her shoulders.

"Sure I can," I said, falling back against the Blazer. Passenger seats scared me as much as hospitals.

Fumbling my keys, I stared at the ground. It seemed *very* far away. Nguyen scarfed up the key-ring and dropped it in her purse.

"You're grounded, Mister!"

"C'mon, Doc! You said it was just a crease."

"Will you accept a *shrink's* assessment of that, Mr. Pinel?"

The argument was persuasive. I let her squeeze me into a two-seater Jag parked near my Blazer and crossed my fingers.

Although the rain had stopped, the streets were still shiny and slick and Nguyen was a red-blooded driver. Reluctant to nod off and miss my demise, I rolled down the window to let fresh air clear my head.

"Kling had handcuff burns," I blurted as if the airstream had dislodged a thought. "Camino isn't into cuffs, is it?"

"It's not a *jail*."

"You said he escaped this afternoon?"

"That's when he was missed. It may have been any time after lunch."

"And he called you this evening."

"Around eight. I came immediately."

"So somewhere in those six to eight hours someone cuffed him. Probably the ones who stormed my office."

"How would they know he was missing?"

"Someone at Camino?"

"It's *possible*, I suppose, although it's illegal."

"So is kidnapping."

"But how would they find him?"

She punched the gas and slewed right through a yellow light, puckering my sphincter.

"Well, uh …" I was blank for a moment. "Did you talk to anyone after Kling called? The hospital, maybe?"

"No. I should have, but I didn't."

"Would he have called anyone besides you?"

"I don't *think* so. I've pretty much become his world, and even that link has frayed."

"*Bad* memories are harder to lose," I said. I had a point to make, but it got lost in my thoughts.

"And ...?" Nguyen said, nodding as if filing some mental shrink-note.

"And what?"

"Bad memories are—"

"Right, right. What was my point? ... Oh, yeah, the kidnappers! Maybe *he* called them."

"Why would he call the people he was fleeing?"

"That's a mystery." I took a different tack. "He might have been bugged. He considered the possibility."

"That's a common paranoid delusion."

"Yeah, but in this case, someone *was* out to get him. He escaped. They found him. He escaped *them*. And they found him again."

"Perhaps they followed him?"

"He said they were waiting outside my building. I think he was right. That means they *knew* where he was going."

"No." She shook her head emphatically. "Walter might *wander* through an unlocked door, but ... evade desperate criminals? He was incapable of outsmarting *anyone*."

"How about you?"

"What are you suggesting?"

"Maybe his matrix is more functional that he lets on."

"I see Walter every day, Mr. Pinel. I've examined his records and tests. His EEG's are almost flatline. I'm very good at what I do."

"Stipulated, your honor. But you don't need a weatherman to tell which way the wind blows."

"Okay. You've said that twice now. It must mean something to you. What?"

"Well ... the Kling *I* saw was spry for a catatonic and gabby for a mute. He escaped a lockdown, commandeered supplies, planned a little trip, made phone calls, figured out bus routes, gave the slip to whoever cuffed him, and showed up exactly where he said he was going. Any reason to believe my Kling *wasn't* your Kling?" She got the point, but I enjoyed rubbing it in. "*Res ipsi loquitor*," I smirked.

I expected the snooty dismissal doctors always give lay opinions, but instead she said, "You're right. Sudden lucidity is inconsistent with end-stage dementia."

"Elementary."

She smiled.

"So he's faking it," I said.

She swung the car north on Memory Lane.

"No ... malingering doesn't explain it either. Too many observers for too long a time. PET scans and all those EEGs."

She turned right on City Drive.

"Could he have snapped out of it?" I said. "Or been cured somehow? You mentioned that *lethargica* thing."

"How much do you believe in miracles?"

We were passing Olivewood Children's Home where Ronnie had worked as a psychologist. Behind Olivewood, the San Dismas River Trail wound past the stadium where the Angels sometimes played. Beneath the tall, haloed "A" sign was a stand of eucalyptus trees. Ten years earlier, in the blessed shade and damned concealment of those fragrant trees, chance or design had brought together Ronnie and El Tigre's Fallen Angels. Just ahead was San Dismas Medical Center. My eyes were drawn to a dark sixth floor window – the room where Ronnie had died holding my hand.

"I don't believe in miracles at all," I said.

Chapter Six

Nguyen pulled into the hospital complex, swiped her card key at a gated, staff lot next to the ER and docked in a slot near the ramp.

"I hope Hiatt isn't on duty tonight," I mumbled.

"Steve Hiatt? He's the best doctor I know."

"Me, too."

"Then why—"

"He sewed me together a few times and counts my carcass as half his. He reams me royal when I abuse it."

"Steve does have a healthy sense of his own importance," she chuckled.

Nguyen climbed from the car, removed her bloodied silk jacket, and dropped it in the space behind the seats.

"I think club soda will take that stain out?" I said sheepishly.

"Scissors might."

She came around the car to pry me loose.

"You know ..." she said thoughtfully. "You probably want to leave that."

"Leave what?" I said, grappling with a seat belt that wouldn't let me go.

"Your weapon. The open back gowns aren't tailored for it."

I let her lock the gun and holster in the glove box. She had to help me up the ramp.

"I'll take care of the paperwork if you'll trust me with this," she said, producing my wallet.

"Hey! How did you get that?" I patted my empty seat pocket.

"Misspent youth," she said without smiling.

Inside, Nguyen's faculty ID earned me cuts in line. I asked the nurse who whisked me away about Hiatt. She said he had been booted upstairs a few years back. He was *Chief* of Trauma Services now, no longer a minion who took routine night call. She made me strip, covered my front half with a hospital gown, and parked me on a gurney surrounded by green drapes. On either side I heard groans and labored breathing. I closed my eyes and tried to think happy thoughts.

The doctor who came had already reported the gunshot wound. He said he had an okay to release me if I lived.

Comforting.

He shined lights in my eyes, tapped my knees, and ran me through the rest of the neuro gauntlet – squeeze his finger, stick out my tongue, puff my cheeks, shrug my shoulders. I think I passed, but he sent me for a head scan anyway. When an aide wheeled me back to my curtained cubby, I saw the doc scrutinizing what looked like x-rays of walnuts – my head shots. I took his yawn as a good sign. He stitched my scalp, covered my head with a gauze turban like those you see in cartoons, and left. A nurse appeared with a sheaf of instructions for concussion and wound care. She also gave me a vial of codeine tablets to ease the pain of my bill. The label read one every four hours, as needed, so I swallowed two. Thinking twice, I downed another.

As I was struggling with my shirt buttons, the curtain whooshed open like the bridge door for Captain Kirk. I could have been bare-assed, *in flagrante delicto* for all the newcomer cared, which was not a whit, because it was Hiatt.

"Goddamm it, Pinel! You're too old for this."

"Good to see you too, Doc. How long has it been?"

"When was the last time you were shot?"

"This one's just a scratch," I said.

"If you want to play doctor, stick to gynecology."

Thumbing through my chart, he stopped and shook his head in disgust.

"Your liver enzymes are elevated. How much are you drinking?"

"Six-pack?" I said sheepishly.

"And *after* breakfast?" He riffled pages, almost ripping them. "Who's your doctor?"

"You."

"How many times have I told you I'm *not* your doctor?"

"Every time you think I'm well enough."

"Exactly. It's a handoff, see? I'm a quarterback. I can't run every ball. I hand you off to your regular doctor who scores the touchdown."

"I guess I'm a fumble."

Hiatt whipped an ophthalmoscope from his white, lab-coat pocket as if to smite me. Instead he pushed me down on the gurney, peered at my eyes, inspected the skin of my nose, and examined my palms and fingernails. Lifting my shirt, he prodded stiff fingers so deep under my right ribcage I half expected him to remove viscera. He lingered a bit, examining the old scars he had made on my chest and belly.

"Who can resist his own face in a photograph?" I said.

He looked up. "If you ever stop being a wise ass, I'll be *really* worried. Okay, it's not cirrhosis. Not *yet*. I'm ordering you to cut back on the booze, though. Preferably, *quit*. Will you need help with that?"

I considered it a moment. "I think it'll be alright now."

"Why should I believe you?"

I shrugged. "I don't know. It's just a feeling, I guess, but ... that's how I feel."

He ran a hand through his hair. Since hesitation was not Hiatt's nature, I assumed he had something important to say.

"You're getting old, you know?"

It wasn't a burning bush moment.

"C'mon, Doc," I said, sucking in my gut. "I still make five miles most days. And I bench—"

"*Less* than you used to. Just like me. Why do you think they kicked me upstairs? Because hundred-hour weeks just weren't doable anymore. But *other* things are. Other *valuable* things. Are you getting the picture?"

"For a guy like me, Doc, the career track is fast and flat. Race horse, then glue."

"I'm not saying you don't have more races in you, Pinel."

"One more, for sure," I said somberly.

"Then take better take care of yourself. Stop using your Goddamm *lizard* brain exclusively. You *do* have a cortex, you know? Frontal lobes?"

He rapped knuckles on my forehead.

"Ow! I said I'm okay now, Doc. I have a handle on it."

He grabbed the chart again, probably to keep his fists busy. "When was your last colonoscopy?"

"You're kidding, right?"

"Wrong. You're *sixty*, Pinel. You should've had one ten years ago." He brandished his pen. "Call the hospital tomorrow and talk to my nurse. She'll tell you when to come in. I'll say it's a volvulus so I can finish cleaning you out and do it right here in the ER. You won't show otherwise."

"I won't show *regardless*. Look, if there were *anyone* I'd let ram a fireplace poker up my ass, it'd be you. Honest. But it's *not* happening."

"We don't use pokers anymore. Flexible fiber optics. So smooth, you'll want seconds."

Hiatt ignored my objections and scribbled a couple of prescription slips. All his whoop-de-doo had riled me. Granted ... a few hours ago, before the madman came, I was feeling like Methuselah. But I *wasn't* anymore. Tired and achy, yes, moving rapidly *past* groggy from the pain pills, for sure, but ... *different* somehow. Maybe because I was hunting again, *working*, doing what I used to love as much as Fred loved his work.

Yet along comes Dr. Buzzkill to tell me how past my expiration date I am. I looked at the prescription slips and shook my head. *Laxatives* for Christ's sake! What next? Daily prunes? Mush for dinner?

"Take those tonight. And make sure you call," Hiatt said.

Call this! I almost blurted. I had more hair on my head than *Hiatt* and less belly oozing over my belt. And who the hell was kicked upstairs? He could stick flexible fiber optics up his own ass.

"*Call*, Pinel," he said with the solemnity of a sentencing judge.

I crammed the papers in my shirt pocket.

Writing a note in my chart, he said. "Are you seeing anyone?"

I glanced at the wedding ring I still wore. "I'm not a *monk*, Doc."

"Are you *seeing* anyone?"

" ... Not recently."

He sighed. "The man had come thither and had died there. When they tried to detach the skeleton which he held in his embrace, he fell to dust."

"Quasimodo," I said. "I always liked the guy."

"You would," he said. "That antidepressant I prescribed ... did you take *any* of it?"

"Sure. It was worth a try."

"And?"

"It sucked."

He nodded. "Yeah, I tried it myself." He glanced at the Timex I'd always known him to wear.

"Little lady waiting up, Doc?"

The question was facetious. I presumed Hiatt was still single and that he would stay that way at least until he retired, because, marriage would be cheating. And, frankly, the idea of him retiring was funny.

"Wide my world, narrow my bed, Pinel. But I did just buy a hi-def, sixty inch flat-screen to fill all my new free time and I'm missing *Real Housewives.*"

When he wheeled to go, his long coat flared like a cape. The flourish was a little creakier than the last time I saw it, but he could still pass for Cyrano.

Who also grew old.

"You've never owned a TV in your life, Doc," I shouted as he marched away.

"Call," he said, not looking back.

"Yeah ... I've missed you too," I said.

Chapter Seven

The three codeine tablets had been overkill, a conclusion I reached when I couldn't find the lobby. Despite color-coded lines on the floor, I stumbled up and down identical hallways. When I started to recognize particular scuff marks, I knew that I was traveling in circles. Since begging directions was unthinkable for a master sleuth, I pressed on, albeit as edgy as point man on a recon patrol. When a hand touched my shoulder from behind, I whirled.

Woe betide skulking assassins who misunderestimate the feral instincts of Pete Pinel, Private Investigator!

Reeling drunkenly, I saw the tile floor rising to kiss my face. Nguyen grabbed my waist, but –a foot shorter and half my weight – she fell, too.

"I'm *so* sorry!" she said, struggling to help me up. "I … I didn't mean to startle you."

I stared dumbly at the wallet in her hand as if it were a rabbit she had pulled from a top hat.

"This? It's yours. You let me register you."

I took the wallet and tried to put it in my hip pocket, but couldn't find the pocket. Looking behind me, I began to twirl like a dog chasing its tail.

"Whoa, Fido!" Nguyen said, grabbing my shoulder. "Let's get you to bed."

I crammed the wallet into my front pocket.

"I'm good. I'm good."

"You don't have your car, remember? *I* drove you."

"You did? That was so damn *sweet*! And you waited, too? Bring it in now. C'mon!" I tried to hug her, but she sidestepped me.

"You're a foxy little thing," I said, sounding ridiculous even to my dysfunctional matrix. Chuckling, I whispered, "Between you and me, I think I'm a little stoned."

"It'll be our little secret if you keep your voice down."

People in the lobby were staring.

"Codeine," I shouted. "Ask for codeine!"

Nguyen prodded me through the door.

"How many did you take?"

"Three?"

"A lot, but not *that* much … are you sure?"

I scratched at my pocket to remove the pill bottle, but gave up, since the wallet was in the way. "Who's counting," I said.

"I am," she said sternly. "No more until I get you safely home."

"Absolutely not!" I said, staggering down the ER ramp. "I have *never* relied on the kindness of strangers."

To me it was a funny line, but perhaps she hadn't seen the play, because she got all priggish.

"You mean you don't *trust* people?"

"*Au contraire!* I trust them to be *people*. Hey, did I say that right?"

"*Parfaitement.*"

"So! It's to be a dual of wits," I sneered, not knowing what she'd said.

"C'mon, *Monsieur* Pinel. Let's go."

"No, no, I'll just get a ... uh, you know, a ... yellow car."

"A yellow car? The seasons will change before you get a *cab* in Orange County."

She flashed a landing-lights smile. I liked smiles. I liked clowns and monkeys and happy faces. Playing follow-the-leader down the ramp was fun, too, but watching her shoe-horn me into her Jag was a crack-up – a slapstick game of twister. I laughed and laughed, although my mouth felt full of cotton. Nguyen finally corralled my flailing appendages inside the car, buckled me down, and slammed the door to keep me put. Before I could crawl back out, she skedaddled around the car and squeezed behind the wheel.

"Game, set, match!" I said, but in the confines of the car I could tell I was shouting, so I lowered my voice. "You called Hiatt, didn't you?"

She craned toward me. "What?"

"You called Hiatt," I boomed.

She flinched. I clamped a hand over my mouth.

"I thought he would want to know," she said. "He did."

"That's cool ... that's cool ..." I chased my slippery-little-bastard thoughts for a moment. "Man-o-man! Always something with that Hiatt. He wants to stick flexible fiber-optics up my ass. Go figure."

The part of me that was listening to myself was no virgin to codeine *or* concussion, but full-blown blasted was a first for either! I started to nod off, but jerked myself awake.

"Wait! I live out in the boonies. Just park me over there." I pointed toward the Doubletree across from the Medical Center and banged my hand into the windshield. "Goddamm glass!" I said, massaging my knuckles.

"I can't leave you out all night, Mr. Pinel. What would your wife say?"

"Wife?" I looked at my wedding band. "Oh, this. No, this is … a habit."

She started the car and glanced over her shoulder to back out. In shadowed profile she *did* look Vietnamese.

"It's, uh … hard for me," I said.

"What?"

"That kindness of strangers thing. Trusting people."

"Mà bên. I remember."

"Cut me a huss! I apologized for that."

She drove forward. "No, you didn't. You said you had scars."

"Sheez! *Forgive* me already."

She shrugged. "I don't fault a fire for burning, so I can't forgive it."

"Jesus Christ … a *Buddhist!*"

Her laughter was more musical than her voice. "Why, Mr. Pinel! Are you, despite your dissolution, still capable of irony?"

"Who knows," I slurred.

She laughed again.

Chimes.

Stuck in a line of cars, we edged toward an exit gate.

"The pursuit of uncollectible debts binds us in an eternal cycle," Nguyen said.

"Like this Goddamm pole here," I said as the gate bobbed. "Samsara as you mystics call it."

Her head swiveled. "Is there more to you than meets the eye?"

My lids sagged shut. "What you see is what you get."

I felt the car accelerate away.

"I'm far from a mystic, Mr. Pinel. Not religious at all. Philosophical, perhaps."

What a chatterbox! Well ... maybe a music box.

"How about you?" she said.

"I'm just ... searching ..." I said with slow, regular breaths. I had more to say, too. Cogent things. Trenchant things. *Ironic* things. Things that flowed from deep springs that didn't meet the eye. But my voice trailed off and sleep erased the slate.

Chapter Eight

The jouncing car woke me. Rubbing my eyes, I recognized a rutted dirt road and its sky-high view of Orange County. Nguyen turned at a numbered mailbox, crossed a plank bridge over a running drainage ditch, and pulled into the gravel drive of a small cabin nestled against Saddleback.

Home.

"GPS," she said before I asked. "I filled out your ER forms, remember?"

"Lucky we made it. A wet, washboard road and a Jag aren't the best match."

"There were moments," she said.

She came around the car, pulled me out, and shepherded me up three steps to the wide, wooden porch. I blushed when she noticed my rusty mountain bike chained to a railing. It's wrong to let things rust.

"Is someone home?" Nguyen said. The cabin lights were ablaze.

"Timers," I replied, unlocking the door and keying in the alarm code – R-O-N-N-I-E. "I hate opening doors on dark rooms."

"I'm surprised you have electricity up here. Is indoor plumbing too much to hope for? I simply *must* pee."

"Bedroom," I said.

She scurried through the only doorway.

I yearned to swan dive into the deep end of the couch, but – made of sterner stuff – I shuffled into the kitchen.

"Sapporo?" I shouted.

I heard the toilet flush and the sink run. "*Not* a good idea, Mr. Pinel," she shouted back.

"I'm tapering off. Besides, all things are Buddha things from your point of view, right?"

She entered the kitchen chuckling. "You do manage a certain insouciance, even in distress. Oh ... all right, it's been a long day. A glass of Chardonnay."

I pretended to check the refrigerator. "Fresh out."

"Red is fine then."

I checked the refrigerator again. "Out of red, too."

She smiled. "No selections from your cellar?"

"I do have a cellar. Lots of spiders, but, last I looked, no wine."

"Have you no guests with taste?"

"No guests."

"Then gimme a brewski," she said.

"Now you're pitching to my sweet spot."

I pried off caps, handed her a bottle, and swigged from mine. Nguyen rummaged through the dish-strewn kitchen until she found what passed for a clean glass. She decanted the beer and sipped.

"In the car ..." she said. "Your dreams were painful."

I studied the label on my bottle. "They always are."

"Who's Ronnie?"

I said nothing.

"I see," she said. "Divorce?"

I followed her eyes. I was thumbing my wedding ring. I nodded.

"And then she died. Her funeral was ten years ago. Today." I had an urge to chug the beer and open another, but instead I sat the half-full bottle on the sink counter.

"You called other names, too."

I still didn't want to talk about it.

"You can't let go?"

"Why do you say that?"

"Look at your hands."

They were clenched.

"Or perhaps you're afraid you *will*?"

"Fixed in a formulated phrase, am I? Look, if I ever want to see a shrink, I'll have my head examined. And don't bother billing me for the psychoanalysis, because I'll ignore it, just like I'm ignoring the damn analysis."

Her voice was light, although her face remained serious. "I could hire someone to collect. Private detectives do that sort of thing."

"Some do. You'd need a tenacious one."

"Ten years ... *you* seem to qualify."

She was making my head spin. "You'd hire me to collect my own bad debt? I'm too tired for koans."

"Oh, that's when they're most useful, Mr. Pinel."

"And you're against chasing debts anyway. That eternal cycle mumbo jumbo."

"Exactly. Your debt would bind us both. Forgiving it frees *me*." She smiled. "But there's nothing to write off. I wasn't making a professional observation, at least not consciously. I merely found your reaction curious. I'm also a woman, you know?"

I took her remark two ways and felt foolish and guilty for one of them. I opened my hands and toyed with my ring again, running it up and down my finger. She nodded. Curiously, not professionally.

"It's been a kick, Doc," I said, "but I'm feeling a lot like Gumby right now. I really, *really* need to be horizontal before my legs bend backwards." I wobbled into the living room, reeled toward the couch and plopped down hard.

"Is this another of your ironies? We shrinks have progressed beyond couches to settees. Even chairs."

She lifted my legs and stretched them out.

"The Sister Kenney act is hard to swallow. What's *up* with you?" I said.

"Kenny was a *nurse*, Mr. Pinel. And *you* are paranoid."

I noticed that I was in the dark again. My eyes had closed.

"Of course, suspicion is a tool of both our trades. And neither of us can *completely* turn off our professional selves, can we?"

Was the woman planning to talk all night? Couldn't she take a hint? The sound was nice, though, especially in the dark. Lilting.

"We both doubt what we see and hear," she went on. *And on and on.*

"We search for things lost or hidden. We find clues that uncover answers … sometimes even truth. We solve mysteries. I hate to discomfit you, Mr. Pinel, but in a parallel universe you might be a *shrink*."

With my eyes closed, I could see the madman clearly. I felt his lips against my ear and heard the wet whisper of his one true answer to the only important question.

They kept you from knowing what really happened to Veronica.

I jerked awake with a cusp-of-unconsciousness start.

"No! A surgeon."

"Interesting! So was Freud's first collaborator. Fliess." She shook her head. "Cats and dogs. It didn't end well."

I was so fatigued, I actually growled when she stooped to remove the .45 from my shoulder holster.

"See?" she chuckled. But she persisted with a mussed and blood-stained ferocity that was more than adrenalin fierce, but not quite testosterone fierce. Strangely protective.

Estrogen fierce.

"Tôi đứng về phía bạn," she said softly. "I'm on *your* side."

I closed my eyes and let her take my gun.

"What's your *first* name?" I mumbled.

"My mother called me Xuân."

"Springtime." I couldn't tell whether my words were audible or merely in my head.

"Xuân means springtime. Most people won't pronounce it. Or if they've heard me and try, they pronounce it Xuâ which means—"

"Old."

"I *dislike* being called Xuâ."

"Goddamm language. Can't tell your ass from your elbow."

I imagined her smiling in the dark, although, of course, *she* wasn't in the dark. I imagined that her smile was ironic. I made a yeoman's effort to speak aloud.

"Well, Xuân ..." While I was forty years rusty, I thought my pronunciation was passable. "I'm Pete. No tricky sounds or double meanings. Simply Pete."

"Things are *rarely* simple. Isn't your name actually Peter? From *petra*? In my birth country boys are named to mark their character. Is Pete also a rock?"

I was sinking deeper into the darkness and, as always, sound was the last to go. Her voice was like a thread she spun, a thread so strong it held me for a while. But finally the thread broke and I was nothing.

When I woke several hours later, it was with a tranquil dawning of awareness minus the usual hoopla – no choked screams or slamming doors. Xuân sat curled in the stuffed chair beside the couch. Her eyes were closed, but when I gently brushed her toe with my toe, her eyes opened. She wasn't asleep.

Which seemed to say that I could be.

And within a breath or two, I was.

Chapter Nine

I woke to sunshine.

Now *that* was new.

For years dark windows and glaring houselights had greeted me. Unable to sleep again, I usually parked at the kitchen table, smoked cigarettes, drank coffee, and re-read the *Banner* from the night before. Other times I merely stared into a black windowpane and watched a world slowly develop like a print in a darkroom tray.

For whatever reason – too much codeine, too little beer, enough sleep – I felt better. The sunshine was a pick-me-up, especially after days of rainy gloom.

Xuân had finally draped a quilt over her shoulders and fallen asleep, cocooned in that knees-to-chin posture wispy Asian women adopt in airport lounges when trying to nap among strangers. Given my age and circumstance, I was flattered that she'd considered disrobing imprudent.

Despite regular breathing and motionless eyelids that suggested a deep, dreamless state, her face bore a curious, tranquil smile. The expression was unconscious, unbidden, seemingly natural and inherent. Her *original* face, a Buddhist might say – the face she wore before her parents were born.

My gaze moved from her mouth to the open vee of her white, silk blouse, sliding further along the coil of her belly, around her hips, up to the hem of her skirt – riding well above her knees – and down again to her stockinged toes.

"Xuân?" I said.

"Yes?"

Instantly alert, she tugged at her skirt. I chuckled.

"Do I strike you as a voyeur?"

"You strike me as a *man*," she said, uncurling. "Besides, detectives watch. Chances are they *like* to watch."

"Impressive."

"What? Deep thoughts before breakfast?" she said.

"No. Your *instant-on* switch."

She patted her hair and retrieved her shoes. "A trait honed by internship and residency. Thirty-six hour shifts."

"Takes me an hour to get going *with* coffee," I said.

"I couldn't tell by looking at you now."

I stood, raked my fingers across my hair, and padded into the kitchen. "I *am* feeling pretty good today. Must be the extra sleep. How do you like your coffee?"

"I prefer herb tea."

"Herb tea, huh?" I banged cabinet doors. "Chamomile or Lemongrass?"

"You're kidding," she said, joining me in the kitchen. "You have those?"

"Of course not!" I guffawed. "Fresh out of aioli, too. I do have some tea, although I can't remember *why*."

"Tea is fine."

I sniffed the box. "Does tea go bad?"

"Whatever you have."

I put a saucepan of water on to boil and readied the coffee pot. Xuân nudged aside dirty dishes to make elbow room at the kitchenette. I dropped into the opposite chair.

"I need to repay you for all you've done. Starting with your jacket."

"You don't owe me anything, Pete."

"*I* determine my obligations. Paying them is another path to freedom."

She thought for a moment. "All right. Find Walter."

"*Count* on it."

She glanced at her watch.

"I have to shower and change before rounds. Do you want me to take you back to your office? Or will you get…" she paused. "A yellow car?"

"Yellow car? What do you mean?"

She grinned. "Just something you said last night."

"A lift would be great. You can freshen up here if you like."

"I will *not* go back in that bathroom, Pete. Even the *water* is dirty."

"It's well water, okay? It stains the sink and toilet. Iron or something."

"Or something."

"Consider it super-water. Mineral fortified."

"You're *boiling* it for tea, right?"

I showered quickly, smell-tested clothes from the bedroom floor, and threw on what passed. She was right about the bathroom, but her sentiments applied to the rest of the cabin and to me as well. I remembered my embarrassment at the rusty bike on the porch. I'd been neglecting things.

When I returned, she was drinking tea.

"Don't pick the flowers behind that first big tree on the right," she said.

"That's a patch of poison oak."

"Very funny."

I looked around. She had cleared the table and stacked the dishes neatly in the sink.

"Okay, okay, I'll clean the place up," I said.

"*Mens sana in corpore sano.*"

"Enough already, Cicero. You made your point."

"I used your phone to call the hospital. No cell service out here."

"Any word on Kling?"

She shook her head.

"No news is probably a *good* thing. Do I have time for a quick cup?"

She glanced at her watch and nodded. I poured coffee and sat.

"I'll start with Rick and Tim or they'll hang wanted posters. They'll probably stonewall me, but I know someone who might not."

"What should I do?"

"Who knows Kling best?"

"Me. Walter has no family."

"Old college buddies? Lifelong pen pals?"

"I don't think so."

"Friends?"

"Walter was—" She stopped. "I *despise* using the past tense. Walter was a unique man. He didn't *require* friends."

"Always alone and never lonely."

"A part of genius sometimes."

"There's a flip side. Never alone and always lonely?"

"A different kind of genius. A writer, a poet, an artist, perhaps. Certainly not Walter."

She sipped her tea.

"Then I guess you're his only witness, Doc. Brainstorm what might be behind this. Dark secrets? Revenge?"

"Nothing like that, I'm sure."

"He talked in riddles, Xuân, but when I asked who handcuffed him, he said the *past*. He said the Stone was his *dharma*, but also his *karma*. Something caught up with him. Something he saw coming. I have to consider everything."

She dunked her teabag a few times, removed it from the cup, and placed it on a saucer. "But ... *enemies*? It's so hard to believe."

"An ex-wife?"

"No."

"Angry husbands? Jealous women?"

"Certainly not."

"How about *you*?"

She leaned back as if pushing away from the table. "I see what you mean by consider *everything*."

"What I don't know can hurt me. Kling, too. You said he recruited you from Stanford, a mentor or something, but you had some kind of falling out, right?"

"Not at all. I said I left the field of research, not Walter. *Never* Walter." She sighed. "Our relationship is ... complicated. But not what you seem to imagine. Regardless, it's impervious to other women. *Or* other men. Jealousy is just another uncollectible debt. Walter shares that philosophy."

"*Two* Buddhists. You could start an ashram. My experience, however, teaches that hatred trumps philosophy every time."

"Not necessarily."

"How about love?"

"A stronger force in the long run, yes, but still ... Love, too, may yield to right and wrong."

I snorted. "Like you said last night – cats and dogs. I can't swallow – or *stomach* for that matter – a philosophy that dismisses what makes the world go round. *In the beginning was desire.* That's how the Greeks put it."

"Really? How interesting. Freud said the same thing, only he called it libido. He also saw it as the source of endless grief for which philosophy was a remedy. *Where id was there ego shall be.*"

"I'll have to remember that one. Okay, forget revenge for now. Even served cold, revenge is usually rage. Kidnapping is much more ... philosophical. How about a work-related motive. Kling was lead dog. Other dogs get tired of the view."

"Walter is no longer an obstacle to anyone. What would kidnapping accomplish?"

"Obtain that Philosopher's Stone."

"I thought cocaine made no sense?"

"He never actually said the rock was the Stone. I just assumed. Regardless, they also wanted something in his head. Try to figure *that* part out." I downed my coffee and stood. "Ready?"

She rose, rinsed her cup, and placed it upside down on the drain board.

Shrinks and their Goddamm mind control tricks. Left sitting on the table, my cup seemed to shout slob!

I swiped up the cup, rinsed it, and placed it beside hers. Later I'd dig out my old copy of *Hints from Heloise* and brush up on housekeeping skills.

"Let things percolate in your head," I said, drying my hands on a paper towel. "Pondering a mystery is like looking for a target in a dark landscape. You scan things with the corner of your eye. Central vision is weak in the dark. Stare and everything runs together. Peripheral vision is sharper for anomalies."

"Once again, Pete, advice worthy of a shrink."

I shrugged. "Sure. As you said yesterday, the subconscious gives you a clue."

"Good recall for someone who *was* subconscious."

"I'm *better* now."

There is was again. Better.

And it was true.

Chapter Ten

Surrounded by gray, stone siblings, the glass-walled San Dismas police headquarters building stuck out like a milkman's child in a family portrait. Some forgotten, mid-century pied-piper had touted a re-engineered "commons" as spawning a new social order. Mesmerized, the city council had bet a gallon of red ink that a building with strong, young lines and transparent planes would beget a department of simplicity, efficiency, and openness.

They lost the bet.

Worse yet, the design had proved faddish and expensive to maintain. A complicated, exterior louver system intended to shield the exposed interior from blistering sunlight hadn't functioned in decades. A water shortage ten years earlier had given City officials an excuse to drain the chronically malfunctioning fountain. It now sat dry and dust-covered. Gaps in the irreplaceable custom tile-work reminded me of missing teeth in meth mouth. The building looked not only decrepit, but a little silly – like a balding, old man in a faded leisure suit.

Rick Waggoner's eighth-floor desk sat baking in morning sunshine. His window seat was a perk of seniority. A minion's placement against an interior wall spared Tim Mulligan.

"So, what's the skinny, guys?" I said, sauntering in and plopping into a folding chair next to Rick's desk.

I had abandoned the silly turban in favor of a four-by-four and tape, but the bandage wouldn't stick. Tim eyed the cornrow of stitches across a cleared patch of my scalp.

"You look good, Pinel," he said.

"I'm a new man."

"New look, anyway. Should have ducked, though. *Back* of your head, you'd have some Friar Tuck action going. Bald spot on the side looks like mange."

"Sage sartorial advice, Tim. Any leads yet?"

Tim let Rick answer. "With the average-height, average-weight crap you gave us? I figure our first lead comes when we find the body."

"How about the slugs?"

"Guns were cherry. No matches."

"And no witnesses, of course."

Rick wiped his sweaty forehead with a paper towel torn from a roll on his desk. "Tell your landlord to spring for a nighttime guard. We're looking at cameras – an ATM and a traffic monitor might've caught something. So far, *nada*."

Squinting into the sun, I found myself wondering about the incidence of melanoma in the building. Parking at Tim's desk would have been a healthier move, but not a wise one.

"Nguyen says the guy has no enemies," I volunteered.

"That checks," said Rick.

"No threats reported anyway," added Tim.

Rick scowled at the qualification.

Taking Tim's comment as an opportunity to swivel a quarter turn, I said, "How'd he get loose to begin with?"

"You asking him or me?" Rick said. "I can't tell."

Goddamm egos! I turned back.

"An orderly got pulled into a take-down just as he was coming in. Left the door unlocked for a sec," Rick said. "All eyes were on the fracas and no one saw Kling bolt, but he was missing at the next head count an hour or so later."

"No ransom demands?"

"We're waiting for one of those letters with the words cut out of magazines."

"I had one of those once," I blurted.

"Bullshit, Pinel. No one does that," Rick grunted.

"Bullshit, yourself, man! Dude saw it on TV. Figured that was how it was done. Wanted to look professional. Christ. That must have been ..." I tried to remember the year, but it was slow coming to me. "I dunno, seventies, sometime."

"You old farts and your war stories," Tim guffawed.

Rick's face did all the talking for a while. I busied myself scratching the itchy edges of my bald spot.

"That orderly sounds dirty," I said when Rick looked at me again. "Someone snatches Kling when he *accidentally* leaves the door open? Chance favors the prepared."

"Pithy," Rick said, still glaring. "Who said that?"

"Fleming."

"Fleming who?"

"Wrote the James Bond books," Tim smirked.

Nodding, Rick blotted his forehead again. "You know, Pinel, you got a whole ass-full of great ideas.

Lucky for us you're not dead or we might never solve the case."

"Only the orderly's record is clean," Tim said. "We're cross-checking calls out of the hospital that morning, but that's a week of work, and every cock-sucking miscreant has a throw-away cell anyway."

"Miscreant?" I said.

Tim shrugged. "Sensitivity training. It's mandatory now since that incident with the towel-head."

"So we wait for a break," I said.

"No, Pinel, *we* wait for a break," said Rick. "*You* slither on down your slimy little path and stay out of it."

"But, guys, that's the good news! Nguyen is Kling's court-appointed guardian. She hired me to find him." I was bluffing of course, but I figured she would play along. "So it's like we'll be working together. How great is *that*!?"

The room suddenly felt cooler – as if those broken louvers had kicked in.

"Work *your* side, Pinel," Rick intoned.

"Cherchez l'homme," I said.

Rick glared at me.

"It means *look for the man*," Tim chuckled. "He's making a joke about—"

"A cop with your education is stone wasted in San Dismas, Tim. Maybe you should check out Interpol."

"It was *sort* of funny, Rick," Tim said sheepishly.

Rick took his time moving the paper towel roll from one side of his desk to the other while he did a staring number on me.

"Okay, Pinel. Guy has to make a living. Looks like you got yourself a missing person case. So look for the man." He shot a scowl toward Tim and turned back. "*Just* look for the man."

"Yeah, we don't need any more kids killed," Tim growled.

"They were miscreants, Timmy, me boy. And it's ancient history. You were still in high school."

"Yeah? Well, school is out, Pinel. See?" He stood and stepped forward, offering a hand as if to show me his heavy college ring. Close enough, he flicked his wrist to thunk the ring against my stitches. "And *you're* just a boozy, washed-up, old man."

Rick bristled at the "old man" crack, but Tim was his partner while I was lower than whale crap. If his partner wanted to play bad cop, Rick could look away. "You heard him, Pinel," he said. "Scram."

I touched a finger to my stitches to check for blood. "That's it? Why the hell have me come all the way down here, Rick?"

He leaned back in his swivel chair and casually scratched his balls.

"Because I can," he said.

Chapter Eleven

As Deputy Chief of Police, Manny Vasquez had risen as far as he could go in San Dismas, bumping against the *ass ceiling* – a Peter Principle level above which jobs like Chief, Commissioner, or City Supervisor all demanded an incompetence he wouldn't feign. Born in San Dismas to upwardly-mobile Mexican parents, Manny was – among eight kids and countless cousins – the first to finish high school. Dirty-hands day-labor bought him night-school at San Dismas Community College. With a two-year degree in criminology, Manny joined the force as a beat cop and finished college on the job. Thirty-five years later, he occupied a top-floor office bigger than the bungalow that had housed his whole family. The overhang that anchored the useless louvers blocked the sun, and a uniformed woman at a reception desk shielded him from riff-raff like me.

"You have no appointment," she glowered as if about to write me a ticket. The lady was new and it'd been a while since I'd dropped by.

"Yeah, well, we have this open door thing between us."

"How lovely for you. But I'm the door and without an appointment, I'm closed. If you want to park it, I'll check."

I *tried* to sit, but the extra sleep had me wired. The uniform took my pacing as suspicious. When I lied that I'd just had a colonoscopy, she relaxed. Cops *hate* mysteries.

Waiting for Manny, I ticked off a list of my other friends. It was a short list, grown shorter over the years. Some had moved on. Blake the bartender retired to Phoenix, but still sent Christmas cards. Fred Lynch *didn't* send cards. Some of my friends were dead. Like Jesus. Or Ronnie – my best of best friends, although sometimes, when I was drunk, I recalled that the divorce decree had read irreconcilable differences.

With whom did I *not* have irreconcilable differences anymore?

Manny Vasquez.

Manny was the best cop I'd ever known – another reason he would never be Chief. And since everything important about a man is summed in how well he does his work, he was also the best *man* I'd known. Cops see life as choices or they couldn't do what they do. Some see only the big choices – you pull the trigger or you choose not to. Manny, however – a stickler for detail – saw *everything* as a choice with a right or wrong answer. You might argue with his criteria, but you never doubted that he always chose what he thought was right. If he bent iron rules – and certainly for me he'd bent enough to make an ornamental fence – it was only because he knew that the rules of law were merely the shadow of justice. And while Manny worshipped justice, he also loved mercy. That's a rare combination, sometimes worth its weight in gold.

Ages ago, Lemon Tom – a good cop who went bad and was well on his way to becoming Chief – tried to muscle me into betraying a client. In a near fatal demonstration of disrespect, I'd broken Tom's nose. Manny stepped in on the side of mercy and likely saved my life, since even Tom couldn't stand against Manny when Manny knew he was right – not without killing him, and Tom wasn't that far gone yet.

Lemon Tom went on to choose crime chief over police chief. Eventually, I chose to kill Lemon Tom, a shudder that engendered my marriage breached, El Tigre dead, and Manny – a half-foot shorter than me – rising out of a roiling deathtrap one impossible ladder-rung after another, legs quivering from the dead weight of me clinging to his back. Manny's choice of mercy bought me ten more years. I grimaced considering how I had invested his gift. The uniform's wave was a reprieve.

Manny's windows, facing Saddleback, overlooked San Dismas. On the opposite side of the building, the Chief's ocean view was, undoubtedly, a perk of rank, but Manny would have chosen this office anyway. He liked to keep an eye on his city.

I dropped into a chair while Manny made final scribbles on a stack of papers.

"Goddamm coke trade is turning into a civil war again," he muttered without looking up. My conversation with Manny was always in progress.

"The *Banner* doesn't even front page the shootings anymore," I said.

"Tell me about it!" He capped his fountain pen and slipped it into an inside coat pocket. "Global warming is affecting the harvest or something. We had years of feast when, no matter how much we seized, the market was glutted. Pushers were giving toasters away with the crap. Now it's famine time, and rats are fighting for scraps."

He tapped the side of his head, indicating my stitches.

"You were lucky again, Pete."

"I think my luck has changed, Manny. I think it's going to run good for a while."

He nodded noncommittally.

"You *look* different, if that's a sign. Still dressing like a bum, but ... something."

I surveyed my frayed-cuff jeans and scuffed cowboy boots. I scraped at a faint stain on my shirt pocket as if my ragged thumbnail could make it disappear.

Manny's hands were manicured. Gone were the calluses and dark crescent nails he had known as a kid. I couldn't see his shoes, but I knew the toes were spit shined mirrors. The old shine man in the lobby was his first stop coming to work. And his clothes were more than a costume like Tim's; more than knock offs or overpriced labels. They were *right*. Although Manny, too, had added a few pounds, his blue blazer and creased khaki trousers fit perfectly, because clothes were supposed to fit. That's what tailors were for, to make them right.

Since I was fashion blind in the way some people are tone deaf, Manny's jibes about my appearance had always been background noise. This time, however, I tuned into something extra. Casually dressed and unconcerned was one thing, but *carelessly* dressed suggested I was unconcerned about something that *should* have mattered.

"Are you off the beer? You look antsy."

I looked at my hands. I wasn't shaky, but I was definitely fidgety.

"Let's say *it's* off me," I said.

"Sure ... one day at a time. Did that bullet send you toward the light last night? You see Jesus or something?"

"Why not Moses? Or Buddha? Cops can't show bias, Manny. Didn't you have the sensitivity training?"

He snorted. I'd never known him to take much stock in the idea of a God who gave a Goddamm for human affairs – a big leap for *any* cop – but at his core, Manny was Catholic.

"You *sound* different, too, Pete. Playful. Like you used to sound. I hope it lasts this time."

Although I couldn't imagine why, Manny had never given up on me. For years he had loaned me money when I was broke and steered cases my way when he thought he could count on me. He'd kicked my ass a few times and dragged me home to dry out. He'd sat with me saying nothing when that helped, and other times he'd said all the right things. He rescued me from the shipwreck vortex of Ronnie's death, kept me afloat for a time after that, and dived in again each time I sank.

It was *me* who had given up on me, I thought – something I'd told myself innumerable times – but, suddenly, I rejected the idea. Manny wouldn't let a friend drown as long as one them could hold on. He'd *proved* it. But so had I. With Jesus and Ronnie, for example. So maybe the last few years had been less giving up than holding on. Maybe *I* still liked me, too.

"What's with Rick and Tim," I said to change the subject. "It's like they both went to prick school and got A's."

Manny smiled. He enjoyed watching people prove his points. "College kid teamed with a hard-knocks veteran. They scare each other and it keeps their hackles up. Takes a while to shake out, but it usually does. Did they lean on you?"

I waved it off. "Nah ... just pissing contest stuff. So what do *you* know that they won't say?"

"Check the *Banner* for updates. Fifty cents."

"C'mon, Manny. It's personal."

"That's the problem."

"I won't muck up the investigation."

"Hell you won't! But that's not what's gnawing me."

Stalling to choose his next words, he drew a cigar from a four-slot leather case – his day's ration, no more, no less. He snipped the cigar tip with a pocket gizmo, licked the leaf wrapper, and struck a wooden match. He puffed the cigar to get the ember right, making blue clouds.

"You can't smoke in city buildings," I said, realizing I hadn't had a cigarette all morning.

"The Mayor does. Three supervisors do. So does the Chief."

"Arrest them."

He smiled cryptically, rolling the cigar between his thumb and forefinger, studying the ash. Finally he said, "You're not the man you were, Pete."

"What the hell is it lately? Somebody hang an AARP sticker on my back? Jesus!"

"See? You're more hot headed than ever and still a bad listener. But your mouth is writing checks your ass can't cover anymore."

"That remains to be demonstrated."

He tapped the side of his head again.

"So I lost one. So I'm no Marciano. It was three against, Manny."

"That hasn't improved since yesterday."

"They missed, didn't they?"

"A *head* shot, Pete! For once without the double tap. Better not ask for a rematch. You lucked out."

"Chance favors the prepared."

"What a Goddamm bullshit artist! *You* didn't discover penicillin."

I was steamed – only partly because he knew the quote. "They snatched a guy who was relying on me, Manny. Right from under my nose. That's *rotten* for business."

"Suddenly your reputation is bugging you?"

"What's bugging me is gorillas who figure I don't know what's what. Waltz in and play me for some fucking *citizen*?!"

"A *senior* citizen. Something you should reflect on."

I was out of the chair, needing some distance. "My ass is no older than *yours*, Manny."

"But mine sits behind a desk. *I'm* not still playing street cop."

"Damn it, Manny! You're right, and I know you're right," I said, close to launch and trying to slow the countdown. "But too old for grabass and gunplay doesn't make me senile. I'll poke around a little, see what I see. I have a client."

"A client? In *writing?*"

"I wouldn't lie to you. The doctor. Nguyen. She's Kling's conservator."

He puffed his cigar some more. "Okay, Pete. Always good to see you working. Keep a copy of the contract for Rick and Tim when they ask."

I waited, but he didn't say anything.

"C'mon, Manny. High profile case like this, you've been briefed. Give it up!"

"You sound like you're hitting on some debutant," he muttered with disgust. "Okay, fine, I'll put out for what good it does you. Aragon Pharmaceuticals."

"The drug company?" I looked out the window at a taller building several blocks away. "You're neighbors, Manny. Close enough to peep on whatshisname counting his money."

"Les Burdick."

"A string of misfortunes was quite fortunate for him, as I recall. He still shoot big money pool in Newport?"

"The Cue Tip? No way."

"Colombians owned it, as I remember. The Feds hit it a couple of times."

"Then someone hit the Colombian's. It's 12th Street's place now, although they shed the moniker not long after Frankie Mendez died in that fire."

"Pure waste of a match."

His eyes narrowed. "Why match?"

"C'mon, Manny. Maybe it was a Zippo. How would I know?"

"12th Street goes by Mendez Holdings now. That's Frankie's brother, Sheik."

"I thought he was dead."

"Not from want of efforts."

"*Sheik?*" I said sardonically. "What is it with Mexicans and nicknames?"

"We're *colorful*," Manny said stonily.

"Sheez! I didn't mean anything. So why did Burdick give up pool? Someone break his thumbs?"

"He gave up low life ties when he tried to take the company public. At least he did publically. *Privately* he and Frankie Mendez did more together than shoot pool. *Un*-patent medicine. Sheik continues the business relationship."

"Where does Burdick hang now? The Cheesecake Factory?"

"Built himself an oceanfront fortress at Pelican Point."

"Probably has a billiard room."

"It does. I got the tour once when we went to talk to him about some of his fortunate misfortunes."

"What's Kling's connection?"

"Les Burdick was his sugar daddy. Aragon backed his research; endowed a chair for him at UC San Dismas. Kling's reputation buoyed the company."

"Did Burdick snatch him?" I tried not to show the heat rising in me again.

"Goddamm it, see what I mean! I didn't say that at *all*. Nothing, and I mean *nothing*, supports it. All we have is Kling's connection to a tainted big money guy whose business is faltering."

"How's that?"

"Aragon was built on copycat drugs and generics. Kling made the company sexy – not enough to save Burdick's IPO bid, but venture capital bought in. Blockbusters take years, so most of the money stuck around, waiting for Kling to lay some golden eggs. We *thought*, but couldn't prove, Burdick was laundering his *illicit* income through Aragon, padding the balance sheet to give investors reasons to keep nibbling."

"A Ponzi scheme."

"When Kling wigged out, the money tried to bail, but Burdick had managed to freeze the assets. His lawyers have stalled, but they're running out of motions. He's going down. Soon."

While he was talking, my mind was darting ahead, backtracking, taking new turns to find connections of my own. Ronnie worked just down the street from San Dismas Medical Center, but she had trained at UCLA and didn't teach or do research. Propinquity to Kling by itself was a slim connection. She *was* a psychologist, however, and Kling was a psychiatrist. That path was more promising. And while she'd never mentioned Kling or Burdick or Aragon that I recalled, the company was new back then. Maybe I wasn't paying attention.

"What's up, Pete? You have that look."

I shook my head. "What look?"

"You're hunting."

I laughed it off. "C'mon, Manny! I'm thinking. I'm allowed."

"Thinking or jumping to conclusions?"

I wished I could run my thoughts by him to see what trails *his* brain would follow, but this hunt had to be solo. If Ronnie's name came up, Manny might bend a few iron rules into a cage just to keep me off the streets.

He eyeballed me for a moment, then shrugged. "Your client probably gave you that much already and it's public record anyway." He glanced at his watch and I knew our time was up.

"Thanks for talking to me, Manny," I said, standing and moving toward the door, but I stopped to look back. "It's good seeing you."

"Watch yourself, Pete. You're not a kid anymore."

I was still *partly* a kid, the smart-ass part anyway, so I said, "Some work of noble note may yet be done." I pronounced it No-bel, because I wanted to be doubly clever.

"You always had a Jeopardy memory, Pete, but Wheel of Fortune judgment. You ignored the line right before that one."

"What line are you referring to, Manny? Peanut sittin' on a railroad track?"

Manny balanced his cigar like a teeter-totter on the lip of a large ashtray.

"Death closes all," he said.

Funny. Yesterday I had remembered the death line and not the *other* one. Something to do with my account book, I recalled. Maybe memory works that way, summoning things that have a similar color or tone to what you're feeling already, like watching a rainbow with colored lenses and seeing a single hue. I left Manny's office humming.

A man hears what he wants to hear and disregards the rest.

Chapter Twelve

The Aragon Pharmaceutical building was only a few blocks past the meter where I'd stashed my Blazer, so I plunked in a few quarters and kept walking. I was pent up. Movement felt necessary. Later I'd take a long run to vent some steam. It was a good day to be outside anyway. In fact, a *great* day. Seventy degrees. Buttery sunshine. Rain-scrubbed air lemony fresh. The cloudless sky was tinted that trademarked blue reserved for glossy magazine shots of Caribbean cruises. Joggers, bikers, walkers, talkers. The air hummed with voices and laughter and music.

I had no particular plan in mind – eyeball the building, maybe go inside. Sometimes detective work is like a kid with a chemistry set. Mix things together and see what happens. It's fun!

Although I rarely paid attention, I caught my reflection in a row of store windows. A working detective needs to blend in, but, Manny was right. I looked like a bum! Passing a men's store, I decided to buy some clothes. Off-the-rack suits were hard for me to find because my shoulder, waist, and thigh proportions don't conform to the master templates. Casual clothes were rarely a problem, however – at least not during the previous administration, which was the last time I'd bought any.

Ignoring the natty little clerk's haughty gaze, I found what I hoped was still my waist size on a circular rack of pants, and threw several pairs of black slacks over my arm. My boots merely needed polish and my black belt went with anything save a tuxedo. I grabbed three knit pullover shirts from a nearby display, and – long overdue for new underwear – added two packages of white briefs and some plain, black socks. Next to the socks was a shelf of handkerchiefs. Who the hell used handkerchiefs anymore? I snatched up a couple anyway and toted the armful into a dressing room. I put on new underwear, new socks, new pants, and a light blue shirt – one with a horse logo where the pocket belonged. Although I hated shirts without pockets, I hated shopping more. I stashed my belongings and crammed a silk handkerchief in a hip pocket. Wadding all the old stuff into a ball, I tied the shirt tails and sleeves together to make a hobo's bindle.

The snooty clerk – *way* too put-together for my taste – saw the commission I dumped on his counter and began gabbing like an old pal. He brandished a spray tester-bottle of some chartreuse liquid, but wisely read my face before he spritzed it. Goddamm if I would go *that* far! Ringing the sale, he stalled over the total button to tout his sweaters and sport coats, and then made a last-second, hail-Mary pitch for a *lint roller*. Sheez!

My Visa was long dead, but I thought I might have some leeway with American Express. When the card-swiper beeped the wrong beep tone, however, the blossoming friendship with my new buddy wilted.

"Your card has been declined, sir."

"They're always losing my payment."

"Yes … of course."

My cards were over limit because my bank account was tapped, but what the hell. Something would turn up.

"I'll write a check," I said.

"You *do* have identification," the clerk said suspiciously, as if he thought I were some pod-person born without a navel. I almost lifted my shirt to show him.

"*Yes*, I have ID," I said, snatching the card from his prissy little fingers.

The clerk took his time scrutinizing the check and my driver's license. I felt a little like a cat being rubbed the wrong direction, and had to remind myself that he was just doing his job. When he bagged my purchases, I asked him to toss the bindle of old clothes. Recoiling as if it were a soiled diaper, he pointed at a sidewalk trash bin. I thanked the little shit and left.

Ditching the rags, I strolled back to the Blazer, jauntily swinging my handled shopping bags. I *liked* bags with handles! The store windows told a good story this time, particularly when I sucked in my gut. I looked *great* for sixty! Better than Manny in some ways and a *lot* better than Rick or even Tim who was thirty years younger.

I plopped the clothes bags in the back seat and from habit scratched at the non-existent shirt pocket for a smoke. Cursing the shirt-maker, I dug the crumpled Winston's from a pants pocket, but realized that – three hours without one – I was half-quit already!

I flicked the pack toward a trash can like a playing card at a hat.

Score!

I pumped my fist over my head and let out a whoop. No booze. No smokes. Fresh clothes. Man-oh-man, I felt *reborn*. Like a virgin. Like Madonna, shiny and new!

God, I hoped I didn't find religion.

Chapter Thirteen

Outside the Aragon building, my cell phone rang. I didn't recognize the number.

"Pinel Investigations. The eye that finally sleeps."

"… Pete? It's Xuân."

As if I could mistake her lilt.

"This isn't Yogi Berra?"

"No. It's Xuân."

"Just joshing, cutie. Zup?"

"You sound … different."

"Better or worse?"

"Better?"

Question marks! What the hell was it with people?

"I just finished rounds at San Dismas," she said. "Something occurred to me."

"Great! I'm dying to talk. Swing by my office?"

"I'll have to backtrack. Give me twenty minutes."

I launched the Blazer, but caught a Starbucks' sign in the corner of my eye and skidded into a red zone out front. I darted inside but stalled behind a man flummoxed by the menu. *Is the caramel swirled in or on the bottom? I don't like hazelnut. What's a Frappuccino? Can I get a medium instead of Grande?* I was about to pick him up and set him aside when he settled on a half-caf latte mocha frappe something, which was probably my justice. Thinking I should cut back on the caffeine, I ordered two large herb teas and came close to popping the guy when he rattled off a dozen choices. Waiting, I almost fell victim to a lonely cinnamon roll pressing its wet little nose against the pastry case. My new pants felt snug, however, so I left it for the next chump. Snatching a racing thought, I punched a button on my phone to save Xuân's number.

The daytime lobby guard in my building was a white-haired retiree from PG&E who wouldn't fancy the idea of shooters. He frowned when I pushed through the revolving door, probably hoping the landlord had bounced me. Upstairs, however, the crime scene tape was gone, and my key still worked the lock. Eviction or not, twenty-plus years in the same building must have counted for something. I went inside, sat the drinks on the window sill, and surveyed the damage.

Things looked better in sunlight. If I paid my rent the landlord would replace the window and fix the broken door. The rest was just housekeeping. I righted the desk, scooted it back in place, and arranged the chairs. I'd need to find something to cover the bullet holes, a blotter, maybe, or plants. Yeah, plants! Give the place some color, some pizzazz. I banged file drawers shut and stacked scattered papers atop the cabinets. The orderly stacks reeked of purpose and progress. I whipped the handkerchief from my pocket and began to dust. Buying the handkerchief had been a good move. I knew it. I just *knew* it!

With a pretty client due, I decided the wastebasket brimming with empty Sapporo bottles had to go. I covered the bottles with the threadbare, blood-stained throw rug and carried the basket down the hall to the waste bin. Returning, I met Xuân getting off the elevator. She wore another snappy suit, blue this time, with a bow thing at the neck of her blouse. She had to be a size zero – right out of a Fashion Island display window.

"Pete!" she said, giving me a surprised once over. "You clean up nicely. I almost didn't recognize you."

"New clothes aren't *that* big a deal," I huffed.

"You sound ... you sound great?"

"What's with the damn question marks? I *am* great."

"Sometimes a concussion—"

"I *said* I'm great! I dodged a bullet, right?" I choked on a laugh. "Oops! I guess I didn't. C'mon in. I brought you an herb tea."

Inside I noticed her taking stock of the office.

"Run your finger over the cabinet tops. Go on. Do it."

Looking puzzled, she did.

"I dusted! It's better with a white glove, though. C.O.'s in the Corps make inspections with a white glove to catch the dust. You don't have a white glove with you, do you? No, of course not! Why would you. That's silly."

I slid her tea and a napkin across the desk. She thanked me, sat, and sipped the tea through a hole in the plastic lid.

"Hey! No lipstick marks. I hate lipstick."

That look again. I felt like a specimen.

"Any news from the police?" she said.

"Those numb-nuts? They're waiting for a body."

She stared at me.

"Kee-rist, that was blunt, wasn't it? ... What did *you* come up with?"

Still X-raying me with those freakish eyes, she said, "Last night you mentioned following the money."

"From Deep Throat," I said, but added quickly, "No, no. Not what you're thinking. Watergate. That Watergate guy."

"I, uh … understand the reference. Anyway, Walter has become quite wealthy over the last ten years."

"Mega-bucks in that Nobel deal, I hear. Say, does he pay taxes on that? I always wondered, I mean, it's a gift, right, so maybe Sweden pays the taxes. *Huge* taxes over there. Fucking welfare state! But how about US taxes? If he had to pay both, he'd be left with bupkis! Wouldn't that be a drag? Like those guys on quiz shows you hear about who go bankrupt winning a—"

"The Nobel *is* substantial," she interrupted, "but he also had a consulting relationship with a pharmaceutical company. A lucrative relationship."

She meant what's-its-name, of course, but I played it coy.

"Consulting is common, even necessary" she continued, "but a scientist of Walter's stature would normally have *many* such relationships. It's prudent not to appear beholden. His agreement with Aragon Pharmaceuticals, however, was exclusive. Do you know Aragon?"

"Local. Not in the Merck or Lilly league."

"Which was odd enough when I started to think about it. But something else caught that "corner of my eye" you mentioned. Walter has been at a posh, private hospital for more than a year. No insurance company would cover that."

"So what else should he spend his dough on? Crayons?"

I needed to watch the dumb remarks.

"But that's just it. He's *not* paying for the hospital."

I took a drink of the herb tea and choked.

"Are you all right?"

"How do you drink this swill?" I sputtered. "Goddamm elixir of dog-park weeds!"

"You're drinking herb tea?"

"Not anymore!" I dumped the cup in the vanity sink. "I was cutting back on caffeine, but this stuff is poison!" I started to pace. I was more than wired, I was downright antsy. Her eyes followed me around the room.

"And I was saying ...?"

"What?" I snapped. "Oh, yeah. Okay, okay, so who *is* paying?"

"Aragon. Actually, the owner, Les Burdick. His firm leases a small ward at El Camino for clinical research. I'm sure the hospital gives him a favorable rate for Walter's care, but Mr. Burdick's personal expenditure has been substantial, I'm sure."

"Just *now* you figured this out?"

"Of course not. I manage Walter's affairs. But Burdick's involvement never seemed strange before. I assumed Walter was a business asset."

"Makes sense. Big bat in the lineup sells tickets."

"But that's what suddenly struck me. Walter's condition has been hopeless almost from the beginning. The university gave him an emeritus title and a small stipend because a Nobel laureate, even a demented one, confers prestige. But to a business concern? Walter adds little or nothing to a profit margin."

"Maybe Kling and Burdick are buds."

"Walter hated the man and Burdick cares for no one."

"Guilt trip, maybe?"

She sipped her tea. "I haven't examined him, but I *know* Les Burdick, and I can't ignore my instincts. He's incapable of guilt."

"Pretty successful for a sociopath."

"Oh, you'd be surprised. The term describes a spectrum ranging from street thugs and serial killers to managed healthcare executives and politicians. Burdick falls at the upper end of that spectrum. Machiavellian."

"So Burdick's a *Prince* of a guy with no reason to spend … what, hundreds of thousands?"

"At least."

The room was too small to pace in. I deserved an office like Manny's with big windows and views and a sexy woman out front to screen calls.

"Bingo, Xuân!" I exclaimed, punching my palm. "Kling disappears. Burdick cuts his losses."

"But he has no *legal* obligation to pay anyway."

I slapped the side of my head. "Right, right. Stupid idea!" Remembering the stitches, I checked my palm for blood.

"He must have *some* reason to keep Walter at Camino, even if I don't see it," she said. "In my field what you *don't* see is usually the key."

"In my field, too."

I grabbed my empty cup from the vanity and two-pointed it into the wastebasket. Yanking open a file, I snared a blank client contract, dug a pen from the desk drawer and printed Xuân's name in the space at the top.

"I'll be tripping over cops on this, Xuân. A paying client buys me some leeway. I need you to hire me."

"I intended to."

"On paper. Legit."

Watching me write, she grabbed my hand.

"One dollar? You will not!"

"A *paying* client. A fee makes it valid."

"Then make it believable."

"C'mon, Xuân! You saved my life!"

"You're exaggerating. Besides, *Walter* is hiring you."

I felt guilty at the way my heart jumped at the thought of money, although it might have been the touch of her hand.

"Whatever the state of his brain, his *heart* had a reason to find you."

I wasn't ready to share that yet.

"Is … is he still alive, do you think?" she said.

"If they're hot for something he truly can't remember, it buys him at least a few days. *Unpleasant* days, no doubt, but until they lose hope, they'll only press him so far."

"A few days! Can you postpone your other work?"

"I'll swing it so I'm full-time on this."

When she squeezed my hand, I thought I might squeak like a chew toy. She pulled a checkbook from her purse.

"You'll need a retainer. Say ten days to start? $1,000 per day?"

I coughed.

"Too little? I don't know usual and customary in this situation. "

"It's Kling's money?"

She nodded.

"Then it's just right," I said.

"Plus expenses, of course," she said, writing the check. "Including your hospital bills from last night. Clothes, office repairs, ongoing incidentals. I'm afraid you'll have to itemize, though. What I spend as Walter's conservator is audited."

"Sure. Receipts and stuff. That's how I always handle expenses."

She separated the check and slid it across the desk. All the zeroes made me dizzy. I folded it and automatically tried to tuck it in my non-existent shirt pocket. I settled for a pants pocket, crumpled the unfinished contract and began a new one.

"Indicate Walter Kling, MD as your client. I sign as his conservator."

I filled in the blanks, signed, and let her sign. I gave her one copy, pocketed one for the police, and stashed the original in a file drawer.

"What now?" she said.

"I'll scope out Aragon and do some digging on Burdick. Do you have Kling's files?"

"His personal things and financial records. Clinical files are in his lab at the university. His graduate students are trying to continue his projects."

"Go through what's handy. See if that subconscious of yours catches anything else."

She stood and dropped her paper cup and napkin in the trash. "I'll look over Walter's chart again, too. Should I question the hospital staff?"

"No. We already know how bad the bad guys are and they won't be wearing signs."

"Will you be in danger?"

"From those monkeys?" I laughed. "They'll never get the drop on me again."

"Beware of hubris, Pete."

"Hubris, hell. I'm big, I'm bad, and I'm *back*."

Another question mark in her face!

"For Christ's sake, what now? Everything's Jake."

"You're ... loud."

"If I were a font, I would be bold-faced caps."

That time she actually frowned.

"Lighten up already. I've been down longer than Australia. You have a problem with me enjoying myself?"

Once again it came out harsher than I intended.

"Whoa! Too much coffee, see?"

She turned to leave, but looked back from the door.

"Call me later, Pete. Please?"

Chapter Fourteen

Things to do.

Lots and lots of things to do.

And busy for a change felt *damn good*.

I chose a press pass from a batch of phony credentials I had used over the years and suddenly I was Ralph Reese, mild mannered reporter with a secret identity. I glanced at the mirror over the sink and flexed my muscles. I was big enough. All I needed were the long-johns.

Impatient with the elevator, I galloped down the fire stairs, jumped into the Blazer and barreled toward Aragon. Screeching into a handicapped spot in front of my bank, I rushed inside to deposit my check, but kept $500 cash. The wad of bills – mostly tens and ones – felt like a lucky charm in my pocket. Next stop was a drugstore for a steno pad. I also snagged a pair of reading glasses from a revolving rack, and – since I *did* feel lucky – bought ten lottery tickets, too.

Back in the car I rolled down the windows to feel and smell the air. The great day was even greater! The sky was *bluer* than the Caribbean, blue like blue-eyes. *Sapphire*-blue eyes. Blasting the radio, I slalomed between meandering Sunday drivers, although, actually, it *wasn't* Sunday, was it? It was ...oh, *whatever*! A weekday. A *great* day.

Braying along with Steely Dan – "Cuz he looks so fine, upon that hill. They tell me he was lonely, he's lonely still" – I drummed bumpa-bump on the steering wheel and bellowed – "Those days are gone forever. Over a long time ago. Oh, yeah!" Letting go the wheel to add a little air bass, I almost overshot the building. I squealed up to a fireplug and sat for a moment to reconnoiter.

The Aragon building was hard to look at. *Literally*. It wasn't just the ToonTown curves and goofy angles, but a foil-wrapping-paper façade that blinded drivers with reflected sunlight. I laughed aloud when the word *eyesore* popped into my head. Confronted by the *Banner* about a rash of accidents, the architect had replied *"reroute traffic."*

I left the holstered pistol in the Blazer lockbox since Ralph Reese would hardly pack heat to an interview. I breezed into the building lobby and chatted up a young, skin-head, security cop who pointed me toward an express elevator to the C-suites.

The 12th floor was a single expanse partitioned by suspended, odd-sized panels of frosted or mirrored glass. Here and there the glass was etched with images of molecules, chemical formulae, coils of what I took to be DNA. Reflected reflections reminded me of an arcade fun-house. I chuckled imagining some goof smashing face first into a clear panel trying to navigate the maze.

A sexy, redheaded receptionist – I just *had* to get me one of those – took my name and directed me to a circular, slate-colored settee. Unwilling to sit, I flitted like a hummingbird between framed articles and photos of a healthier-looking Kling and Les Burdick. The wait was excruciating. I felt like a fly trapped in amber. Eons slipped by. Numbers on my digital watch advanced at a glacial pace. Goddamm new species were appearing and becoming extinct, stars were born and died.

Somewhere after the heat death of the universe, the receptionist escorted me to Mr. Big. I kept falling a step behind so I could watch her sway. Her fashion-model legs shushed faintly from real stockings, not panty hose, a secret I knew because, like everything else on the floor, her desk was also made of glass with a glass ... what would you call it? An *immodesty* panel? In the sanctum sanctorum Burdick held court behind an even larger glass desk. Thank God he was wearing pants! His throne chair was made of brown leather that looked as rich and smooth as Godiva chocolate. I had to get me one of *those*, too. Swiveling the chair, Burdick leaned back and steepled his fingers beneath his chin. Maybe he was praying.

Behind him stood a bad mother-fucker in a business suit. I gave him the dismissive look mother-fuckers share in such situations and eyed his boss.

Burdick was only 5-11, but as buff as Conan – the barbarian, not the late night host. His hands, while pampered, sported permanent calluses from a lift bar. When he moved in the chair, cords of shoulders and biceps twined beneath a pearly-gray Italian suit tailored to accentuate just that play of muscle. His black, shiny hair was greased straight back. His eyes were black and shiny, too, like onyx. His posture was relaxed, nothing overtly sinister about him.

Nevertheless, some aura he radiated made me want to kick his capped teeth down his throat.

"Ralph Reese, mild-mannered reporter for a great metropolitan newspaper."

I smiled big and stuck out my gladhand. He squeezed it … hard. I squeezed back until he let go.

"You like that gym? Like those free weights, do you? A lot of you short guys do."

"What do you want, funny man?" he said.

"Just the facts, ma'am."

Burdick's aide-de-chump whispered in his ear.

"Who's the fucktotum?" I laughed at my joke.

"Mr. Armstrong is my Chief of Security. He wants to see your credentials."

"*No problemo*, Strongarm." I pulled the press pass from my pocket. The photo was old, but it was me. Armstrong gave it a glance.

"You can read without moving your lips?"

"What do you want?" Burdick repeated.

I launched into a rambling spiel about Kling and his connection to Aragon. Why did Burdick think he was snatched? How did it affect the company? Did it delay plans for the new drugs everyone was buzzing about? The irony of *drugs* and *buzzing* made me giggle.

Burdick gave a sourball pucker that nudged some sleeping faculty of my brain. Why the hell was I giggling? *Girls* giggled. Plus I was jabbering. Talking too fast. Talking – Xuân had said it as well – too *loud*.

"Is this your idea of undercover work, Pinel? Your picture was in every morning newspaper."

"Busted!" I chortled. "Should have worn my big nose glasses with the mustache."

"He's *stoned*, Les," said the goon.

It felt as if a flash bulb had frozen an image of something that had been moving invisibly in the dark. The son-of-a-bitch was right! I was *flying!* It was as if, last night, some draft had parted the curtains of my insomnia, my addictions, my grief, but now, become a tornado, it was kiting me up and away. I started to hoot like a hyena.

The long-leggedy redhead poked her face around a frosted glass partition.

"Peek-a-boo, Cutie Patootie," I cackled.

"Is … is everything all right, Mr. Burdick?"

"Mr. Armstrong is about to show him outside," Burdick said, waving her away.

"Outside my ass!" I snarled, squaring off. "No *one* guy shows me anywhere I don't want to go."

"Guess I should call for backup then," Armstrong said, moving around the desk with the dispatch of tree-sap.

I couldn't wait a week, so I took it to *him*, ignoring a bank of caution lights: he was as big as me; a professional; probably in practice; and half my age.

Sure enough, he oozed inside, slipped my roundhouse with a raised shoulder and crashed a locomotive fist into my gut. When I folded like a bellows, he braced me with an uppercut just hard enough to ring my bell without crumpling me. Well played! Why carry dead weight when the dead weight can walk? Besides, he was having fun.

Spinning me around like a blindfolded birthday boy at a piñata party, he slapped a cuff on my wrist. I jerked away, but he slammed a shoulder into my back, pitching me onto my stomach. He dropped a knee between my shoulder blades and rode my back while he dragged the cuffed arm behind me, trapped it under his knee, and jerked my other arm around to finish the job. The whole thing could have been a training video.

"You ridiculous old fart," he snickered, standing. "Guess I can cancel the back-up, huh?"

He wasn't breathing hard. *I* was hardly breathing. I tugged at the cuffs.

"Hey, Les, look. He's doing the squirm. Man, oh, man! I *never* get enough of the squirm. Always a riot."

I tried to lie still, but couldn't. Gulping breaths, I wheezed, "Okay, okay, you win. I'm getting up."

Armstrong placed a foot on my back.

"You didn't say mother-may-I?"

The foot was a boulder pressing me flat. "May I? ... *Mother*," I said.

Chuckling, he rolled away the stone. I struggled to my feet.

"Will you need a walker?" he said, grabbing the cuffs and jostling me toward the elevator. Reflections in the glass maze offered kaleidoscopic perspectives.

Armstrong manhandled me past the redhead's desk. Her lowered eyes expressed what I took to be pity. That's the worst part of shame – the eyes. Mercifully her eyes disappeared when the elevator door slid shut. And Armstrong's eyes were focused on things of consequence like the floor indicator. The only staring eyes I had to contend with on the long, ride down were the ones reflected in the mirrored door.

Mine.

At the sight of his boss elbowing an old man across the lobby, the guard sprang unnecessarily from his perch. Armstrong merely muscled me through a revolving door, removed the cuffs, and sent me sprawling with a kick in the ass.

I hit the ground on all fours and froze, mainly because I hated to see the smirk on Armstrong's face as he moseyed back inside. When his laughter died, I plopped down cross-legged. Passers-by passed by. Thankfully, no one offered a helping hand.

The pebbly, decorative sidewalk had scraped the butts of both palms and bloodied my knees. I daubed at the oozing flesh poking through the legs of my new pants.

My Goddamm brand new pants!

My head was racing like an engine with a burned-out clutch. I wanted to go, I wanted to stay. I wanted to shout, I wanted to hide. But what was so soul-shaking about torn pants? I could patch them. As a little boy I had worn patched pants. As an old man I could wear them again. Lots of use left in a pair of patched pants. Wear them to putter in the garden. Wear them to get that colonoscopy.

Face it. What does an old man need with new pants anyway? It's a waste of good resources. Pure economics. A simple truth.

So why was I sobbing?

Chapter Fifteen

"Xuân?" I'd slinked back to the Blazer to call.

"Pete? ..." Her answer was whispered. "My cell is for emergencies. I'm in a staff meeting."

Kicking up outside the car was a Santa Ana – a hot wind that clears the smog and makes for an Indian summer. It's also called a *devil wind* for what it makes people feel and do – something about negative ions. Tucked beneath my wiper blade, a parking ticket fluttered and threatened to tear free. Staring at me from the open lockbox was the .45.

"Something's wrong. *Bad* wrong. My *head* is loose! I ... I think this *is* an emergency."

I heard a muffled aside and the sound of a door. I glanced at my Timex.

Always there.

"Okay, I can talk now," she said. "What is it?"

"I feel miserable. And ... and *good* at the same time. *Too* good and real, real bad. I'm laughing and ..." I hated to say it. "... And at the same time, Christ, I'm *crying*. I haven't cried for 10 years."

"Slow down. It's hard to understand you."

"I know, I know! My thoughts are zooming and I'm making dumb choices. I just got my ass whipped."

"Are you confused, Pete?"

"Jesus Christ, I just said that! I didn't call to fucking talk to myself!"

"Let me *help* you! Are you disoriented?"

"Like, you mean ... who, what, when? No ... no, I think I'm good. Not disoriented."

"Have you taken drugs?"

"I'm no Goddamm hippie! Booze. Smokes. Coffee. A little Vicodin sometimes for the knees, but *drugs*? Hell, no!"

"Not amphetamine?"

"C'mon, speed kills! I'd never – Hey! That's it! I'm *speeding*."

"Could someone have slipped you something?"

"*Starbucks*. The sons-of-bitches dosed me!"

"Hold on, just hold on. Two teas. You dumped yours and I'm fine."

"Man, that stuff is *horrible*. How can you drink it?"

"Focus, Pete. Did you take more pain medicine?"

"No. I was great. And ... wait, wait! Yeah, that's what I was thinking about! I think this started last night and picked up steam. How about someone in the ER? That one nurse looked just like an old girlfriend. Rotten mean. I mean *rotten*."

"All the staff I saw were familiar. It's unlikely."

"The thugs then. They gave Kling a needle. Maybe they shot me up, too."

"That would have been a sedative, wouldn't it?"

"Yeah, right! A sedative. Goddamm it! See? My head isn't working."

I was pounding my fist on the steering wheel and kept glancing back at the Aragon entrance. I couldn't keep my knees still.

"Has this happened to you before, Pete?"

"No way!"

"Milder, perhaps. Think about it."

I squeezed my eyes shut as if the pressure would muscle my mind in a single direction.

"You mean like, maybe ... high on life? Ups and downs? Sure – more downs than ups – but never *this*. How about concussion?"

"Your tests were clear and concussion would cause depression and confu ... uh, *disorientation*, if anything." She hesitated. "Are you a heavy drinker, Pete?"

"What are you saying? Like DT's? I'm not that far gone, for Christ's sake. I quit all the time, *no problemo*."

"Calm down. We have to consider *everything*. Remember?"

"Don't talk like I'm *senile*."

"Pete, I'm only trying to ... What's that noise? That banging."

"I, uh ... I was hitting the steering wheel."

"Tell me what you're feeling right now, Pete."

"What I'm *feeling*? Fucking female questions! How am I supposed to know what I'm—?"

"Forget that. Just forget it! What are you *thinking*?"

"I'm thinking it's go-time, baby! I'm thinking I'll take this .45, head back inside, and shoot me some fuckers."

"You can't say that!"

"Oh, cool your jets. It's just *thinking*, right? You asked."

The fronds of the palm trees lining Main were doing a hula in the wind. The fluttering ticket fascinated me. The wiper blade was losing its grip.

"Do something for me, Pete."

"Man, that wind is blowing," I said. "Feel it?"

"I'm indoors, Pete."

"Oh, yeah, yeah. You wouldn't feel it that way."

"I want you to do something."

"Go fly a kite?" A laugh exploded from me.

"You're in a storm, Pete."

"Damn right. It's gusting maybe 30-40—"

"A *chemical* storm. In your brain."

"Oh, Christ, no! ... Wait. What is that, a chemical storm in my brain?"

"Drugs, hormones, neurotransmitters."

"Hey, that's Kling's gig. I remember you saying—"

"Stay with me, Pete. You have to find a storm cellar."

"We ain't in Kansas no more, Toto."

"Inside yourself, Pete. Go inside."

"Damn it, I don't know what you're talking about. What the hell do you want me to do? Spit it out!"

"Somewhere inside you is a safe space. A space you go to regroup, to heal. A place that's always there for you."

The words jolted me like a slap. I thought of Ronnie who wasn't there, but the feeling was still there. And the *need* for it. I took deep breaths and tried to hold Ronnie's face in my mind. Xuân's face was there, too. I barely knew her, but it *seemed* as if I knew her, as if I recognized her from the past, although I knew we'd never met.

"Okay ... okay, I get it. I'm riding the brakes hard," I said.

"Now listen. Who do you trust *absolutely*? Trust with your life? Trust beyond *any* appearance."

"Hiatt."

"Can you get to the Medical Center?"

"I got *here*."

"Without killing yourself or anyone else. I can send paramedics."

"I said, I have it covered, damn it!"

I knew how I sounded. I just couldn't do anything about it. She let it slide, though. Maybe she understood.

"Ask for Hiatt. Have him—"

"Wait, wait! In case I forget before I forget. Armstrong, head of security for Aragon. Definitely a cop one time. Expert with cuffs. And I think I recognized his voice."

"Thinking you recognize things is part of the syndrome. Like that ER nurse."

"Bullshit! I tell you he's the one. Burdick has Kling, Xuân. I need to go back and—"

"Pete! Pete!" She was shouting.

"What?"

"San Dismas. Ask for Hiatt. Have him call me. Say it."

"He'll stick a tube up my ass."

"Let me guide you. Just for now, Pete. Say it. San Dismas. See Hiatt. Call Xuân. One, two, three. Say it."

"San Dismas. See Hiatt. Call Xuân."

I turned the ignition key. The engine caught. I shot from the curb. She must have heard the squealing tires.

"Pete! Are you driving?"

"Hah! I can thread this sucker through the eye of a needle."

"You *think* you can."

"I think I can, I think I can! Hey! The other cars are all slowing down. I think they want to help me get there. It's so damn cool!"

"Say it. Say it with me. Aloud. San Dismas. See Hiatt. Call Xuân."

"San Dismas. See Hiatt. Call Xuân ... What's with the mantra? Some hypnosis thing?"

"Just keep saying it."

As I chanted, I noticed everything around me lagging. A part of me – maybe a part holed up in that storm cellar – knew that speed was relative, and suggested that, relatively, mine was far too fast. I noticed the Blazer's roar and eased my foot off the gas.

"Goddamm it, Xuân! Am I ever going to be the same?"

"Of course," she said.

"You're blowing smoke!"

My mouth was like an M-16 stuck on auto-fire, but my ears *heard* what I said, and the hunkered down part of me reacted to what didn't sound right.

"That's not me, Xuân. Not even me *exaggerated*. Am I ever going to be *me* again? Am I—?"

I veered onto the City Drive exit ramp and almost rammed a Caddy oozing along in front of me. I slammed the brake, slewed sideways, and snapped back as I hauled on the wheel.

"Pete! What happened? Pete?"

"Am I ever going to be the *same*, Xuân?"

The hollow silence of the cell phone was like the sound of a seashell held to my ear. An ocean sound. The sound of the tide. A retreating tide. A sigh.

"The more things change, the more they stay the same, Pete."

It threw me, but maybe that was the point.

"You're saying that regardless, I'll be alright. Is *that* it? That I'll be alright?"

"Wait and hope," she said.

Chapter Sixteen

Wait and hope was Monte Cristo's mantra, but the words were immediately lost in a buzz of words and pictures and willy-nilly choices swarming through my head like bees. But – as if echoing from some deep cellar – I heard myself repeating aloud my own mantra.

San Dismas.

See Hiatt.

Call Xuân.

I exploded over speed bumps, careened into the hospital lot, and skidded into the first open slot. Jumping from the car, I streaked up the emergency room ramp. Figures on the ramp were turtles and patients in the waiting room were leaden. My mind was accelerating so rapidly, the world's slow motion was becoming static.

Time was about to stop!

But ... if I *had* seized control of time, why stop at zero? Perhaps my mind could spin fast enough to *reverse* time. I flashed on a herky-jerky image of people skipping about backwards, talking in Swedish, flying up out of swimming pools.

Fuck the future! All shifting sand. The past was rock solid. Moving in reverse, broken things reassembled and returned intact to careless hands. Somewhere in the past – somewhere between the almost frozen present and the oblivion before breath – beckoned a perfect instant whose perfection I had missed the first time around. Could I return and freeze-frame *that* moment? Trade all my tomorrows for a single yesterday? Exist as a perfect snapshot?

Should I?

Confronting an admitting clerk, I forced myself to utter aloud the categorical imperative.

"San Dismas. See Hiatt. Call Xuân."

The clerk stood frozen. It was done. I had stopped time!

But no ... his lips were moving, he was talking into a telephone. To what conceivable end? Had I not said the words? What more could be said than *the words*?

"San Dismas. See Hiatt. Call Xuân," I repeated like a Tibetan chanting *Om Mani Pedme Hum*. I reached across the counter, grabbed the clerk's shirtfront, and pronounced the words more precisely, expecting tumbrels to click and the gates of heaven to swing wide.

Nothing.

Perhaps the words were tonal, the sesame secret in their sound.

I tried to mimic the words exactly as Xuân had pronounced them, but a security guard gripped my shoulder. Amused at his presumption, I swatted him away like a helium balloon. The reinforcements who tackled me were funnier still, unaware that I was faster than a speeding bullet and able to bend steel in my hands. Guards flew from the pile atop me, rolled away, jumped up, and leapt back into the fray. I roared with laughter watching some Keystone Kops Kommotion whose tinny score sounded like *See Hiatt. Call Xuân. See Hiatt.*

Pinned finally beneath a half-ton of bodies, I was less angry than disappointed – like the time I was six and broke my collarbone leaping from the roof in my new Superman costume. *To Hell with magic* I'd sworn that day and to Hell with it now. Not Superman, but equal temper of heroic hearts, I readied myself for a shudder that would blast the lot of them airborne.

"Pinel! Pinel! Stop it or I'll let them beat you to death. Do you hear me?"

Arms and legs and torsos held me like cement. My head was frozen, my cheek squashed into the linoleum, but I caught the cape-like sway of a lab-coat and tried to look up.

"San Dismas. See Hiatt. Call Xuân," I spluttered.

Hiatt squatted into my line of sight. I felt fleece-padded leather restraints encircle my wrists and ankles. A few yards behind Hiatt stood an orderly dangling leather belts like a fistful of snakes.

"Check for a gun and carry him inside," Hiatt said.

Hands scurried over me like rats. Cops grabbed my limbs and head. One cop was a woman. I hoped I hadn't slugged her. Face down, I rose from the floor, a rope of slobber dangling from my mouth. I floated through double doors where they flipped me like a flapjack onto a gurney. Since my mission was accomplished, I tried to be accommodating. My muscles had joined the anarchy of my thoughts, however, leaving me twitching, grunting and braying. Cops threaded belts through the wristlets and anklets and buckled me to the bed frame.

"H..hey, c..c..cutie," I managed to stutter at the lady cop who was cinching my right ankle. The tics distorted my sexy wink into something she responded to with a jerk of the strap that almost took off my foot.

Hiatt double-checked the restraints and dismissed the guards.

"What the hell is wrong with you?" he said, shining a light into my eyes.

"San Dismas. See Hiatt. Call Xuân." I had a thousand jumbled things to say, but that was all I could squeeze past the grunts and grimaces.

"Nguyen?"

I stitched together a flurry of twitches that I hoped was a recognizable nod and not a belated sexy wink.

Hiatt shouted orders at the universe. A nurse appeared with a bulging IV bag. Hiatt saw the bag, and that it was good. He grabbed a slew of rubber-stoppered, test tubes from a bedside cart and tossed them onto the gurney between my spread legs. He twisted a sheathed needle onto a plastic holder, then smoothly looped an elastic tourniquet around my bicep and poked the needle into the crook of my arm. Blood gushed into the vacuum-tubes as he thumbed each one into the plastic sleeve.

While Hiatt drained me from one arm, the nurse jabbed an IV into my other arm and hung a saline refill. I felt like a superfluous middleman.

Hiatt spoke. A nurse holding a syringe materialized. While Hiatt squirted the syringe slowly into the IV tubing, the first nurse scissored open my brand new shirt. Screw the shirt. No pocket anyway. The whole fucking outfit was jinxed!

When the nurse slapped electrodes on my chest, the monitor above my head began to beep a crazy paradiddle. Hiatt studied the screen as he scribbled orders on a blank form.

"P-I-N-E-L, Peter," he said to the syringe nurse. "Here last night. Get what you need from the old chart."

"Call Xuân," I croaked, sounding surprisingly clear. The warm syrup oozing through the IV line was a sweet, gooey sap engulfing my thoughts, my senses, my movements, and my will.

Hiatt ignored me.

"Call Xuân!" I said again. The encroaching quietus allowed me to add, "She can ... fill you in."

Hiatt squeezed my shoulder, a tolerant gesture given that my talking was interfering with his work.

"I'm putting you out, Pete. I need to get a handle on this thing."

"I'll wait ... and hope, Doc," I whispered as the warm goo brought everything to a perfectly viscous halt.

Chapter Seventeen

The door at the end of the hall was closed. I tried the handle, pushed inside, and eased the door shut again. Despite utter darkness, I *knew* the office was Ronnie's by a lingering scent of soap or shampoo; a trace pheromone, perhaps. Or was it something else?

The water in a homeopath's tincture of hellebore – diluted until no single molecule remains *but* water – is said to *remember* the hellebore, to retain its quintessence. Do we imprint our surroundings? Do they resonate with that memory?

Or was it simply that I couldn't let go.

I watched myself switch on my pocket light. Among the photos and posters on the walls was a portrait of Ronnie done by a talented kid she had saved from suicide. The portrait captured the devouring look Ronnie sometimes—

No.

Devouring was the wrong name.

Ronnie's gaze neither threatened nor violated. It encompassed, it illuminated, it revealed. Things about yourself. Things about her. Not everything, of course, but what you hoped was *enough.*

Since I *was* watching myself, I knew that I was dreaming. But I was also *remembering*. While Ronnie lay dying at San Dismas, I had searched her Olivewood office for a connection to *El Tigre* and the Fallen Angels. Remembering, I watched myself tip the file cabinet to free the locking bar, then right the cabinet and open drawers.

El Tigre's name anywhere in that cabinet was his death sentence. I found an entire case file. I remembered mouthing his name aloud as if the sounds were an incantation from whose utterance he would wither and die.

El Tigre – Ramon Guiterrez.

He had known her.

And *still* he did that thing!

Why was irrelevant, but I remembered skimming the file. The dream of a memory had become *merely* a dream, however, because all the pages I saw were blank.

"What you *don't* see is often the key, Pete."

As if her voice had tripped a switch, light filled the room, the kind of enveloping glow you remember later when the neglected importance of a moment shines through. I saw her leaning back in the office chair, her feet propped on the desk – just the way I remembered her from my first hello and first good-bye. As always I felt a gut connection to her – that nameless recognition creatures have for their own kind.

"It's not here, Pete."

She visited my nightmares constantly, but rarely my dreams anymore. I missed the dreams. They were precious chances to see and hear her as I wanted to remember her: without pain or fear or guilt.

"Of *course* it's here," I snapped. "I remember."

Her laugh was tinkling, warm, radiant, like silver wind chimes swaying on a sunny day. She was a psychologist, after all, and knew the double meanings of all the unsaid words.

"You're angry," she said. "That's good."

"I'm *not* angry, Goddamm it! How in hell *could* I be? It's just that ... I need your help."

"To find the connection? I said it's not here."

"Then why are *you* here?"

"Curious, isn't it? ... Freud himself posed the question. What do women want?"

"No. What do *you* want?"

"I told you in the hospital."

"Sure, you said you wanted me to end it. But that wasn't what you wanted. Not really."

"No?" Her eyes were alight. "What *did* I want?"

"You wanted me to be there, but *let* it end."

"It's not too late, Pete."

She smiled that smile that I would die for. No ... not die for. *Live* for. That magic-mirror smile that revealed who I was, who I could be, who I ought to be. I reached out to trap her hand like a dayfly between my own hands. But as always, she vanished, leaving me in darkness again.

After a moment I watched myself stoop to retrieve the dropped flash and the file. I thumbed the pages, although what good were blank pages, but I noticed stapled to one blank page, small slips of paper like itemized receipts. A memory can contain detail that's unremembered, yet suddenly recalled. Were the paper slips a real memory or a fiction of the dream?

Like the pages, the slips were also blank, except for signatures, what looked like the *same* signature at the bottom of each slip. I strained to see or recall or even imagine the name.

Was it ... Paul Malek?

Paul Malek! Finally I was getting somewhere.

But who in Hell was Paul Malek?

Chapter Eighteen

"Everything is perfectly fine, Mr. Pinel."

The voice rubbed me wrong. It was affected like a ham actor essaying Shakespeare. And since nothing was *ever* perfectly fine, the reassurance rang false. Expecting the worst, I opened my eyes. My gaze caromed like a Pong ball, settling finally on a lean, smallish, middle-aged man hovering uncomfortably close. His hair was see-through on top, brushed forward over pink scalp. His nose was thin and pointed. A bushy mustache hid a cleft-palate scar. I gave him back a few points, figuring the affected voice represented hard work to overcome a nasal lisp.

"I'm Dr. Malek," he said. "Paul Malek."

I lurched upward, trying to sit, but found myself still strapped to the ER gurney.

"This bondage action is *really* not doing it for me, man," I growled, straining against the chest belt.

"Not doing it for me, *Doctor*. I'm a psychiatrist."

"You gonna fix this or what?" I grunted, tugging at straps

He smiled coldly.

Seeing that brute force was useless, I studied the restraints. The locks were sturdy, but simple, like locks on diaries. I could break into a diary with one hand tied, although *both* hands tied presented a problem.

"That's better," Malek cooed. "I'm here to *help* you."

"A government man," I muttered.

"Are you referring to the university?"

A 60 watt bulb in a 100 watt fixture.

"Listen, Paul Malek, I just dreamed about you."

"Really?" He seemed pleased.

"Yeah, go figure. But the thing is, I don't know you from Adam's off ox."

He smiled condescendingly. "Sometimes, especially right after we awaken—"

"Stick to the singular, Doc. You're creeping me out."

"After *one* awakens ... memory is quite plastic. One remembers dreaming, but not the dream. The subconscious seizes some immediate experience – a face, a name, a snippet of a news broadcast – to fill the vacuum, as it were. One seems to remember dreaming *about* that person or even dreaming the news before it happened."

"I don't buy it."

"Does that really matter?" He flicked a strap like a rein to make his point. "Perhaps a nurse spoke my name. Your unconscious mind incorporated it into a dream. Haven't you ever awakened to a knock at the door while dreaming about, say, a woodpecker?"

"I don't dream much about woodpeckers. Do *you*?"

He scowled.

"You assaulted people, Mr. Pinel."

"Yeah? Well, it happens. Call a *cop*."

"You were hallucinating."

"Call a cop *anyway*. And screw yourself, *Paul*. My mind redlined and I popped a gasket, but I wasn't seeing ghosts or listening to Satan."

"That remains to be determined, doesn't it? I'm ordering confinement for observation and ..." I felt a sadistic caesura. "*Treatment*."

"Places to go, Doc. People to see."

"You fail to grasp the word *order*," he said, leaning closer.

Jerking up against the chest strap, I snapped my head and caught the point of his chin with my forehead. Yelping, he grabbed the bedrail to keep from falling. Thank goodness whatever was wrong with me had passed. I was back to normal again.

"Sorry, man. I was just getting comfortable. These damn belts, you know?"

"The injections you received were obviously insufficient," he hissed, his eyes watering. "I'll correct that on the psychiatric ward."

"I wouldn't go on a psych ward to watch someone piss on you, *Paul*."

"Doctor!"

"Uh-uh, you said psychiatrist. Hiatt is my *doctor*."

"No longer." He took a triplicate form from the wheeled tray beside the gurney and began to print. "I'm giving you a 5150."

"I don't *want* a 5150!" I bucked against the restraints, bouncing the gurney. "Hiatt! Hiatt!"

Metal rings screeched across the curtain rod as Hiatt parted the drapes.

"Pipe down, Pinel. You're disturbing the sick people."
He gave me a quick once over. "No more gibberish. Feeling
better?"

"Better?" Malek interjected. "He assaulted me!"

"In five-points? Definitely on the road to recovery. What
are you doing here, Malek?"

"Security suggested I 5150 the man, *Doctor* Hiatt."

"Did the janitor suggest some meds?"

"Make your jokes. As a psychiatrist at this hospital, I
have the legal power to detain—"

Hiatt snatched Malek's form and read aloud. "Persons
who as a result of a *psychiatric* problem are dangerous to
self, others, or gravely disabled."

"This man is all three!"

"*Tell* me about it. But his problems aren't psychiatric.
He has end stage cirrhosis. Needs a liver transplant."

I tried to sit up again.

"Hepatic encephalopathy caused the agitation. Probably
triggered by a GI bleed. I'm admitting him to my service for
an emergency colonoscopy."

Malek spluttered an argument.

"C'mon Malek … Blood, guts, germs, crap. If you could
stomach that, you'd be a *real* M.D."

Malek ignored the bait. "I'll still need to clear him
before discharge."

"You got it, man. When all the doctoring is done, you
can read the bumps on his head and check his Orgone."

"Just make sure I see him!" Malek said, stamping away.

"What a tool!" Hiatt chuckled.

"Doc! Doc!" I stammered. "W..what's with this transplant?"

Hiatt grinned and lowered his voice. "Relax, Pinel. God knows how, but your liver has survived you so far. And you're not bleeding that I can tell. *Yet*."

"Then why the—"

"Dance with the one who brung ya. Or would you rather go home with *him*?" Hiatt pulled a restraint key from his lab coat pocket and undid my left wrist. "Keep your cool for a while, and I'll undo another one."

My wrist was sweaty from the cuff. I rubbed it against my scissored shirt and noticed my watch was missing. My ring, too.

"Where's my stuff?"

"I gave it to Nguyen. She said you're working for her."

"I can't tell what time it is."

"Four-ten in the afternoon."

"Same day?"

"Same day."

"Five lousy hours? That's not so bad. What was wrong with me?"

Hiatt opened my chart. "Your workup was negative so I asked Nguyen to consult. She thinks you had a drug reaction exacerbated by your cyclothymia."

"Bullshit!"

He chuckled. "You don't even know what I just said. Maybe it means well-hung."

" ... Okay, what's cyclothymia?"

"It means you're moody and a hothead. Do you concur? Also that certain drugs can send you ballistic."

"You believe any of that? She's a *shrink*."

"A damn good one, too."

"All I took was the codeine they gave me last night."

He flipped through the chart. "That wouldn't do it. Probably a stimulant we don't test for."

"Then I'm okay?"

He tossed my chart onto the rolling table. "Unless you die."

"Work on the bedside manner, Doc."

"You want it straight, don't you? Drugs cause intoxication. The effect depends on how long it takes to penetrate your brain and how long it takes to clear. Once it's gone, the buzz is over."

"So I've heard."

"But some drugs are poisons, too."

"Hangover."

"That's the concept. Brain damage, liver damage, heart damage. Temporary or permanent. Depends on the drug."

"And you don't know yet?"

He shrugged. "You're looking good so far. The tranquilizer I gave you blocked the tics and let you sleep. Quick response is a sign that whatever caused the meltdown is out of your system."

"Great!" I wiggled the other wrist. "Then how about—"

"On good behavior, Pinel. The last one comes off *after* I do the colonoscopy."

"What the fuck! You said that bleeding story was–"

"I *also* said that you're sixty and need a colonoscopy."

"Maybe *you* gave me the drug, you bastard! Look who gets his way."

He roared with laughter. "Our minds do work alike, don't they?"

"You *did!*"

"Oh, Pinel, think about it. Would I risk having *you* on the street out of control? But since you're *here* ..."

My free hand was still half asleep. I pumped the fingers making a fist.

"Swing at me, and I'll dose you with crap that'll twist you like a pretzel."

"Doc, you're getting paranoid in your old age. We're *buds.*"

"So why are you smiling?"

"That's a grimace. My hand is killing me. I'm still reined in too tight on this side."

Not about to show caution, Hiatt leaned across the gurney, as if daring me to clock him.

"Plenty loose," he scoffed. "Quit your bellyaching."

"Check it again," I grumbled. "I can't move my fingers."

I was older, slower, weaker, and damn rusty at being smarter. Still – like the old guy in the poem – much abided. While Hiatt was distracted, I slipped my free hand into his coat pocket and palmed the restraint key.

Chapter Nineteen

Run, run, run, as fast as you can. You can't catch me,
I'm the gingerbread man.

Strains of *that* in my head as I skedaddled down the
hospital fire stairs had me thinking my escape was
premature. Testing the mental brakes, I found them mushy,
but felt a grip. Fortunately, people I encountered in the
parking lot ignored my bare feet and gaping shirt as signs
of homelessness. Fetching spare keys I kept in a magnetic
box hidden in the Blazer's wheel well, I fired the engine and
headed home.

Mulling my Twilight Zone encounter with Malek, I
admitted that hearing his name in my sleep made sense.
But might the name have triggered a *memory* and thus the
dream. Had I *actually* seen his name in El Tigre's chart? I'd
taken the chart with me at the time, but it was
incriminating evidence that I might have shredded later. If
I hadn't, however, I'd find it in the cabin storage cellar. I cut
over to the east corridor toll road, an eight-lane mainline to
the sprawling, beige stucco terminus that used to be the
outland of Trabuco Canyon.

Malek and Kling were both psychiatrists at UC San
Dismas. Was Malek in bed with Aragon, too? Such
questions always called to mind Fred Lynch who knew
everything and everybody. Before he stopped talking to me,
a phone call or a visit to the *Banner* newsroom often saved

me a week of legwork. But who could say *what* Fred knew now – if anything. A memory nagged at me – the goodbye I had said to Jesus too late for him to hear.

I pulled a throw-away, cash-as-you-go cell phone from the console and rang information for Xuân's office number. Saving it to speed dial, I called. Her message greeting squeezed an FM voice through an AM filter, but the lilt was still unmistakable. I also perceived a subtle sultriness that struck me as too raw for a shrink's business phone, but then, sultry is probably in the ear of the beholder. I left the cell number for her to call back.

I punched 411 again and scribbled numbers for Paul Malek on the suction-cup notepad stuck to the dashboard. I told a secretary at the first number I was a patient with forms to complete. The address she gave me was at San Dismas medical center.

"I think I need his other office," I said.

She gave me one at Camino by the Sea.

Fancy that.

Xuân rang just as I disconnected. She probably had her voice mail set to page her.

"Pete? You're not at the hospital?"

"My insurance balked. HMO's, you know?"

"That's preposterous!" She sounded ready to fight.

"Hiatt will fill you in. I'm okay now. Honest."

"Okay? ... Not *great*?"

"Some have greatness thrust upon them," I said. "It sucks."

"Great," she said, chuckling. "By the way, I have your personal things. Hiatt gave them to me earlier."

"Thanks, I need them. I'll pick them up this evening."

The cell was warming my ear, so I switched sides. I hated holding the damn thing against my head, imagining microwaves nuking my brain when I preferred it Sushi style. My earpiece had been in my pants pocket, though.

"Dr. Malek," I said. "Know him?"

"Paul? He's Walter's attending psychiatrist."

Bingo.

"Know him well?"

"Not really. Paul started at the university a little after I did and he was in a clinical track from the beginning. He's a unit chief at the med center. He publishes occasionally, but he's not academic faculty."

"Is he also in that facilitated neurotransmission racket?"

"It's *not* a racket," she huffed.

"I'm just *teasing* you, okay? But if they're both sniffing around the same hydrant, it could be important."

"Paul's expertise is in electroencephalography. EEG mapping?"

"EEG ... brain waves, right?"

"Yes."

"Which Kling doesn't have. You said he was flat-line in that department."

"Exaggerated, but yes."

"The ones you saw were done by...?"

"Well ... Paul, of course."

"Was he tight with Kling?"

"No. Very different circles."

"Any connection with Burdick or Aragon?"

"Some. Paul has privileges at Camino, of course. He doesn't treat patients on the research ward, but his EEG lab is there. I think he brain maps study patients in return."

My engine gave a harbinger cough and stuttered as I zipped down the exit at Margarita Parkway. I sputtered past the toll booth in the Fast-Pass lane, exhausted the fumes left in my empty tank, and coasted into a Chevron station.

"So how did Malek end up Kling's doctor if they didn't know each other? Did you pick him?"

"Technically, yes, but mostly it was chance."

"Chance is a mystery," I said.

"And detectives hate mysteries."

"That they do. Listen, can you hold a sec? I need gas."

"I'll wait."

Without my wallet and pocket cash, I had to rummage through the console to glean a handful of coins. Inside the mini-mart a turbaned attendant swiped up the change as if robbing piggybanks to pay for gas were routine. Of course, with gas worth gold, it probably *was*. I found myself wondering what tangle of government red tape had snared the fuel cells I kept reading about? Water to energy – a *real* philosopher's stone. Outside, I plugged the economy-grade nozzle into the tank.

"I'm back," I said into the phone. "So Malek is Kling's doctor because…?"

"The night Walter fell ill, he was taken to the university emergency room. Paul was the psychiatrist on call."

"Why not Camino or South Coast? More chance?"

"Walter was in his office at the hospital."

"Did Malek 5150 him?"

"Yes. Gravely disabled."

"Which made him Kling's doctor?"

"Until I was appointed conservator. But I saw no reason to change."

"Did Malek balk when you transferred Kling to Camino?"

"He suggested it."

I had the self-fill catch pumping slowly, since I prefer a little foreplay with a screwing. Nevertheless, my five bucks whooshed by with a whirr, purr, thank you, sir – barely enough gas to get home, find some money, and get back.

"Hold on again," I said, squeezing the phone against my shoulder to replace the nozzle. A warning sign on the pump pictured a stick man holding a cell phone as he filled his tank. Lightning bolts shooting from the phone had exploded the gas.

Good safety tip!

Back in Saigon I was told that all things were Buddha things, including suicide, particularly self-immolation. I disliked the notion then and, despite the passing years, I still resisted enlightenment. I hopped in the car and squealed away before I was blown to Nirvana.

"One last thing," I said. "Olivewood."

"You're breaking up, Pete.

Picturing lightning bolts zigzagging through the already troubled contents of my skull, I was keeping a few inches of air between my head and the cell phone as insulation.

"Olivewood," I said, jamming the phone against my ear. "The County children's shelter. Does Malek work there, too?"

"Is it important?"

"It's a connection I'm looking at."

"I don't think any San Dismas doctors are *employed* there, but a few consult *pro bono* for the kids' sake. I know Hiatt does. Paul never struck me as charitable, but I could check."

"Do that."

"I'll let you know tonight at dinner. I finish at Camino around six."

I could almost hear her smile at my hesitancy. "Oh, come on, Pete. You can *expense* it."

" ... That might be a conflict of interest."

"Seven o'clock. Pick me up in San Clemente."

A straight-up answer to where and when. The woman was a keeper, but the thought was seconded by a stab of guilt.

"Okay ... you win." I looked at my bare feet. "Seven o'clock gives me time to buy new boots."

"Not on my account, I hope."

Irony. I could almost hear her smile.

"What I'm wearing right now isn't appropriate for the restaurant I have in mind."

"Not formal, I hope?"

"No, but dressy."

"Then suit yourself," she said.

I chuckled. "You're good at this game. Let's do Thành Vì. It can't be far from you. Near the back gate of Pendleton. Do you know it?"

The phone seemed to go dead against my ear.

"Xuân? ... Did I lose you?"

"I know it," she said. She gave me her address and disconnected.

Something had happened.

But what?

Was a Vietnamese restaurant a bad choice? Had her shrink senses detected some unconscious meaning in the choice, like maybe I *wanted* it to be bad? After all, this *meeting* – I refused to call it a date –*was* a conflict.

I glanced at my wrist for the words on the watch that was always there.

But it wasn't.

Chapter Twenty

Hinges groaned and a stale, pent-up sigh escaped the darkness when I swung open the lean-to doors over the cellar stairs. I switched on a flashlight, descended four steps, and stood hunched beneath the ceiling. The cramped space was cold, musty and earthen.

My flashlight beam picked out the usual detritus that collects in such weirs – corroded lawn tools, broken discards, clotted cans of paint. Against one wall leaned rickety, rust-pocked, metal shelving sagging under the weight of white, cardboard file-boxes. A marker-pen inscription on each box named the year it contained – 2010(1), 2010(2), for example – or, on the first shelves, series labeled *Childhood,* or *Marine Corps,* or *College.*

Most of the boxes – my life before I met Ronnie – held no *physical* trace of her, of course. And although she was undoubtedly the regnant element of *all* the boxes since her death, *El Tigre's* file, if anywhere, would be in a box from eight, nine, ten or eleven years ago.

Seven boxes were few to exhume. I could autopsy them in the warm, brightly lighted cabin where I could smoke cigarettes, have a beer or ten. Nevertheless, I placed the flash on a shelf, slid the oldest of the four boxes onto the cold, slab floor, and dragged over a shaky chair I'd never gotten around to repairing.

No visible malignance escaped when I opened the box.
The contents were merely a benign, manila chronology of
letters, photos, records, receipts, tax forms. I thumbed to a
folder labeled Olivewood – my case records for the weeks I
had spent undercover investigating computer thefts. My
write-ups included a police-blotter description of my first
meeting with Ronnie – words that assiduously avoided
emotion. In subsequent notes, she appeared with a now
obvious to me, song-stuck-in-my-head crescendo. How
invisible *then* was that foreshadowing of a life-long
campaign for autonomy tottering toward surrender as
unconditional as Hirohito's.

Glancing unconsciously at my empty wrist for the
engraved promise *Always There*, I marveled at a sudden
recognition: the words that had precipitated from a fluid,
never-*named* feeling – the words *unconditional surrender* –
were wrong.

Always there.

Yes. But with *terms*.

I pounded my fist into my thigh. Goddamm it, I wanted
to miss her! No, I *did* miss her, but I wanted it to *hurt*
more. I wanted it to throb like a swollen, bruised muscle,
not ache insubstantially like a phantom, amputated limb.
The pain I inflicted merely made me feel foolish. Job to do, I
returned to my files.

Just past the Olivewood folder, I discovered a photo of a
woman I had known at the time. Mim was her name; her
last name escaped me. Why had I buried her picture in the
file drawer as if her lifeless image were a sin to discard?

Rifling subsequent boxes, I lingered over unused tickets to a play; my marriage license; a receipt for a weekend at the Ritz Carlton; and, tucked inside a first anniversary greeting card, a Timex watch warranty. One folder recounted my shootout with Lemon Tom. The contents were newspaper clippings rather than case notes, since watching over Jesus was friendship, not business. From the yellowing newsprint, Tom's blank face resurrected the hungry leer he had worn when he shot me, and the falling-angel grimace he made as he died.

Another box held my thick, hospital-bill folder; a few inches farther, my divorce papers. Soon after came society-page squibs – Ronnie and Sharfstein, their engagement, their wedding.

Their honeymoon.

And near the end of that box, Ronnie's obituary. Her funeral.

The rest, continuing into the final box was mostly folders related to the deaths of *El Tigre* and his gang – notes, clippings, depositions, inquest records, lawyer bills, doctor bills. I peeked inside each manila folder, but knew the search was pointless. I remembered shredding a sheaf of text that Ricky the computer whiz had gleaned from a stolen hard drive, information that led me to *El Tigre's* den. The file I took from Ronnie's office was equally incriminating. Undoubtedly, I had shredded that, too.

The folders in the last box slumped backwards because the box was half-empty. I closed the lids, looped the red, string closures, and replaced the boxes on the shelves in order. The emptiness of the last box, however, made me curious. I lifted the next in line. It, too, was lighter than the box I'd started with, and the following box was lighter still.

In the flashlight beam, the white boxes, rising to the overhead, looked like the foundation blocks they obscured. Cement endures, however – always there – while corruptible things interred in a dank, airless place rot. The boxes were splotched with blackish mildew. When I poked at a stain, my finger easily made a hole. Brushing cobwebs from my face to shoo-away any errant brown recluses or black widows, I switched off the flash and climbed back into daylight.

So.

What was the point of all those boxes anyway? Taxes?

The Taxman was a caller you could count on as certainly as the Reaper. And despite any *death closes all* sentiment, the Taxman's bony finger reached *beyond* the grave. Just so far, however. Absent fraud, ten years was a limit that came to mind. Older debt was forgiven.

Late autumn is chilly on the mountain, sometimes freezing at night. The Santa Ana had been a hot wind, however. The morning frost, even that which was usually preserved in shadows and crevices, had melted. Low in the west the afternoon sun still shone bright and warm. Dormant live oaks wore a smattering of waiting leaf buds.

I banged a cellar door shut, then swung it open again to air things out. Not today, but in its season, I'd do some spring cleaning.

Chapter Twenty-one

Doors.

Things known; things unknown.

And in between? The doors.

Entrance doors.

Exit doors.

Doors and choices. Doors and deals. Make the deal. Chose the door.

Free a lady.

Loose a tiger.

Xuân's door was green; a thick, dark, over-painted enamel that gleamed in twilight like polished jade. I jabbed the doorbell and heard a muffled bing-bong like lobby chimes that signal the end of intermission.

The house was a tri-level stack of oblong boxes anchored to a steep hill rising from San Clemente Beach. Two redwood-door, single-car garages sat almost flush with the street. Between the garages, a redwood stairway led to a second level deck and the green entrance door. Red and yellow Impatiens billowed from flowerboxes hanging from the deck railing. Above me French doors opened off a balcony. Beyond those doors, I imagined, was her bedroom.

Perhaps Xuân was also having second thoughts. I rang the bell again and turned to take in the view. Framed between a "V" of downhill houses, the sky was a bruised red-yellow-purple that bled into an indigo void of ocean. The beach was a beige ribbon serrated by orange cones cast by a row of pole-lights. The San Clemente Pier was a narrow, illuminated thrust like an airstrip.

I wheeled at the sound of the door and rediscovered – it had been a long time – that a brilliant thing could still make a catch in my breath. Xuân wore – so feeble a word – she *infused* a neck-to-toe, embroidered silk sheath, an Ao Dai. Although I might ballpark an ordinary one haggled for in a Saigon stall, hers was ceremonial – something a queen would wear and probably *had*. Gold threads and tiny rainbow jewels sparkled in the delicate, dazzling embroidery. The white silk shimmered like a mirage.

"You'll cause a Sigalert in that," I said when I could talk again.

"You chose the restaurant, Pete. I chose my ... costume. It was a gift from Walter. He bought it as a wedding dress, always hopeful I'd marry someday."

"Someone else?"

"Yes, someone else," she said tolerantly. "That story was not written for me, however."

"Stone waste of a gown."

She smiled. "There's always my funeral."

"You Buddhist's are a fun crowd."

"We accept what was written."

"But no one knows what was written, right? So it's not over till the fat lady sings. Maybe at your wedding. Besides ... we write our own stories. And if I'd known I was escorting royalty, I'd have written myself into something suitable – say, my old dress blues."

Her face had a faraway look. "That would have been *wondrous.*"

I laughed. "That would have been *impossible.* Long gone *that* light-foot lad."

"But you still have the uniform?"

"Somewhere."

"The sword, too? That magnificent, pearl-handled sword? What is it called?"

"The Mameluke. The handle is ivory, though, or used to be anyway. Probably some cue ball composite these days. Yeah, I have it."

"Were you a general?" she said, turning her back to lock the door.

In its own way, English is a tonal language, too, and I was missing something. She'd made it clear that we all have scars from that time. I felt as if I were point-man on a punji-spiked trail, but tried to keep it light.

"No stars," I chuckled. "One gold bar for the duration. Attitude problems, they said."

Facing me, she ran a finger over the point of my shoulder as if tracing a gold bar.

"Second Louie ..." She seemed to savor the words. "Isn't that the term of endearment? Second Louie?"

"Not many Leathernecks would call it *endearment,* but, yeah, it's a friendly term. Like *Doc,* I suppose."

I extended my elbow to her for the stairs. She stood fast.

"Many men see a woman in an Ao Dai as vulnerable." Her face was opaque. "She seems bridled by it. The long-sleeved, neck-to-toe tunic, prudishly high-buttoned, tight like a binding over the arms, the abdomen, the breasts."

"Covers everything, but hides nothing is a phrase I remember."

"Exactly. The silk is so thin, translucent. The side slits so revealing – the line of the legs, the swell of the hips, the peep of naked flesh above the waistband of the leggings. A woman seems bound and exposed. That image titillates many men."

I laughed. "I've cuffed and been cuffed by too many bad guys to get off on bondage."

"You don't find the Ao Dai alluring?"

"You in yours? Most definitely. But the base model I know from women wielding AK47s. Those slits gave them the freedom of movement of a queen on a chess board. I mean, it's a pants-suit, for Christ's sake. *Work* clothes. Gloria Steinem probably wears one."

She flashed a smile. "So I've heard," she chirped, skipping down the stairs.

"My car is over the hill," I said when I caught up. "Street parking around here must be bequeathed."

"We can take mine."

"Only if I drive."

"Men!" she huffed, handing me her keys. She nodded toward a telephone style keypad mounted on the right hand garage. "648936."

I punched in the numbers. The redwood door clattered up its tracks. Since the space was compact even for a compact, I squeezed along the wall, scrunched under the

Jag's steering wheel, and backed the car into the street. Xuân shimmied in and slammed her door.

"So, how long have you lived here?" I said.

"Do you mean this house?"

I jerked the floor-shift into drive. The car groaned up the steep incline.

"This isn't *my* house, Pete. How could I afford it? It's Walter's."

Chapter Twenty-One

Thành Vĩ was on Basilone, a short hump from the rear
gate of Camp Pendleton. Although it was a public
restaurant, the words meant *For Members* – a sign common
on the doors of private clubs in Saigon. I'd discovered the
place back in the day during a stint at the base. The
Vietnamese food at *Thành Vĩ* was as close as I had found to
what I ate *in country*. And while only the oldest salts would
remember *that* experience, the Corps' nostalgia kept the
place busy. There wasn't a hippie-haired head in the joint.

No Ao Dais either. When we entered, women scowled at
their gaping dates. I expected excitement from the ancient,
Vietnamese maître de, but his greeting was stiff. He
escorted us to a table next to the swinging kitchen door.

"What about one of those?" I said.

"Reserved," he answered, walking away.

Xuân sat stone-faced. My attempts at small talk stalled.
When I tired of playing with my fork, I barked toward the
maître de, "We need drinks over here, pal."

A waiter – also ancient, but younger than the maître de;
about my age – trudged to the table and greeted me with a
bow. He turned to Xuân, placed a hand on her shoulder and
greeted her in Vietnamese, using informal pronouns in a
worse than informal way. I remembered enough of the
language and customs to know what it meant to touch an

unfamiliar woman and address her in that fashion. I rose from my chair like a missile rising from a silo.

"You meant *Kinh chào quý đàn bà*," I corrected.

He set his jaw obstinately, a step shy of having it set surgically. I called him a few things in Vietnamese that would either make him fight or surrender. He lowered his gaze and repeated my first words – the formal greeting appropriate for a lady.

"Now apologize."

He did, but to *me*! The guy had brain damage or was about to have.

"Apologize to the *quý đàn bà*."

Choosing discretion over valor, he saved me from an assault charge. He bowed to Xuân, and apologized. Formally.

"Bring me a 333," I said, as if daring him not to have it. It was the Saigon brew I drank in strip clubs back then. It was lousy beer, but I was feeling nostalgic. "And a bottle of good chardonnay for the lady with a *clean* glass, got me? Open them both at the table."

The waiter slinked away. "What the hell was that?" I said to Xuân. "Your outfit?"

Her chest was heaving against the bodice of the Ao Dai as if the tight fabric *was* some kind of bondage. She closed her eyes, and I imagined her employing some psychiatric or Buddhist trick, because her breathing slowed.

"The dress merely made the inevitable worse," she said, opening her eyes. "My kind does *not* wear a royal Ao Dai."

"Your *kind*? What's that? Women? Psychiatrists?"

"*Bui doi.*"

My face burned as if she had slapped me. "Mixed blood," I whispered.

"No, mixed blood was *con lai*, the less-hateful term, the one officials used."

"Xuân ... We ... I ..." I had no words. All I could do was wait to see if she would speak to me again.

She reached across the table and touched my hand.

"It was war, Pete. Americans waged it as honorably as possible against a merciless enemy. We were ... collateral damage. The bastard children of mothers vilified as whores. But at least they were *Vietnamese* whores, which in a racist culture left them *something*. The children were nothing. Dust of the earth ... *Night-soil*! *Bui*—" Her voice cracked trying to say it again.

"Just words, Xuân."

"Some words are *actions*, Pete. *Bui doi* was a nightjar emptied over me again and again. The world's disgust with my very existence. Only my mother called me Xuân. After she died? *Bui doi* was *all* I heard."

Some of the gray-haired men around us looked down when she said it. I reached across the table to cover her hand.

"Children left behind. Left homeless. Left alone," she said. "Children left illiterate. Left to starve. Children ... *used.*" Her voice broke again. "Children beaten, murdered, mutilated. Children *blinded*!" I felt her fist clench as she looked up. "Because of our eyes."

When the waiter brought our drinks, *my* eyes sent him scurrying away without opening the bottles. I used the corkscrew on the serving tray for the wine, carefully examined Xuân's glass, and poured. As demurely as possible, she downed half. I pulled my keys from my pocket and used one to pry off the beer cap.

"The generations born here are still nursed on old ways, but an ocean of strangers dilutes the poison. Such concentrated venom is now rare. The old man who owns this place, however, boasts of membership in the royal lineage. His family is steeped in that history."

"You've been here before? You should've—"

"I welcomed it, Pete."

"But ... the Ao Dai? You knew they would—"

"I wanted you to see who I am. I wanted to see who *you* are. And because ..."

A visible shudder jarred the mental fire door she had shouldered shut. I felt a hot blast escape those cool sapphire eyes.

"Đụ họ!"

Conversation ceased. Plenty of people around us knew the phrase. Xuân blushed, but held my gaze.

"I ... I don't usually use such language."

"Don't sweat it. I do."

"This was madness. I should have said something."

"You just said *everything*."

"We can go," she said.

"No way!" I summoned the waiter.

"But why?"

I glared at the waiter and repeated Xuân's words in English.

"Cause fuck, 'em!"

Chapter Twenty-Two

Having made a separate peace, the waiter's cessation of hostilities permitted a fragile armistice. I asked Xuân if she was vegetarian. She said yes, but that she ate meat. That probably made sense to a Buddhist.

I chose dishes typical of the Saigon region where Xuân had lived – a lot of fresh vegetables and less of the fiery chilies that whetted spice-scarred tongues farther north.

In the center of the table were placed assorted communal dishes – some of the no-meat vegetarian kind, others with pork, chicken, a little beef, and, I hoped, no dog. Surrounding the communal dishes were small dipping bowls filled with fish, soy, mint, and peanut sauces along with condiments such as shredded cucumber, bean thread, and cilantro.

After politely slurping bowls of Pho – a rich, noodle soup – we plopped chopstick sized helpings from the communal dishes into our individual bowls of white rice. Dining in Vietnam demanded an etiquette that befuddled chiefs of protocol. I knew the rules no better than I knew my own culture's manners – don't use the table cloth as a napkin, for example – and consequently took my lead from Xuân. Hardest to master, but clearly wise hygiene, was the use of both ends of the chopsticks, the broad end for selecting bits from the communal bowls, the narrow ends for placing morsels in the mouth.

"I spoke with Hiatt," Xuân said between bites. "He told me what happened and said ... should I repeat it?"

"Why not? I've already heard you swear. And *believe* me I've heard Hiatt swear."

"He said to tell you that a tough monkey like you always ends up in the ER sooner or later. One day they'll roll you in and he'll be waiting. Then he acted like he was slapping something against his palm."

I almost sprayed tea laughing. "Flexible fiber optics."

"What does it mean?"

"It means he's doing Ernest Borgnine in *From Here to Eternity*." I tasted the pork *Dhin Gua*. "So explain what happened to me. Hiatt said you thought it was a drug?"

She bowed her head. "Am I not but a shrink?"

"A damn good one according to Hiatt."

She glanced at her tea glass. I inferred that I was supposed to refill it from the ceramic pot on the table without her asking.

"Given the negative tests and the fact you seem fine now, intoxication is the best explanation."

"Cocaine?"

"It can cause similar symptoms."

"I scraped a bit off Kling's rock and tested it on my gums, but that wouldn't light me up, would it?"

"No. What you experienced would take a unique predisposition or a massive dose, probably intravenous. Plus, cocaine would show on the drug screen. Are you sure it was cocaine?"

I shrugged. "Sure that it *seemed* like it."

"Could someone at Aragon have given you something novel? Something they were developing?"

I shook my head. "It started last night. I know it. My sleep was different. I woke up different. It pyramided. Aragon was just the apex." I fell silent for a moment remembering Armstrong's gloating eyes. "Goddamm I showed my ass!"

She gave me a silent space to say more, but I changed the subject.

"No word from the cops? No demands yet?"

"Nothing," she said, placing her chopsticks across her bowl. No wonder the Vietnamese were petite. They were probably starving!

I backhanded another sliver of pork through a translucent brown dipping sauce and plopped it into my rice bowl.

"Did you check into Malek and Olivewood?" I said,

"No mention on his C.V."

"What's that?"

"*Curriculum vitae.* A doctor's resume. As Walter's conservator, I'd asked for one to file."

She seemed to hesitate.

"Something else?"

"I also looked through Walter's charts again."

"And?"

"Well … Paul *is* a colleague. I'm reluctant to mention this in so serious a context. It's probably nothing."

"Let me do my job."

She sipped her tea. I set my chopsticks down on the tablecloth, caught her glance and laid them across my rice bowl. Her smile was my *A for effort*.

"Sometimes doctors ... *massage* records," she said.

"Nice euphemism."

"Usually it's defensive – putting the best spin on what might turn into an unjustified malpractice suit or to get a reasonable fee from the managed care company."

"Like the 45 minute hour."

"Exactly. It's just the way it's done. But looking more critically at Walter's records, I saw things that disturbed me."

"Like what?"

"Remember I said Paul's subspecialty was EEG mapping?"

"Brain waves."

"It's not a mainstream technique in psychiatry, but some investigators believe brain wave patterns can indicate a diagnosis, suggest treatments, demonstrate response. Walter had regular sessions in Paul's EEG laboratory at El Camino. Far too many, really."

"Would it hurt him?"

No, not that, but ..."

"You think Malek's padding his bill?"

"It's possible. I think I already suspected it. I mean, EEG is not a treatment, but since it's harmless and Burdick was paying ..." She shrugged. "But there's more."

I waited. She looked at the half-full dishes and said, "Please, Pete. *Eat*. We can't leave all this. Somewhere children are hungry."

"Someone's hungry right here," I said, shoveling the remainder of each dish into my rice bowl and getting busy with the chopsticks again.

"First, it struck me that Walter was transported to every session by the same orderly. "

"That's unusual?"

"Orderlies are ward staff. Not assigned to a particular patient repeatedly. And when I checked Walter's chart, I found that sessions were cancelled when that orderly was out sick."

"Okay, that sounds unusual even to me."

"Plus, he was the orderly who left the door open when Walter escaped."

"You know how I feel about coincidence," I said, pushing my empty rice bowl away. I arranged the chopsticks on the bowl again, and downed the remainder of the 333. "Do you want anything else, Xuân?"

"An Ao Dai discourages gluttony."

I signaled the waiter for a check.

"I, too, dislike coincidence," Xuân said while we waited. "I looked more closely at Walter's progress notes and noticed behavioral changes on days he had EEG sessions. Small things that wouldn't register unless you focused only on those days and suspected a correlation. Sometimes Walter would sleep through the day or perhaps he wouldn't sleep at all. A few times the nurses noticed him vocalizing. One time he sat making loops on a pad with a pencil as if trying to write."

"His functional matrix was surfacing."

She laughed. "You'll be taking your boards soon, Pete. No. It was minor, but unusual. I mean, an EEG is merely a measurement. Nothing should be changed by it at all. My curiosity, however, led me to something that was *more* than unusual."

"Hold the thought," I said as the waiter came, left the bill, and retreated quickly. Glancing at the total, I peeled currency from the new wad I had withdrawn from the bank on my way over. I dropped the cash on the table and stood.

"Did you leave him something, Pete?"

"Yeah. His teeth."

"I would consider it a favor."

"He should, too."

She took my hand. "I so look forward to seeing you with your sword," she said with a smile I couldn't quite fathom.

"Good thing I didn't bring it tonight, though."

"I felt as if you had ..." She paused. "Nevertheless. whatever I imagine these people owe me is unrecoverable. They're who they are; my anger made me something I don't wish to remain. Help me let go."

Snorting, I fished out a few more bills, and tossed them on the pile. Xuân made a slight bow. I took her arm and escorted her smartly through the door as if she *were* an Empress and I was her Honor Guard.

"Okay. What'd you discover?" I said while the valet ran to fetch the Jag.

"Are you familiar with EEG tracings?"

"From movies. Scribbles to me."

"Scribbles to everyone. They lack the kind of recognizable shapes you see on a heart strip. But many of

Walter's strips were *identical*. I checked carefully. Exact duplicates are impossible."

The Jag squealed to a stop. I opened Xuân's door, slipped the valet two bucks, and squeezed behind the wheel.

"So …" I said, mulling it over. "Kling was going regularly to Malek's EEG lab, yet Malek was putting copies of *old* EEG's in his chart." I dropped the shift into drive and accelerated away. "But if Malek *wasn't* doing EEG's—"

We said it simultaneously.

"What *was* he doing?"

Chapter Twenty-Three

Her lacquered door, jade at sunset, was now hunter-green, a darker, deep-forest hue. We stood outside the closed door, bathed in a footlight glow of deck lights lining the railing. We chatted – the woes of beach traffic, the 'infelicities' of my 'mountain retreat.' The topic of dinner jogged falling-domino memories of Vietnam and left us tiptoeing around dominoes too unpleasant to disturb. I sensed the universe rolling toward some overwhelming question and talked to fill time, buy time, deny time. Inevitably, however, came the caesura.

Keys jangled, a lock turned.

A door opened.

So.

"You should invest in a clapper," I said, peering into the shadows beyond.

"What?"

"You know ... clap on? For the lights. No more entering dark rooms."

"Allow me," she said, stepping inside to flip a switch.

I crossed the threshold and shut the door behind me.

"I bought Sapporo," she said. "Would you mind pouring me a glass of chardonnay? I simply *must*—"

"I know, I know. Some reflex you have to front doors."

In the kitchen I pulled a Sapporo and an open bottle of Kendall-Jackson from the fridge. Finding an opener and a wine glass, I popped the cap of the Sapporo, poured the wine, and carried the drinks into the living room.

Along the beach side of the deck, an L-shaped couch faced a wall of sliding, glass doors. Ocean and sky had merged into a black void penetrated by the thrust of the pier. Clinking the drinks on a glass coffee table, I meandered around the room.

The place was indeed Kling's. Xuân might have chosen modern décor, but nothing so masculine – all straight lines, stiff fabrics, poker-faced colors. I knew she could be linear enough, even hard; I'd seen her meet crisis. But she still had curves. A light side, a soft side. Yin *and* yang.

Bookshelves covered almost every wall. A man's bookshelves are like an x-ray that reveals who he is ... or who he hopes you'll think he is. I noted the absence of knick-knacks and decorations. Kling respected the singular importance of the books. Opening a few volumes, I saw underlining and margin notes. The books were important enough to read, even understand.

The titles were arranged with a fussiness that befit a scientist – alphabetically by topic, alphabetically by author within topics. Chemistry, physics, biology, medicine, and psychiatry predominated with astronomy, geology, and engineering also represented. A selection of history books, mostly about Indochina, was an island in the sea of science. Nowhere did I see a novel.

The bookshelves revealed a man who had little interest in art, philosophy, music, or poetry, and no interest at all in fiction. I felt sorry for him. Without science we die, but without the humanities, we never live. And good fiction – imaginary gardens with *real* toads in them? Fiction shines an essential light on facts. Not simply what they are, but what they could be; what they ought to be; what they mean and how they matter. How false is a world without fiction.

My musing was interrupted when I noticed a small, solitary object adorning a far wall, one I had initially taken as blank. What treasure would Kling so enshrine in white space – his Nobel medal? I went for a closer look.

The artifact was merely a small, framed snapshot. The background was out-of-focus – a squalid, third-world street that could have been anywhere. The hair on my arms, however, told me it was Saigon.

The man in the picture was an old, but much younger Kling, tall and beefy as I had suspected he once was. His hand rested on the slight shoulders of a raggedy child wearing a stained and tattered Ao Dai tunic – no sandals and no trousers. Her almost-almond eyes were Sapphire.

Chapter Twenty-Four

"I changed."

Her voice startled me.

"Sorry. I sneaked up on you again, didn't I?" She wiggled her toes. "I like to go bare."

She had donned a short wraparound. The white fabric, filmy and clinging, was revealing in a way beyond sight, revealing like Braille. I turned back to the photo to keep from staring.

"This is you and Kling."

"I was twelve."

"Saigon?" I said glancing back.

She nodded, but I noticed that she avoided looking at the picture. "Let's sit," she said.

Moving to the couch, she passed a table lamp whose backlight seemed to strip the filmy wraparound from a naked silhouette. We sat on opposite sides of the sectional where the limbs came together. Leaning forward for her wine glass, she pinched her gaping neckline a second too late, an inch too low. Sitting back, she crossed her legs and studiously repositioned the white fabric to cover her thigh. Extending her arm in a toast, she touched the lip of her glass to the neck of my Sapporo bottle.

"What was Kling doing in Vietnam after the war?"

She sighed. "So long ago. Is it relevant?"

"To his kidnapping? I don't know. Frankly, it's you I'm interested in."

"You mean my relationship with Walter."

"He seems a big part of you."

She took another deep breath and a drink of wine. "Walter was invited to study mental illness caused by defoliants."

"Agent Orange."

"Actually a rainbow – Silvex, Super Orange, Agent Blue, Agent Pink, Agent White, Agent Green, Agent Purple. Americans in Vietnam were rare. Walter was useful to the Central Intelligence Agency. He still is at times ... or was."

"Agent Kling. Were you part of either activity?"

"No."

I waited. "... And?"

"Walter brought me here."

I tried to recall a timeline. "Let's see. That would have been ... the American Homecoming Act?"

"Years before. Right after I met him." She glanced involuntarily at the photograph. "The C.I.A. arranged asylum. Walter found a foster family for me in Westminster, and became ... *You* would probably call him my Godfather."

"You think he saved your life?"

"I *know* he saved my life, but my life was nothing. Walter saved my soul."

I chewed on it a moment. "Why would he do that?"

"He was—" She caught herself. "He *is* a *good man*. The children he saw devastated him."

"Okay. But the country was full of kids. Why *you*?"

"We incur some debts before we're born."

"Like Original Sin?"

"Or Original Virtue." The leaden finality in her voice said move on.

"Were you living here with Kling?"

"No. He's a private man. I often stay now because it's convenient. Walter wouldn't object. Before his illness, I often stayed."

"As a God-daughter?"

She toyed with her neckline. "You're obsessed with the idea of me sleeping with him."

"Gratitude sometimes knows no bounds."

"My gratitude to Walter *certainly* knows no bounds," she declared defiantly. "For what it matters, I wasn't asked."

I think I blushed. Whatever was going on, if anything, I'd lost the knack for, but I tried to sound grown-up.

"A detective considers all the possibilities. But that idea you're picking up on? *He's* not part of it."

Her eyes sparkled with an eerie, blue fire.

"Listen, Xuân—" My tongue was dry and my voice cracked. I gulped my beer. "I know we only just met, but you're ... quite a package."

"*Really*? Like a Christmas present? Or more FedEx?"

I chuckled nervously.

"No. Tell me, Pete. How so?"

"Fishing for compliments is hardly like a psychiatrist."

"I'm also a woman, Pete," she said, re-crossing her legs. *That was true.*

"I think the usual script has you say that I'm bright and ironic and...?" She made a coaxing gesture.

"Cool and quick and funny," I chuckled. "What's par on this hole?"

She pouted. "You omitted ... how would you put it ... a *knock-out*?"

"Well, see ... I'm a feminist."

She laughed. "In for a penny of objectification, in for a pound, I always say."

"Smarty. Okay, so you're one darned knock-out and you saved my life, too."

"Flattery will get you places, Pete, but you needn't ..." She smiled. "Strain credulity."

We both laughed. "Fine. I don't *know* that you saved my life, but you watched over me. So, sure, maybe there is some of that ... what do you psychiatrists call it?"

"Lust."

"No! I was thinking transference."

"The feelings of transference are displaced from the past, shadows of illusions. Lust – whatever its roots – is here and now and altogether real. Does that disturb you?"

"All things are Buddha things." I was trying to sound cavalier. "...Only it's ... it's been a while since I lusted."

She leaned forward. "In your heart?"

"In my anywhere."

"Ten years?"

"Get real! A Hall-of-Famer horn-dog like me?"

"I don't mean sex. Has it been ten years since you *longed* for anyone? Anyone *else*?"

I shrugged. "Ten years since I could feel okay about it."

"Suggesting you feel okay about it *now*?"

Damn, she was good!

"Not okay, but ... less *not* okay. Does that make sense?"

"Perfectly. What was your wife's name?"

"I, uh ... I told you."

"I remember. But I want you to say her name."

I took a deep breath. "Ronnie. Veronica Lamb. Sharfstein when she died. She was a shrink, too. A psychologist. She worked with kids. Loved them, but scared to have any. She left me and married another guy."

"You must've been enraged."

"Damn straight. I wanted to kick his ass. At *first*, anyway."

"You weren't angry at ... may I also call her Ronnie?"

I nodded.

"You weren't angry at Ronnie?"

"Nah ... How could I be? I knew it was me. She was great."

"Some have greatness thrust upon them. How did you put it, Pete? It sucks?"

Our knees touched as she swiveled to face me. Reprising the now-you see-'em, now you don't-trick with the wraparound, she picked up her wine glass from the table.

"Was there ... infidelity?"

"No! I *loved* her. She loved me. No, nothing like that. It was my work. She couldn't handle my work."

"Isn't your work part of *you*, Pete? Isn't it the most *important* part of you?"

A feeling stirred. A feeling buried long ago without a funeral. A feeling still too deep to recognize. I was pissed at myself for burying it; pissed at Xuân for disturbing it. I wanted to grab her. I wanted to make *her* feel something, too. I think she saw how close to some edge I was, but her sapphire gaze was unflinching. She rose, stooped for her glass, and silently walked to the stairs. As she ascended, I watched her legs through the suspended redwood risers. Her naked feet paused for a moment near the top. The white wraparound fell and draped the step.

I'd slept with women since Ronnie – more than I cared to remember. A preponderance of pick-ups. Faces I couldn't recall; names I rarely knew or cared to know; no one I wanted to *be* with. How could I *be* with someone when I was always there with Ronnie?

What I imagined in the restaurant *could* happen; what I suspected entering the house *might* happen; what I knew when our knees touched *would* happen, was happening. I crossed the floor – basic instinct, I plead; not from choice. I climbed the stairs – irresistible impulse, I argued; no criminal intent..

No mens rea, I maintained. *No guilty mind.*

Halting, I balled the wraparound in my hand, and pressed it against my face to inhale the smell of her body.

I decided I needed a better lawyer.

My mind was as guilty as homemade sin.

Chapter Twenty-Five

In the dark at the top of the stairs, Xuân lay propped on her side across a low platform bed. Broken light through vertical blinds splashed her body with zigzag shadows like camouflage paint. All she wore was her wine glass – a pose straight from a 60's men's magazine, which was a better time for men's magazines, but then, old men always think such stuff about something.

Words were superfluous and mine would've been wrong, anyway, so I crossed to the bed. Dropping her eyes – black in the dim light – she allowed me the icy pleasure of watching without being watched. And when she looked up again, her flashing gaze kindled me with the fiery pleasure of discovery. She stretched languorously to place her wine glass on the nightstand. Light and shadow played across the hills and valleys of her body.

She was a lot younger than me and I was as old as I had ever been. Hand on my belt buckle, I paused. Noticing the hesitation, she rolled onto her stomach, resting her head in the crook of one arm. The privacy felt strangely intimate. I kicked off my boots, shed my shirt and tie, and wriggled from my pants.

Sitting on the side of the bed, I watched the regular rise and fall of her back and imagined for a moment that she had fallen asleep. My flash of relief irked me. I touched the curve of her waist, felt her respond, swiveled to stroke the swell of her hips, and discovered – God-almighty! – like some ludicrous TV repairman in an old stag film, I still had on my socks! I yanked off the socks, but stalled at my skivvies. The erstwhile inevitability of the moment had abruptly sicklied with the pale cast of thought.

The problem was software, as it were, not hardware – I had ways of knowing *that*. And although it had been a while, this particular ability was one *honed* by disuse. Excuses swirled in my head like disturbed bats in a cave. I felt laughable, but told myself that, when you look at it, everything about sex is laughable. Except the sex.

I try to treat worries like dairy products. Let them sit, if necessary, but an expiration date gets them tossed. This one had curdled. I pulled off the skivvies.

Having seen the elephant – although no elephant was *then* to be seen – I fell back on experience and grit. I bobbed and weaved, feinted, moved inside and clenched, but each stratagem suffered in its execution.

Backpedaling, dazed but game, I told myself I could still go the distance, win by a decision. I'd been in trouble before and I'd fought my way out.

Cover up, Champ. Keep your head down. Use the ropes. Wait for the bell and hope for a break. You can still pull this off barring a below-the-belt 'what's wrong?' No foul drops a guy as surely as that low-blow 'what's wrong?' But otherwise? It's still yours, Champ, all yours, as long as she doesn't—

"What's wrong, Pete?"

And that was that. Lights out, no eight count. I flopped onto my back.

With any respect for Queensbury rules she would have retreated to a neutral corner, but no – she curled herself around me like a snake on a caduceus. Gratefully, her eyes were closed; at least I think they were. I wouldn't look.

"Listen, Xuân—" I said to the ceiling.

"Shhhhh. We're new to this with each other, Pete, and … well, I've not been with many men I wanted to be with."

I turned to look at her. "What do you mean?"

She shrugged. "All things are Buddha things. I just felt uncomfortable for a moment. I'm sorry."

"But it's—"

"Shhhh." Her head was resting in the hollow of my shoulder. "I'm listening to the music of your heart."

"It's … it's not *you*, okay."

"Oh, Pete, I know *that*. You're probably gay."

I tried to bolt upright, but her twined limbs restrained me. Her laugh was a kaleidoscopic sound-burst. Helplessly I laughed, too, because a lot of tragedy is pretty Goddamm funny. Our laughter was not *joyous*, not *free* of pain and fear and guilt, but momentarily we were beyond their reach. Like kids at a pajama party, we sputtered and rolled with tears in our eyes, held our sides, and tried to catch a breath. And when I did, I kissed her until I had to breathe again. I rose onto my knees and looked down at her legs spread like wings around me. I leaned forward, clutched her wrists in my hands, and drew her arms over her head. Sinking onto her body, I pinned her, supporting myself on my elbows, but letting her feel my weight.

"Turn over, love," I whispered in her ear. "Make your voice real deep and speak to me of football."

We laughed again. Two ironic souls playing bowls on a splitting wreak. But it was all right then. Everything was all right. I got the decision. And made a good showing in the rematches.

Chapter Twenty-Six

Seeing her naked in daylight, I regretted promising to let her sleep. I crept from the bed, dressed quietly, checked that her alarm was set, and tiptoed downstairs.

Rummaging through cabinets looking for instant coffee, I turned up a half-dozen varieties of herb tea and – I smiled – an unopened bag of Starbuck's French Roast. Retrieving my discarded coat from the couch, I paused a moment before the framed photograph.

The hand on the tiny girl's shoulder might have been a wing she was tucked beneath. Xuân looked up at Kling with a wide-eyed stare that could only be called adoration. Kling, however, was tough to read. His posture was straight, but not rigid or frightened, not braced like a boot in front of a drill instructor. His face was equally cryptic. I sensed a shadow of pain and noticed in sunlight a fresh cut over one eyebrow and another on his lip. I wasn't reading physical pain, though – more a heaviness. Was it the pain of burden? The weight of the responsibility he was about to assume? At the same time, however, I sensed something light and soaring; something that transcended burden. I thought I recognized that look from somewhere back, but couldn't quite remember where or give it a name.

Sunlight seemed to burn in the blurry storefronts. I saw neon – bar signs, probably. Directly behind Xuân, on either side of the black doorway, several indistinct female figures lounged against the wall. Their poses were universally recognizable. The doorway was that of a whorehouse.

I closed my eyes for a moment. When I reopened them, the photograph had developed a strange sense of depth that took a moment to identify as merely the room reflected in the glass of the picture frame. Glancing back, I caught something in the corner of my eye. Hooked to a charging cord on a small writing desk sat a Kindle Reader.

It was hardly odd – people with Kindles also have books – but I switched it on. The Kindle was Kling's: the titles mirrored the topics on the shelves. Buried in the middle, however, was one that didn't fit.

Harry Potter and the Sorcerer's Stone.

A single novel was curious enough and Kling was an unlikely Potter fan. Of course, Xuân might also use the Kindle. After all, it was charging. Nevertheless, *Sorcerer's Stone* was a coincidence hard to ignore. I slipped the Reader in my coat pocket.

Humping the hill to my parked car, I found myself whistling. If it meant anything, the Kindle was a lucky find since hiding things in plain sight often works. Chance does favor the prepared mind, however. Eager to see what I had, I jumped in the Blazer and headed for my office.

Feeling good in what I hoped was a normal way, I let myself smile at women stopped for traffic lights and even had a few smiles returned. I blamed the distraction for overlooking the car following me until I was pulling away from Starbucks.

Chapter Twenty-Eight

A black Expedition, piloted by two Latino skinheads, was keeping an amateurish distance. For confirmation I drove about a mile to allay suspicion and stopped for gas. The Expedition continued past, circled the block, and reappeared on the side street behind me as I pretended to top off my tank.

Sometimes you want to be spotted, but I suspected my shadows were merely lousy tails. Regardless, I retrieved my shoulder rig from the lock box where I had stashed it when I picked up Xuân for dinner. The goons might have skills not yet demonstrated.

Driving to the office, I timed stop lights to help them keep up. Normally I use the outside lot to save money, but this time I chose the building garage. Eyeing my mirror at the ticket-spitter, I saw the Expedition pull into the lot across the street and park facing the garage exit. I was tempted to roust them just to feel tough again after Armstrong's ass-whipping, but opted instead for a potential freebie. If the skinheads were dumb enough, they might lead me to Kling.

For that gambit I needed a new ride, but I was years rusty stealing cars. I could get inside easily enough, but once there, electronic theft devices could stymie me without time and tools. I prowled a few levels and spied an ancient Impala that any self-respecting boy from my era learned to hot wire by fourteen. I stowed the Blazer a floor below and stashed the Kindle in the lockbox for safekeeping. Disguising myself with a black watch-cap pulled over my ears, I hoofed it back to the Impala with a Slim-Jim and a screwdriver. Low rent buildings forego security cams, but a surprise witness was always possible, so I moved quickly. I shimmied the Slim-Jim into the Impala's window well, tripped the door lock, bypassed the ignition, and was gone in sixty seconds.

My conscience rebelled, however, reminding me that I was a thief, not a repo-man. I pawed through glove box papers and found a name, address and phone number to square things with the sad sack whose car I had conscripted.

Near the exit I grabbed an open slot with a view of the Expedition across the street and waited twenty minutes. When it drove away, I averted my face, paid the attendant with the ticket for the Blazer, and eased into traffic.

The skinheads took I-5 south and veered toward the ocean on the 55. When the freeway ended near the fairgrounds, they continued along Newport Blvd and turned into a place I recognized by its lighted sign – cotton swabs crisscrossing a pool table. I drove past and circled back.

Perhaps the goons were killing time, but Manny had mentioned the Cue Tip's new owner was Sheik Mendez, so I assumed he had sent them. Whether their mission had anything to do with Kling and Ronnie was a mystery, but Sheik's brother once shot pool with

Burdick, and Manny had alluded to a continuing business arrangement. The coincidence – I chuckled at the phrase that seemed to be trending – *strained credulity*.

Beyond the red double-doors was an answer. This time, however, the old man would have an equalizer. I donned the holster, chambered a round, and clicked the thumb safety in place. I wiped down the Impala in case I had to ditch it, and left it idling since I might be running if I returned. Pulling on my coat again, I went inside.

Although my familiarity with the Cue Tip was nodding and strictly business – tables and drinks were a lot cheaper everywhere – I was glad to see that Sheik had let the place be. It was hard to find a *real* pool hall anymore – one without a juke-box or noisy, family-friendly video games. The Cue Tip had neither. I took a moment to savor the gentle click of balls colliding and the soft plops they made dropping into leather pockets.

Above each green table a shaded fixture cast a bright cone of light. Elsewhere the room was shadowy with secluded nooks perfect for making bets, exchanging money or drugs, closing deals of any kind. In one of the nooks – a booth along the rear wall – sat the skinheads, big and round like fat spiders. Both sported unzipped red and black Angel's jackets to cover the hardware.

Ambling back to their booth, I saw how much uglier they were than I'd imagined. Their globe-like heads bore black stubble shadows that reminded me of continents. Puffy scars looked like mountain ranges in relief. The goons blanched when they recognized me, but awaited orders from the tall, wiry *hombre* squeezed between them. Dressed in a shiny, light-blue suit *sans* tie, Sheik Mendez looked every bit the prosperous businessman on casual Friday. You don't buy stock in a huge criminal enterprise, however, and, family or not, you don't inherit it. You *kill* for it. I kept my hand on the automatic.

"Pete Pinel," Mendez said, eyeing me as calmly as a sunning lizard eyes a fly.

I knew him from the media, of course, and we'd come within shooting distance a few times, surprisingly few given our lines of work. His face had always seemed long-ago familiar, though, like that of a movie extra you recognize but don't remember.

"The years have not been kind to you, man," he said. "You're looking old."

"I'm surprised you *are* old, Mendez. Shatters my faith in karma."

"Let's be friends. Call me Sheik."

"Sheik," I snorted. "What's with that? Your mother in love with Valentino? You a fan of Lawrence of Arabia?"

"Don't know Valentino. The movie I liked. Fact is, though, you *gringos* gave me the name. Couldn't say the real one."

"Which is?"

"Xiuhcoatl."

"Right. Let's stick with Sheik."

His eyes looked disappointed, although why a gangster would suddenly get touchy about his name was a mystery.

"So ... you come to shoot pool?"

"Your flunkies were tailing me. Why?"

The skinheads stared at the table.

"I want what Kling had. Do *you* have it?"

Honesty can be quite a time-saver, but it's not *always* the best policy.

"Yep," I exaggerated.

"No joke? Let's see," he said.

"It's safe. Is Kling?"

Sheik's honesty had limits. Copping to kidnapping, for instance.

"See if he's wired, Jorge."

One of the goons stood. Slowly, so as not to startle anyone, I drew the .45 and flicked the safety. English-as-second-language schooled or not, the goon recognized the international symbol for *no* and froze. Not from fear, though. You wouldn't share Sheik's booth if you had much fear in you. It was simply that a public shootout was an executive call, above a goon's pay grade, and he was waiting for the nod. Mendez drew leisurely on a cigarette, blew smoke my way, and signaled his man to sit.

"Smoking is illegal in here," I said.

"I know," Mendez replied indifferently.

What was it with all the scofflaws?

"Why would I be wired, Sheik?"

"You wouldn't. But you've been … I'll say it kindly … semi-retired. Old age changes a guy. I needed to see if you could still be useful."

"So this is what? A job interview?"

"Sure. The tail was a test. See if you would make my boys and follow them back. And showing your dick in my joint rather than take a frisk? You haven't lost your balls, man."

"Tho' much is taken, much abides," I said. It was over his head, but I said it anyway because I didn't like the old age crack.

"*Ulysses*," he snickered. "You geezers love that poem."

I hadn't featured Sheik for a man of letters, but left it for later.

"So what's the angle?"

"Kling had to have a reason to find you. He gave you something, told you something."

"Are you looking to trade?"

"I would if I had him."

"But you know who does."

"Sure I do."

"Can't wait to hear."

"Listen, Pinel … even if Kling told you enough to find what I want, the word is you can't use it. Odds are you don't give a damn anyway. It's just bait to you. This is strictly personal."

"Personal?" I tried to keep my face straight and my voice flat, but I was ready to stomp the accelerator if he said the wrong thing. "How's that?"

He touched the side of his head to indicate my stitches. "The guy was on your turf, *viejo*. Someone snatched him. *Shot* you! Time was, a diss like that was personal."

He hadn't mentioned Ronnie so I backed off a notch.

"Okay. But a smart *hombre* like me could have it all, right?"

"Or nothing," he said. "Brains and balls aren't enough for this one. You need me."

"That'll be a bad day. Need you for what?"

"An army."

I weighed the idea. "That's an unholy alliance, Sheik."

"Sure. Like the Russians and the Americans double teaming the Martians' ass."

"You're too young for those movies."

"Mystery Science Theater 3000. DVD's. Got the boxed set."

"Costco?"

"Yeah."

"Great prices and a gut load of free samples. Steer clear of that Kirkland crab salad, though."

"Good safety tip ... So here's the deal, Pinel. We'll get Kling back and resolve your personal problem. Afterwards I get what he was snatched for."

I ran it forward, toying with the angles.

"Or I could just kill you now," Mendez drawled at my hesitation.

If Sheik had a hand in Ronnie's death, I'd make sure he got his chance. I was pretty sure his gang involvement had come later, however. Innocent would never describe him, but innocent of *that* probably fit.

"Okay, Sheik. You and me against the Martians. But I was a Marine, so *you* have to play the Russians. Where's Kling?"

"Show me yours first."

I rolled my eyes. "Right. I brought it with me."

"Okay, okay, so there's no crazy Pinels. But I won't make a play for a *description* now, will I?"

I gripped the .45 a little tighter, brushing my thumb over the safety to make *sure* it was off. All I had was a hunch. If I didn't convince Mendez I had the Stone or at least a good lead, he might give his goons that nod.

"Computer files," I said.

"Have you opened them?"

I watched the goons tense, probably from a knee under the table.

"Not yet."

"Not *ever* is the rumor. But let's get real, Pinel. I need to see more pig in your poke than *computer files*."

"*No problemo*," I said. "Try Philosopher's Stone."

I felt the tension level drop – from ten to eight, maybe.

"Okay … that name has come up. You know Aragon Pharmaceuticals?"

"Les Burdick's company. He and your brother used to shoot pool."

"Frankie was better. Burdick has Kling."

"Why?"

As soon as it slipped out, I knew I should have kept my mouth shut.

"Maybe he knows the secret formula for classic Coke," Sheik said with a grin. "You're not as sharp as you were, Pinel. Better for me that way."

"What's to stop me trading with Burdick?"

"Self-interest."

"As in, you'd dust me?"

Mendez scoffed. "No, Pinel. I've seen you play. You consider Death a goalie, and you always think you can bend it, man."

That familiarity again. It bugged me.

"You talk like you know me, Sheik, but I don't remember you having the pleasure."

He shook his head with another fleeting look of disappointment.

"Jorge, Luis. Go shoot some nine ball."

The goons got up and moved to a table behind me. I didn't relish their position.

"I'd tell them to shoot straight pool, but I don't think they count to fifteen," Sheik said. "They'd take slugs for me, though. That's worth more than calculus." He dropped his cigarette in Jorge's glass and lit another. "We met a long time ago. Top of the World Park in Laguna."

"Really? I remember meeting your brother there. I bet he pissed blood for a week," I said laughing. "Two other punks, too. One ran like a scalded dog and a tall guy, more balls than brains, totally wasted, he—" My déjà vu made sense suddenly. "That was *you.*"

"That was me. The other one, the runner ... Ricardo? Carjacked an old lady at MainPlace next day. Wrapped her beat up old Vega around a light pole. Served most of three to five and now all he drives is his wheelchair. For me and Frankie, though, that night was an eye-opener. He used to joke that you were our mentor."

"He told me that once."

"He meant it. I quit the crack, finished high school. Even college. Got a degree."

"Criminology?"

"Accounting."

"They're connected."

"Frankie got serious, too. Worked his way up and took over 12th Street. He handled Burdick's distribution."

"Not the aspirin."

"Not the aspirin."

"And now it's your job."

"Off and on. Hasn't been much to distribute for a while. I'm looking at other arrangements. The Stone is part of the plan. I'd say the *critical* part."

"That sounds a little threatening."

"C'mon. How would you take to that approach? If I need to kill you, I'll do it without a threat."

"Noted," I said. "Okay, Sheik. Deal. Where do I find Kling?"

"You're the detective, man. Detect."

"The game is afoot," I said.

"Just remember, Sherlock, I'm lousy at waiting."

"Shame," I said. "Monte Cristo said the key to life is to wait and hope."

Mendez said nothing, which I took as permission to leave, but I backed out anyway. Unholy alliances have a way of unraveling, and I'd never trusted the Russians one Goddamm bit.

Chapter Twenty-Nine

The Impala sat idling where I'd left it. In Newport it might be towed as an eyesore, but – surrounded by a donut shop selection of Mercs, Jags, BMWs, and Escalades – it would hardly be stolen. I highballed it back to the office, but parked at a meter a block away in case the Impala's owner had missed it. I patched the ignition as best I could and crammed the wires in place. Taking my tools and wiping the car down again, I left it locked with $200 in the glove box to ease my conscience.

To retrieve the Blazer, I pleaded a lost-ticket and surrendered the full-day rate ransom. Who said crime pays? I moved the Blazer across the street and pocketed the Kindle. Before crossing, I scoped out the area, realizing I'd be looking behind me more than usual now that Sheik was my ally. Using the service corridor pay phone, I dialed the number I'd lifted from the Impala's glove box.

"Sentry Insurance," chirped a man's voice. "How can I save you three-four-or-even five-hundred dollars today?"

"Mr. Packard?"

"At your service. Call me John. Let me get your name and number."

"You drive a '65 Impala?"

"Did you hit it? I hope you're insured!"

"I borrowed it for a couple of hours."

"What the hell?"

"But I returned it."

"No way, pal! You took it, it's yours. Just make it disappear, okay?"

"You don't want your car?"

"Is this a gag?"

"I left it at a meter a block north. Good as…well, as good as it was."

"Wait, wait!" He lowered his voice. "I insured it as a classic restoration. Dig?"

"Needs some finishing touches."

"Don't get all righteous on me, pal. A guy like you must know what's what."

"Sorry. Can't help you."

"Do the right thing here, man!"

"Wrap some electrical tape around a few bare wires under the dash. You'll find two hundred bucks in the glove box."

"You *have* to be kidding. Listen … go steal it again, and lose it this time, okay? You're two hundred ahead! Easy money."

"I think not."

"You *owe* me."

"Have a nice day, John."

"My damn luck," I heard him say as I disconnected. "An honest thief."

In my office I woke up my computer, but had to wait while the virus valet and various updaters brushed its teeth and combed its hair. Meanwhile, I paged through the Kindle's table of contents again – just books, as far as I could see. I opened a half-dozen titles, which all

looked legit. I went back to the contents, clicked the one of
interest, and *voila*!

Harry Potter and the Sorcerer's Stone by Helen
Rowlands.

Ever the optimist, I expected a pony to accompany the
gift manure. Scrolling the pages, I looked for an inserted
comment, highlighted words, secret code – *anything* besides
Harry Potter. Perhaps the pony was draped in an
invisibility cloak.

When my computer signaled it was ready to face the
day, I typed in my password. From a knot of various cords
and chargers in a bottom desk drawer, I pulled out a USB
connector that fit the Kindle. Since detective work had
become largely electronic – Google, public record databases,
Facebook, Linked In – I was savvy enough to know that an
electronic reader was really just a storage device with add-
ons. When I plugged the Kindle into a USB port on my
desktop, the screen flashed a *loading Kindle drivers* pop up
and then an *autoplay* window. The Kindle was now a linked
external drive. Clicking *open folder to view files* brought up
the Kindle's directory, a list of all its stored files and
programs. I saw four folders. Active-content-data. Audible.
Documents. Music. The music and audible folders – those
would store mp3s and audiobooks – were empty. The
documents folder was a long, scrollable page whose main
entries were the e-books from the contents page. Below each
of those, however, were files with extensions I didn't
recognize – .EA, .HAN, .PHL and others. Extensions specify
which computer language the words and commands of a file
are written in. None of my computer programs spoke those

languages – most were probably specific to the Kindle operating system – but I was able to open them with the Notepad program and read the contained code as plain text. Sometimes that helps if a file has words in it, but most of what I found was gobbledygook – long strings of letters, numbers and strange symbols that might mean something to someone, but not to me. I Googled *Kindle file extensions* and learned that the ones I was looking at were all routine parts of the reader's operating system, including those in the *Sorcerer's Stone* file.

The active-content-data folder contained files identified by long numerical names. I opened those in Notebook, too, and got a lot more of the same gibberish.

Clicking the *tools*, *folder options*, and *view* tabs, got me a list of check boxes. I checked *show hidden files and folders* and unchecked *hide protected operating system files*. No previously hidden content appeared in the four Kindle folders, but the directory now included a fifth folder named *System*. That one, presumably the code to operate the Kindle, was full of undecipherable things. If what I wanted was parked there, I wouldn't find it on my own.

So far, my big clue was a bust. But Mendez had accepted the idea that Philosopher's Stone referred to computer files. How likely was it that *these* files merely evidenced Kling's secret obsession with teenage wizardry?

The thought conjured an image of Ricky, once a *real* teenage wizard, a computer hacker whose feats, although benign in intent, were legendary. Now pushing thirty, he remained every bit the wizard.

We met when he was seventeen, a few years before Ronnie died. Ricky was stuck in a quasi-legal, Federal lock-up, accused of hacking into everything from CIA secrets and his own FBI files to NORAD launch codes. All of that was true, of course, but the evidence was framed. His parents had hired me to help their lawyer spring him. Before we could, however, his Dad – a corporate-weary, IBM drop out in the Age of Aquarius – was murdered senselessly in front of his Waldeneque San Dismas shop, Positively Fourth Street Electronic Repair. Fearing Armageddon if Ricky got access to a computer, the Feds refused to let him attend his Dad's funeral. When I uncovered information that forced his release, Ricky and I became, well ... *something*. For a while I took him to Angel games, gave him advice if he asked, and sometimes when he didn't ask. When I went after Ronnie's killers and almost didn't make it, Ricky's computer genius helped save my life. I hadn't talked to him in a while, though. I had allowed all my human connections to wither. I felt ashamed that I had to look up his number.

"A Little Blue," said a velvety female voice. "Richard Touring's office."

Positively Fourth Street had made Ricky a living of sorts after his Dad died, but kids grow up. Ricky had a second business now, his day job.

"Pete Pinel. Can I talk to Ricky? I'm an old friend."

"Mr. Touring is unavailable. May I take a message?"

"What if I say it's a matter of life and death?"

"I'll include that in the message."

A *human* firewall. It made sense for Ricky to have a good one since firewalls were more than a hobby now. They were that day job – the public part, anyway, the part not classified. I gave the lady firewall my number and, killing time, pecked at my keyboard. Although stumbling on something useful was about as likely as a monkey typing Macbeth, no one stumbles on anything sitting still.

The cell rang almost immediately.

"Pete? Pete, is that you, man!"

The voice was as young as ever.

"Say, Ricky. I didn't mean to interrupt anything. It's not *really* life and death. I can–"

"Bag that noise, man. Hold a sec while I bail from this other call."

I heard him tell someone to keep going, he'd dial back in shortly.

"Central *Un*intelligence Agency," he said, talking to me again. "Conference calls are like soap operas. If I call back a week from now, I won't have missed a thing. No wonder we have high taxes. Zup, buddy?"

"I have a Kindle."

"Techno-Pete! Cool."

"I think it has something stored on it besides books, but I can't find it. Would you look?"

"Good times, man! Way long since I had to worry about prison food. How soon?"

"ASAP?"

He barked instructions. "Jeri's on it. Wait till you meet her. She is *awesome!*"

"Watch yourself, Ricky. People sue these days and I hear you have a little money." I felt silly saying it, but I did.

He laughed. "You'll see. Hold on." I heard him ask *what time* and a silky reply *1:30*. "I'm sending the jet, Pete. Executive terminal at John Wayne. 1:30."

"That's—"

"Don't punk out this time, man! It's faster than FedEx, plus I want to show you what I've done up here." I heard the silky voice again. "Gotta go, Pete. Jeri will blue-screen if I leave the Agency hanging much longer. Christ, I gave them Bin Laden twice before they got him. They'll face-plant on this thing, too. See ya soon."

A private jet was extravagant. But when a hacker kid creates the world's premiere Silicon Valley computer security firm – the guard that guards the guards – and perches respectably on a lower rung of Fortune's rich men's ladder, he could afford to show off.

To an old man who was proud of him.

Chapter Thirty-One

The executive terminal at John Wayne Airport offered valet parking, but I found my own space. Virgin to private flight and ignorant of its handgun rules, I wanted to stash the .45 and pocket my keys. Inside the terminal I discovered that security lines and pat downs were only for the *hoi polloi*. A flirty, red-headed gate attendant glanced at my picture ID and escorted me across the tarmac to a waiting Gulfstream.

Atop the fold-out stairs, a grinning pilot in aviator shades and a brown leather flight jacket flicked two-fingers against his cap visor in greeting. His black, pencil-moustache and slicked-back hair reminded me of Smilin' Jack, a long-defunct, Sunday funnies hero. I was tempted to comment on the resemblance, but the kid looked too young to drink, so I refrained. The older I became, the more my free associations drew blank stares.

The pilot demonstrated the entertainment system and showed me the galley.

"Will you need the seat belt instructions?"

"I'll muddle through," I said, hoping he was joking.

He retracted the stairs, sealed the hatchway, and shut himself in the cockpit. I had eight, king-sized, fully-reclining leather seats to choose from and none were middle seats. Private jet was the *only* way to fly.

I strapped myself in and gaped through a round porthole as the little pony of a plane taxied by the remuda of commercial Clydesdales tethered to jet ways. I had flown puddle-jumpers, but never a small jet. When we reached the end of the taxi way, I felt the pilot flick the reins, trot through the turn, and give Pegasus the spurs. An invisible hand on my chest pushed me deep into sighing seat cushions. The jet climbed at an insane angle – ostensibly to put as much altitude as possible between its roaring engines and the rich Newport PAC contributors below who might be poised to putt. If Smilin' Jack was like other flyboys I'd know, however, noise abatement was merely an excuse to kick gravity's ass. As we rocketed past the shoreline over white-flecked, blue water, the plane bucked a time or two, steadied, and settled into a gentle uphill gallop. Over Catalina we banked north to parallel the ragged coast.

Although the San Dismas storefront of Ricky's Dad would always be there, regardless of profitability, an employee now ran it and a florist dropped the rose on the front sidewalk each morning. Ricky lived and worked in Palo Alto near his Silicon Valley clients. We landed at San Jose where a limo was waiting. The gray-haired driver stood holding an iPad whose screen read *Pete Pinel, President of Vice.*

Twenty minutes away, directly across from the Stanford University main gate – two mossy, stone pillars supporting a weathered wrought iron arch flanked by a giant Mitsubishi electronic billboard – the driver pulled into a parking lot. The complex seemed small for a global firm until I reminded myself that Ricky's product was conceptual, and from that perspective, the whole universe fits inside a skull.

A small obelisk bore a simple plaque: *A Little Blue. Richard Touring, Jr. – Sole Proprietor*. Although Ricky had chosen the name for several reasons, one was his father's former employer. The IBM Corporation is known on the Street as "Big Blue."

Nearing a guard station befitting the Korean DMZ, I decided that the architect of the complex had considered more than feng-sui. The rooftop coping was likely a parapet. The landscaping, while artful, was clearly designed to provide the guard station open fields of fire. The guard quizzed the driver, raised a massive gate, and directed us to a visitor's space. Access to the building was through a ring of attractive concrete planters that doubled as tank traps. Motion sensitive cameras guarded every approach. Outside the entrance, I noticed an entire bank of cameras fix like anxious Meerkats on a bushy-tailed squirrel scampering down a tree.

Interesting.

A sign instructed me to announce myself to a closed-circuit camera and intercom. When the single revolving door was activated, I entered a spare, white lobby containing two arrangements of chrome and black leather chairs. The far wall – made entirely of glass – glowed with the sea-green hue common to armored truck windows. In front of the glass wall stood a chest-high, stainless steel reception desk manned by two uniformed guards. While one guard ran a computer check, the other inspected my driver's license with an ultraviolet light and had me sign a sheaf of stern oaths and warnings. Skimming the paperwork, I let my knee thud against the steel counter – solid enough to stop .50 caliber rounds. Both guards packed 16-shot Sig Sauers. I felt like a boy in the men's shower.

As instructed, I dumped my pockets into a tray along with my phone and watch. I kept the Kindle.

"I believe you have an electronic device for Mr. Touring?"

"I'll give it to him myself."

"Only if he's meeting you outside, sir," he said implacably. Since I was a red-carpet visitor, however, he added, "Actually, it would be rendered quite useless beyond this point. Do you have a pacemaker, sir?"

"Do I look decrepit enough for a pacemaker?"

"I wouldn't say, sir. What I will say is that when the former Vice-President visited, he met with Mr. Touring here in the lobby."

"No, I don't have a pacemaker," I grumbled.

The cop sealed the Kindle in a lock bag made of some metallic mesh. He affixed a tag, and passed everything through a revolving window in the glass wall. I proceeded through a plastic cylinder that was undoubtedly a body scanner and possibly the gizmo that rendered things useless. Nervously I glanced at my crotch, but a *thorough* frisk by a uniformed Amazon allayed my concerns.

Directed into a two-door holding chamber, I found myself searching for gas jets, but that was probably just me.

A revolving portal presented a visitor's badge, the lock bag, my watch and my pocket contents, minus the knife.

"Your knife and phone will be returned when you leave," said a robotic voice through a speaker.

"Don't go making any sex line calls HAL."

"Very amusing, sir."

When the far door buzzed, I scurried through before someone or some*thing* changed its mind.

Interesting.

The gamut was about as secure a setup as I had seen. A frontal assault would cost buckets of blood as direct assaults on fixed fortifications always do.

Very interesting!

The guard who escorted me to Ricky's office was about my age and unarmed.

"You guys must consider me neutralized, but you missed the wire garrote on my watch's winding stem."

"*From Russia with Love,*" he chuckled. "That was a good one, wasn't it? Connery was the only *real* Bond."

Old guys rule!

The guard parked me on a couch next to a table covered with issues of National Geographic and MacWorld. Shame I didn't have my spy camera.

"Someone will come get you when you leave. Don't move from here without an escort."

"What if I have to pee?"

"Do it in the plants or wait for the escort."

"Then why do I need this badge?"

"Allows you to be escorted."

"So if I'm escorted without a badge or wandering alone even with a badge, it would be …?"

"Unpleasant. Cavity searches and stuff."

"Flexible fiber optics?"

"Oh, no, no, no," he chuckled, pretending to pull a rubber glove over his fist. "Strictly old school."

When the guard left, I had unsupervised access to the magazines. I passed on a salacious exposé of partitioning in Windows 8 and took in the waiting room. The décor was high-end, but nothing like Burdick's digs. Conspicuous consumption wasn't Ricky's thing. If he *were* to splurge, it would be on a—

The woman who entered from the inner office finished the thought and almost stopped my clock. She might have been the *real* reason the Vice President stayed in the lobby. More than tall, she was statuesque. And statuesque like Pygmalion's Galatea – perfect in every visible detail, perfect like artwork, so perfect I winced, anticipating disappointment. I hoped she wouldn't speak.

"Welcome Mr. Pinel," she said. Her voice was like hearing stars. "Sapporo, no glass, I believe. Would you care for anything else?"

"I'm good. I'm good," I croaked when I got my breath back.

"Permit me to open your lock bag. Richard will be a moment."

I gave up the bag without protest, glad that she hadn't asked for my blood. She pressed a thumb on an electronic fingerprint lock, opened the bag, and handed me the Kindle.

"You're Jeri," I said.

"Mr. Touring's executive assistant."

She said it as a boast. I liked that.

"Long?"

"Three years."

"You must be *something*," I said, sounding like a letch.

"I am. Not many women could give a man like Mr. Touring what he needs."

I refused to imagine what that might be.

She smiled. More stars.

"*Time to create*, Mr. Pinel. I insure that he need not suffer fools." Her arched eyebrow relegated me to a questionable category. I decided that I would talk fast.

Ricky exploded through a door, rushing at me like a pint-sized linebacker. His hug was a dance.

"Pete, you old boogerhead. Goddamm, it's good to see you, man!"

Still a squirt, of course, Ricky had filled out. His board shorts were old and the waistband snug. His hairline had retreated and soon would surrender. His eyes, however, were eternally fifteen.

"Jeri, did you offer him a Sapporo?"

The look she gave him was the Bryn Mawr equivalent of *does a bear shit in the woods?*

"Mr. Pinel declined," she said.

"Pete! You *changed*!" he giggled like a kid. "C'mon in."

"I stocked your refrigerator, Richard, should Mr. Pinel reconsider. I pried loose *one hour* for your visit, but Symantec cannot be further postponed. The vulnerability is catastrophic."

"I've coded the patch already, Jeri," Ricky snorted "Their only vulnerability is the ass-clown who missed the back door."

Ricky put a hand on my shoulder and propelled me into his playroom.

Chapter Thirty-Two

The gymnasium sized room was strewn with workstations, tools, monitors, and computers; tall racks of server units twinkling with tiny red and green lights; wires and cables twining about like vines; hieroglyphic lined whiteboards. Ricky plopped down at a keyboard. I scooted over a folding chair. He swiveled a monitor toward me.

"What's up with you, Pete? Look at your bank account! Three days ago you were broke." He punched a few keys. A new window opened. "And your FICO? Credit report site kicks it out as an error."

I shrugged.

"It's fine now. Buy a yacht if you want. And don't freak, but I also stuck a little cash in your account."

"Ricky!"

"It's *my* bread, dig? I spend it on what makes me happy. Don't go all gnarly on me."

I counted to ten. "Okay … gift accepted. Thanks. I've had a bad spell. *Quit it,* though."

He sighed. "Ronnie?"

"Worse lately. Old age, I guess." When Ricky grimaced, I added quickly. "But better now. I think I bottomed out. I'm coming up for air again."

"Man, I hear you. Like after my Dad. Everything's different and it always will be, but ... if you last, it can still be good."

"I'm hanging in, Ricky. Really, it's better. So stay the hell out of my records, hear? I'll wake up President some morning."

He laughed. "Probably an improvement over the last dozen. Some of *those* nobs just woke up President, too." He paused. "You know ... I always meant to check it out. Let's see!"

His fingers flew furiously over the keyboard. Files appeared on various monitors. He scooted his rolling chair back and forth, waving his hands over some screens like a sorcerer. Additional screens responded to spoken or typed C:\> prompt commands. Flow-charts, maps, spreadsheets appeared, coalesced, grew, shrank, disappeared in a rapid fire sequence that struck me as projected thoughts. His expression was playful – after all, he was having fun! But his focus was so intense, I pictured the screens glowing from an energy emitted from his burning eyes. The activity slowed. A conclusion crystallized on two large screens. Ricky beamed.

"It's doable, man! I think it's already been done. I found tracks. See?"

I studied – that is to say I *looked* at – a large screen displaying a myriad of incomprehensible files.

"How do you rig a hundred million votes?" Ricky said. "You don't. You don't have to. Votes are just meaningless ones or minus ones that cancel each other out. The *sign* of the total – positive or negative – is all that matters. Cancel out a bit more or a bit less in a few spots critical to the *sum* – say, a few precincts in Florida, Ohio, Chicago – positive becomes negative. What prevents it? Tallying occurs over separate, redundant, near-invincible servers with back-ups and checksums. The outputs have to match exactly. You'd have to invisibly hack and lose the same votes on each server. But look!" He pointed at a screen. "Here. Here … Here. Different servers. But they're all Amazon's."

"The bookstore?"

"The STORE. Amazon's systems are built for infinite capacity. They rent the excess."

"So."

"So things that seem separate reside on a single virtual mainframe. Amazon's maintenance and back-up routines create unprotected portals to multiple servers. Here. And here. See?"

I nodded as if I did.

"The hard part is getting in. Then you have to find the portals. But once you do, you're shredding. I just hacked this one." He grinned. A *big* grin. "I gave Florida to Gore. I hope he doesn't ask for another recount."

"Jesus!"

"So what do you want to be? Red or blue?"

"Red, *white*, and blue. I'm a Libertarian."

"C'mon, Pete. You're making it a lot harder, man."

"If nominated I will not run, if elected I will not serve. And, please, tell me you're kidding."

His face was dead serious. "No, Pete. I'm *not* kidding." He shrugged. "Okay … if you don't want it, you just made me a mint. I'll tell the Feds and the networks I found some chinks to fill before some asshat does it again."

I handed him the Kindle. "Consider this my finder's fee."

He plugged it into a port.

"Check out Harry Potter and the Sorcerer's Stone."

"I *loved* that one. Okay, so?"

"So, I don't know. Something in the text? Some cryptographic thing?"

He spoke commands, brought up Amazon, skimmed the Harry Potter e-book choices, and downloaded one.

"Careless, Ricky. The janitor could order dirty books on your account."

"Not with this, baby. Answers to my voice alone. Recognizes emotion, too. Responds to, say, pain, or fear, or anger."

I started to ask how, but two Potter books appeared on a new screen.

"I'm meshing the files, scanning for anomalies ... Nope. Identical. Nothing in your book that Rowland didn't put in all of them. Is she a suspect?"

I laughed. "Not yet. Anything else there? Hidden files that I can't bring up the regular way?"

He spoke a few lines of gibberish.

"Good call, Pete. You're a natural. See?"

I saw more gibberish.

"The Kindle has a hidden partition. You know what that is?"

"Like two *separate* systems, separate drives on one drive."

"Right. Here's the Potter directory. And this is a partitioned sub-drive. Something huge, man. Gigabytes."

"How come *I* couldn't bring it up?"

"I got mad skills, man."

"So open it," I said excitedly.

As he typed, his brow furrowed. He typed more and frowned.

"Encrypted," he said.

"You can't get in?"

"Sure I can, but I need a bigger locksmith. Size *definitely* matters, Pete." He yanked the Kindle plug and rolled his chair over to the computer racks.

"Is that the mainframe?"

"You *do* try, Pete," he chuckled, plugging in the Kindle. "These are servers. An interface. The mainframe is underground for temperature control and security."

"Oh, that reminds me. Your perimeter security has a glitch."

He smiled tolerantly. "Can't be, man. Feds put all that together. They tell me I'm as tight as a nuke plant."

"Don't say that. I live too close to San Onofre."

He stopped what he was doing.

"You know what you're talking about, don't you?"

"It's security, right? I know *enough*. You have cams linked to motion detectors. I saw them zero in on a squirrel."

"That's sounds good."

"Really? If you don't want to be seen doing something in the back of a room, drop a tray of dishes in the front of the room because—"

"All eyes turn to the noise."

"*All* of your cams zoomed in on the squirrel. They're ripe for a diversion tactic. I saw a fire exit in that area, a vent, some windows."

"I'm vulnerable?"

"I can't say that, Ricky. I don't know what else you have, how many layers. One flaw may not matter, but it *is* a flaw."

"Would Homeland Security be that dense?"

"It's pretty amateurish."

"A Goddammed back door!" Ricky exploded. "You know what that is, right?"

"Learned it from you. Programmer codes a secret entry into a program so he can bypass ..." I whistled. "The Feds want a key to this joint."

Ricky grabbed a red phone and pushed a single button. The other end answered on the first ring, if it rang at all.

"Listen, you bag ass monkeys!" he said, strangling the handset. "You built holes in the site security. No! No! NO! I'm telling YOU! *One. Last. Time.* You really, *really* don't want to piss me off."

The phone buzzed like a mosquito.

"Says my private security consultants. Pinel Investigations."

More buzzing.

"Higher than yours, dickhead. Clearance so high, it's classified. Pete's gonna scrub this place top to bottom.

Everyone connected with it, too, so pucker up. When he's through, you guys can eat breakfast off each other's assholes."

The mosquito buzzed for a long time. Ricky's face grew darker and darker. I had no idea what was said, but I imagined that in some fashion power was invoked or alluded to. And the plain truth was that, buckets of blood they could muster. Security or not, they'd get in if they wanted. *Leaving* with anything was a different matter. Glowering, Ricky toyed unconsciously with his keyboard, his index finger circling lightly over a single key.

Delete.

When the buzzing stopped, an eerie stillness remained, an unnatural calm, the kind of ion-charged atmosphere that would have Oklahomans nervously scanning the horizon.

"Next drone you send by, eyeball the plaque out front," Ricky said. "Richard Touring, Jr., *Sole* Proprietor. Go ask your profilers what that means to me and why you sorry fucks should weigh it *carefully*."

He cradled the phone.

"Damn!" I whispered.

Ricky stood and walked to the window.

"That's where my Dad got his Doctorate," he said, staring a moment at the Stanford gate. "No Mitsubishi sign then. Just the rusty arch." He turned back. "Did I ever tell you why he quit Big Blue?"

"Sixties stuff. Disenchanted with the corporate world. Nothing specific."

"He heard rumors about contracts with the Nazi's. All before his time, of course, and who knows the truth of it, but..." He sighed. "I remember him telling me when I was little that a corporation is a person. Surprised the hell out of me. I mean, it sounded like Pinocchio becoming a boy or something. I thought he was pulling my leg, but he insisted that the law says a corporation is a person so it can have rights, sign contracts, make agreements ... *do things*. But this is what he added – a corporation has *will*, it does things, but it *can't* be moral, because it's a person without a soul and that's *incredibly* dangerous. Dad dropped out when he began to doubt big corporations were the good guys he'd always thought."

He sat down again.

"After that cold stunt with his funeral, I wondered that about the government. It's just a big corporation, right? The biggest. I mean, I was cool with them locking me up. I knew the rules and I broke them. I had it coming. But the funeral thing? Making my Mom do it all alone? That was a *corporate* decision, man. Soulless and *wrong*. *Bad guy* wrong. So whenever some C.I.A. or F.B.I. or N.S.A creep came pouting that I should help save our way of life, I told him to slither on out the door."

"That's putting it mildly as I remember, but it was understandable."

"Sure for a *kid*. But how long do you try to make someone pay for something? How long do you see pure black and white when real stuff is a mixture of colors with lots of gray? Bad guys are real, Pete. Dudes who shoot someone's father for loony reasons, and *scary* bad guys like

Communists and Nazis and terrorists who shoot a
million fathers for equally loony reasons. Our
government isn't so good —none are, no souls – but ... we
need it. And so far ours allows plenty of real souls a
voice so it's usually good *enough*. Better than the rest,
anyway. I finally realized that I could do something
about those super bad guys. Like *you* do with bad guys,
you know? We're individual proprietorships. Solo guys
with souls, right or wrong."

He shook his head sharply to shed the mood.

"Anyway, you'll look things over, right? It's a job. A
real job. You need the bread and it'll probably be a
blast."

"My last security clearance was 40 years ago, Ricky.
It doesn't automatically renew."

"On my task list, man. By the time they check,
you'll rank up there with Elliot Ness."

"How would you know about Elliot Ness, Ricky?"

"You mentioned him once, so I looked him up. I
always look up things you say."

"Try Smilin' Jack."

He turned to a keyboard. "Now?"

I laughed. "Later. But honestly, Ricky, a setup like
this demands expertise. *Special* skills."

"So you'll hire some specialists. You got one *mad*
skill that tops them all, Pete."

"What's that?"

"You won't sell me out."

Chapter Thirty-Three

Ricky glanced at my watch. I'd never known him to wear one himself. I read once that geniuses often have an adversarial relationship with time.

"Cripes! Fifteen minutes and Jeri pulls the plug."

"You're *scared* of her!" I said.

"Way *strong*, man. Not *scared* scared. It's just that … she reminds me of my Mom."

I did a double take.

"Not *that* part! That she keeps an eye on me. Like your watch says. Always there, dig? There to keep me focused, on track, do my best. So let's open these files before Symantec fries the web."

He spoke and typed. Windows opened and closed on a half-dozen monitors. When he stopped, he was smiling.

"What?"

"The encryption. Cool!"

"Way cool," I said.

He chuckled. "You grok encryption?"

"That was your Dad's word, Ricky. Sure, I grok. At a user level. A program uses a key to convert files into code readable only with that key. Like a decoder ring."

"Not sure what a decoder ring is, but it sounds right. Thirty-two and sixty-four bit were early versions."

"Do I need to know what a 'bit' is?"

"Just that more bits is harder to hack. A 128-bit key is virtually foolproof."

"Virtually? Sounds like a challenge."

"It was. One of my first secret contracts. See if 128 was vulnerable."

"Was it?"

"Yep. With mega man-hours, a honking big super-computer, and mad skills."

"Russia and China have a couple of those."

"Israel, too. They *could* pull it off. So for insurance, Uncle Sam, who has more money than God and a bigger mainframe, pushed encryption to 192-bit. It's the lock for things that absolutely, positively *must* stay locked. Your hidden Kindle partition has 192-bit encryption."

"It belongs to a Nobel Prize winner."

"Big whoop. Jesus Christ himself couldn't access a 192-bit encryptor. Not unless he was working for the Feds at an altitude that requires a pressure suit. It's not just illegal, it gets you disappeared. You wake up in Gitmo or you wake up dead. Is your guy a spook, Pete?"

"Do you mean spy or ghost?"

"Either or both from the looks of this."

"I was told that he does things for the C.I.A."

"What's his name?"

"Walter Kling. UC San Dismas."

Ricky nodded. "I'll check him out."

"So what you're saying, Ricky, is that this 192-bit encryption means I'm screwed."

"*Probably* screwed, but let's look anyway. I created it."

Chapter Thirty-Four

Ricky did things with his keyboards that ignited the dormant racks of servers. Linear arrays of tiny lights, like burning fuses, moved across the units in a chain reaction that ignited the next units, the next shelves, the next racks. I imagined the relentless recruitment as some expanding expenditure of energy – ten times ten times ten times ... A *googol* of tens. Enough power to—

A knock at the door startled me. Jeri entered, her eyes aglow with monstrous determination.

"I have Symantec on the secure line, Richard."

Absorbed in the monitors, Ricky was enclosed in a self-made bell jar whose vacuum put him beyond reach of human voice. He propelled his wheeled chair from point to point, typing, observing, thinking.

"Richard?"

"I don't think he can hear you," I said.

"He can't."

Jeri was as transfixed by the sight of Ricky working as *he* was with his work. Noticing my gaze, she blushed as if caught touching herself. Like a person expecting a spark to jump, she hesitantly tapped Ricky's shoulder.

"Richard? ... Richard?"

He seemed surprised by the world suddenly materializing around him.

"What?"

"Your call with Symantec."

He swore under his breath. "Five minutes."

"Richard!"

"Jeri, I found a flaw in the 192-bit."

"My God! I'll cancel the call."

"No, no ... five minutes. I can't solve this now anyway. Five minutes."

"They can wait," she said, exiting.

"Come here, Pete."

I looked over his shoulder at a monitor screen filled with what looked like a long list of file folders.

"This is the directory for the encrypted partition."

My eyes jumped to a folder named Olivewood.

"That one," I said, pointing.

"No can do, Pete. The folders *should* have been inaccessible. That's a bug I'll have to fix before some 99-percenter convinces the exchange he can cybercide Chase Manhattan. But only the folder *names* are readable, the contents are still securely encrypted with a password key. Without it, current state? ... All the computing power in the world combined wouldn't help."

I rubbed my head.

"Try 648936. That opens his garage."

"A security freak, huh? Not a chance. A 192 bit lock needs a 48 character hexdex key."

"So what do I do?"

"Technology is mired in human nature. Hackers count on it. Humans lose keys, so it's common to make a copy and leave it under the door mat. Your Potter fan may have written the password down."

"I would think his C.I.A. pals frown on that."

"Frown with *extreme* prejudice. Forty-eight infrequently used random letters and numbers is no slam dunk, however. If he picked the key himself, he probably chose some pattern that doesn't look like a pattern, something unique to himself or his environment. Something always there so he can't forget."

"I think he did forget."

"Well, if you know the guy, you can figure it out sometimes ... *help* him remember."

"What if his brain is too scrambled?"

"*Harry Potter and the Sorcerer's Stone* is a good book. Might as well read it, because you won't be reading the encrypted part. I've copied the drive and I'll look closer in case I goofed twice, but my gut says it's hopeless, Pete."

He unplugged the Kindle and handed it to me with a print out of the directory.

"If you find the password, the logon program is unencrypted under *settings*. Click *pw.exe* and you're good-to-go. I don't see a screensaver, so it probably stays unlocked until you reenter the password."

The knock at the door had attitude this time. Jeri entered with a scowl that promised any delay on my part would be met with force. "Symantec on the secure line," she said.

Ricky stood to hug me. "Goddamm, Pete, it's good to see you. Get back soon. Jeri will shoot you a contract. What title do you want?"

"I liked your President of Vice gag."

"Right on, man! It'll drive the C.I.Ass nuts."

Jeri urged me inexorably toward the door.

"Your Dad would be proud, Ricky," I said over my shoulder.

"I know," he said.

Jeri followed me through the door and closed it behind us, saving Ricky seconds as valuable as—

I was thinking gold, but that was wrong.

Ricky's time *created* gold.

Chapter Thirty-Five

I spent the return flight milking what information I could from Ricky's print out of the hidden directory's list of folders. One folder was labeled, simply enough, PhilosophersStone. Some folders I recognized as parts of the brain: hippocampus, amygdala. Other folders bore chemical names. Some of the chemicals were drugs. Ketamine, for example, and methylbenzoyl-ecgonine, which I knew was short for cocaine. One sequence began with ClinTrl followed by a nine digit number. Another sequence started with VTAFormula1 and ended with VTAFormula27. Smaller strings included 27SanDismas; 27Olivewood1; 27Olivewood2; 27Camino. Interspersed were folders labeled Burdick_Les, Malek_Paul, Pinel_Peter, and Sharfstein_Veronica. The latter folder shouted guilty knowledge or direct involvement in Ronnie's death. Kling's days were numbered by its contents.

The folder Lynch_Fred surprised me. What was it about Fred that warranted 192-bit encryption? I knew just the person to ask and would as soon as I landed.

If he was still alive.

It's helpful to connect dots to make a picture as long as you remember that, without *all* the dots, your horse may actually be a zebra. The picture I had drawn thus far included a scientist, a legitimate drug company with an illegitimate subsidiary, and a drug-running gang. The cocaine folder was an intriguing connection.

ClinTrl could easily be clinical trial. If the official-looking nine-digit numbers were, say, registrations or grant numbers, the folder contents might be pharmaceutical research. I also had a list of numbered files beginning with VTA. If I could trust the old movie *Silver Bullet*, the first treatment for syphilis, Salversan, was called 606 since it was the 606th formulation after 605 failures. Was VTA a concoction that also went through various iterations? And what was the connection between VTA27 and Olivewood.

Over the speaker Smilin' Jack announced an incoming FAX. I felt as if I were in Air Force One! At a work station aft, a machine was spitting out a contract for consulting services. Ricky had even worked in the President of Vice title. When the fee schedule came through, I found myself chirping *If My Chums Could See Me Now,* but clammed up when I realized Smilin' Jack might be listening.

A FAX was super, but I wanted to make a phone call, too. I popped a handset from my armrest, punched in Xuân's number, and hoped she would answer.

"Dr. Nguyen."

"It's me. Pete."

"You didn't wake me this morning."

"You said not to."

"In certain contexts, no *does* mean maybe. Where are you? I can barely hear."

"I'm on a private jet. Making calls. Getting faxes. If I change my mind, I can be President."

"What?"

"Relax. My matrix is fine. I needed to run a clue by a computer-genius friend of mine. He sent his jet."

"You have excellent friends."

"I'm into quality not quantity. Would you know any of Kling's passwords?"

"The one for the garage – 648936? I think he uses it for everything."

"I tried that. What I'm looking for is a string of 48 letters and numbers. He might've written it down."

"I don't recall anything like that, but I'll look through his desk and files again."

"And see who was admitted to Camino in the last three days?"

"Why?"

"Where better to hide a madman?"

"Camino is a respected institution, Pete."

"I'm not saying it's a co-conspirator, but crooks using the place for cover hardly strains credulity."

"You like that phrase, don't you?"

"Yep. But I should have said *miscreants* using the place for cover. They're both on my Word Power list."

"But Walter is known at Camino. *Well* known."

"Say they dyed his hair, stuck him on a new ward under a different name. Say he's mute again."

"*Someone* would recognize him. Staff rotate to cover *all* the units."

"*Except* for Burdick's, right?"

"Hmm … that's true. Okay. I'll check. Can you meet me at Walter's later?"

"I have to see someone as soon as I land. Tomorrow might be iffy for him. I don't know how late I'll be."

"I'll leave what I find on your voice mail then. But come by if you can. *Any* time is fine." She waited for me to say something, if only good-bye. When I didn't, she said, "About last night, Pete … Are you alright with it?"

"It's been a long time, Xuân."

"For me, too. A *very* long time, I told you. But I'm alright with it."

"Yeah, well, see I'm, uh … rusty."

"Weren't you counting?"

"Not that, although that, too. "I'm rusty at…"

I couldn't quite get it out, so she said it for me.

"Caring. Good-night, dear."

"Yeah. Good-night."

I replaced the phone in the armrest and gazed out the starboard porthole at the western horizon. The departing sun had left behind a red-ember glow. Through the opposite window in the violet eastern sky burned a first bright star.

Chapter Thirty-Six

The hospice Bernie had mentioned was an isolated wing of an upscale nursing home, or, as they tagged themselves nowadays, an assisted living facility. *Maybe* it's living. I'd find out soon enough, unless I got lucky.

The building straddled a prime piece of south Laguna Beach sand. Why erstwhile beachfront condos would morph into a nursing home was a magic trick beyond my grasp of Freakonomics, but business was booming. Perhaps, as Manny had suggested, booming was the key: guilt-ridden baby-boomers offering the greater generation an ocean-view seat on the ice floe.

Inside, however, the place was still just a nursing home. My father had spent a few weeks in one, so I knew the ilk. This one had matched furniture, bright colors, clean paint and wallpaper, but featured the same alarmed doors; the same case hardened staff and hard case patients; the same smells; the same shells – Abishags who had failed to provide; Richard Corys who had waited too late.

Beyond the looking-glass doors of the hospice wing, however, beckoned polished teak floors, soft music, fresh air, and designer furnishings suitable for a living room, ironic since hospice is a dying room. Most hospice care is at home, but sometimes for those last few days or weeks, Medicare offers a perverse upgrade – like a frequent flier club where *fewer* miles earns the first class seat. You sign away all that Federal money squandered in your last days on hope, and a sliver of the savings buys you individual attention, smiles, peace and quiet, clean sheets, warm bed pans, and the smell of roses. Lucky hospice stiffs have everything their equally dying cohorts back in coach lack.

Except IVs.

A sprightly, middle-aged nurse greeted me. Her floral print scrubs were painfully cheerful.

"Fred Barnes?" I said

"Delightful! You must be a friend."

She was chipper to a fault, but maybe chipper is a hospice thing, like the Twilight Zone episode where every day is a really, *really* good day.

"I'm his Dad."

Her *good day* face began to cloud.

"Mr. Barnes is a bit older than you. And black."

"It's a mystery."

Rain fell.

"Do you even know him or are you some cockroach? A bill collector, maybe?"

"Do I look like a cockroach?"

"You could pass," she said.

Her nose and cheekbones bore the ruddy signs of early alcoholism. From what I knew of watching people die, drinking is probably a hospice thing, too.

"Listen, sweetie," she said. "Between you, me, and the bedpost, in the *real* world I indulge a vice or two, and the Indian casinos nurture them all. I've met my share of skip-tracers and arm-benders."

"Close but no cigar. Private Eye."

"Close a damn 'nuff," she said.

I laughed and raised a hand. "I swear on *The Big Sleep*. Nothing like that."

She gave me another stern eyeballing. "Oh, what the hell. Room D. Any pair beats nothing."

"No visitors? That's hard to believe."

"People don't come when you work at it. He talks to his roommate some, but … I think he'll pass alone. I *hate* when that happens."

I could almost *feel* her yearning for a drink.

"How long?"

"Tonight. Tomorrow. Not long."

Outside Fred's open door I halted as if the air beyond teemed with contagion. The room seemed safe enough, however – color splashed walls, vases with bright flowers, large windows that promised a sunlit seascape during the day. But frankly, what did it matter where you fell? I decided Room D was as good a place to die as any.

"What can I do you for?" boomed a man in the bed nearest the door as I stepped into the room. If I were closer, he might've pumped my hand and clapped me on the back. Despite those Goddamm arcs old men get around the irises, his eyes twinkled. A bigger-than-life, large-man demeanor overshadowed how little of him was left.

"I'm here to see Fred."

"Who's Fred?"

Over hospital pajamas, the old man wore a wrinkled blue suit-coat and a stained, white business shirt buttoned to the neck with no tie. Maybe ties were forbidden in hospice or maybe he had forgotten how to tie one. His lapel boasted a half-dozen shiny pins identifying him to Masons, Shriners, Elks and other lodges as a brother.

"Fred's your neighbor," I said.

He turned toward my glance. A brightly patterned drape between the beds was drawn back, but the old man looked surprised as if seeing the other bed for the first time. Fred – if indeed the skeletal figure in the next bed *was* Fred – lay on his side, facing away.

"What's his name again?"

"Fred."

He repeated the name a few times like someone who makes a living remembering names. "Yeah, Fred. He's a good one. Good stories when you get him going. Makes you laugh your head off. I think he's tired now."

The old man was a hand-talker handicapped by a knotted strip of gauze securing one wrist to the bed rail. He kept glancing at the wrist with a puzzled expression.

"Damndest terminal I ever saw," he said. "But I do like these ..." He studied his bed and frowned, struggling to find the word, settling on *seats*. "Did you talk to my boy? He's a doctor, too."

I shook my head.

"I was hoping he'd stop by before my bus came, but I just have to get on home and tend to business."

"I see," I said.

"My helpers are helpless without my help. No telling what mess they've made already." He shouted toward the other bed. "Hey, uh ... um ..."

"Fred."

"Right, right, Fred. Man here for you, Fred. Play dead. Looks like a bill collector."

What was this bill collector thing? I needed to take a hard look in the mirror.

The old man laughed at his joke, wiping tears from his eyes with his free hand. "Go ahead, mister. Shake him. He misses that bus, he'll be sore pissed."

I slid a chair between the beds. "Fred?" I said to his back, waiting anxiously for the movement of a breath that finally came. "Fred?"

"Shake him!"

Still facing the dark window, Fred said, "Our buses will be here soon enough, Colonel."

"Everyone calls me Colonel 'cause I'm an auctioneer. I run three businesses, plus the auction business. Need something? See the Colonel! I used to say that on T.V. See the Colonel. What do *you* need, son?"

"I'm good. Really."

"You could use a new watch," he said. "Timex hasn't made that model since … uh, back when. Even a Timex gets old. Help me find my bag. I had a bag full of watches here." He glanced around for some long-gone sample case and began to tug at the gauze knot on his wrist. "I saw a damn rent-a-cop in here. *He* took my bag. I had good watches in that bag."

"It's okay, Colonel. This one's special."

He tugged harder, not hearing me. I stuck out my wrist. The engraving caught his eye.

"Always there," he read, squinting. "That's fine tool work. Had to cost five times the watch."

"It was from someone ... not here anymore."

He took my wrist with his free hand. A coarse tremor made both our hands shake.

"This old thing won't keep time much longer, son, but..." I heard a slight catch. "Save it somewhere, hear? Somewhere safe 'cause they'll sure as hell take it from you. Save it for that day when memory fails."

The nurse in the floral scrubs breezed in. "Are you selling today, Colonel?" she said, untying his wrist.

"Dollardollardollar who'll give me a dollar," the Colonel rattled in a machine-gun patter. His face was beaming. "Dollarfifty, dollarfifty, two dollardollardollar, I got twoandahalf, three dollarthreedollar, who'll give me three. Three dollardollarthree. Are you all through? Are you all done?" He swung his free hand as if banging a gavel. "Twofifty. Sold!"

"You're not going to break for the door again, are you? I have Tom out there."

"Screw Tom," he said sourly.

"Be nice."

"Screw you, too."

"Later," she said.

He snaked a hand toward her bottom.

"Behave yourself, Colonel," she said sternly, but she let him pat her butt.

He clambered from the bed with a spryness that surprised me, especially when his pajama bottoms rode up and I saw stick man legs mottled with purple blotches like irises.

"Don't forget your slippers," said the chipper nurse.

"Fuck slippers," he blurted, but he retrieved the disposable foam slippers and put his feet inside. "About time that damn bus came."

The nurse escorted him through the door leaving me staring at Fred's back. I waited through a long silence.

"What do want, Pinel? … Absolution?"

"Would you give it to me?"

Silence.

"I thought you might have changed," I said.

"Because I'm knock-knocking on heaven's door?"

"Something like that."

"No, thank you."

"Still not tall, but alone," I said.

"Are we done now? *Via con dios*."

"I want a favor, Fred."

I had planned what to say to bait him. It worked. He labored to turn over. When he did, I had to hide my shock. His eyes and cheeks were sinkholes as if the substrata of his face had collapsed. His dark skin was a color that didn't come with the smaller Crayola boxes – some strange ocher or sienna hue, anemic brown with sickly yellow undertones, a color like rancid chocolate. Hospital pajamas hung from a wasted frame. Meatless forearms and bony hands were dusted with what looked like frost.

He poked a trembling finger at a panel to raise the head of his bed. The hollows in his face flooded with pain. Upright, he labored to breathe while the flood subsided.

"Your balls will be your downfall, Pinel."

"It's for Ronnie."

"She's still dead, right? I'm a newsman, not a historian."

The interest I had sparked flickered, but I was prepared to land him if I got this far. I was about to set the hook when a tornado of flailing arms and legs blasted into the room almost bowling me from my chair.

The Colonel was wind-milling at two refrigerator sized orderlies who could have clocked him with a single swat. Constrained by policy, or more likely, witnesses, they clinched and danced instead, absorbing a steady *thwack, thwack, thwack* of fist to face until the Colonel collapsed beneath their bulk. The chipper nurse rushed in brandishing a hypo, but waffled. She hesitated to jab blindly into the thrashing, grunting tangle of bodies and fill an orderly's ass with a Mickey meant for the old man. Whatever minutes, hours, or days the Colonel had left were being exhausted like jet fuel through afterburners, wasted in a hopeless blaze that could only flame out with a heart attack or the hypo. I started to step in.

"Let him try," Fred gasped.

"Christ, Fred. He's a *dead* man."

"Does he look it right now?" he said.

It ended before I could choose. The orderlies engulfed his emaciated frame like amoebas. The nurse stabbed the hypo through the Colonel's shirttail. He flailed for a time like a beheaded snake. When the only movement was the heaving of his chest, the orderlies stood to knead their bruises. It had been a Goddamm good fight, as futile battles often are.

"That's three for this old fart, Brenda," grumbled an orderly. "Keep his ass poseyed!"

Ignoring Fred – and why not? He was dead too, right? – the nurse looked at me sheepishly. "We're not used to this in hospice, I'm afraid."

"They go gentle, do they?"

"Could you help us lift him onto the bed?"

The four of us hefted the Colonel onto his mattress. He was oblivious, which is a good way to lose a fight, although, unfortunately, you usually wake up. The victorious orderlies marched from the room muttering. The nurse checked for wounds and broken bones, shined a penlight on his pupils, took his blood pressure and pulse, and finally secured *both* of the old man's wrists with gauze strips.

"He's not hurt," she declared, tugging a sheet over his chest.

"Sister," I said, recalling my long elevator ride with Armstrong. "All the dope in the world wouldn't make that true."

Chapter Thirty-Seven

When the nurse left, I dropped back into the chair between the beds and listened to stereo murmurs of uncertain breathing. Fred was conscious, however, despite closed eyelids. I dangled my hook again.

"What if there were more to Ronnie's story, Fred? What if we both got it *wrong*?"

Fred was a newshound in his mother's belly. Getting a story wrong happens, but *leaving* it that way wasn't in his nature. He opened his eyes.

"I'm all out of rollover minutes, Pinel. I don't need any get-it-in-under-the-deadline I'm-sorries or fuck-yous. If you have a *story*, tell it."

I worked my way through the Madman and his Philosopher's Stone; Aragon and Les Burdick; my mental meltdown, the ER dream and Paul Malek. I finished with the Kindle, Mendez, and Ricky's list of file names.

"Just file names?"

"Even Ricky can't hack the encryption."

"And one name was mine?"

"Lynch_Fred. Given the context, I'd say that's you."

He closed his eyes again. His breaths came in shallow sniffs with pauses in between as if he had to work up to each one. Fred's brain had once been a search engine. I hoped it was still on-line. When he opened his eyes again, I knew that it was. He'd remembered something, but he stared at me for almost a minute before he spoke.

"You haven't killed enough people yet, Pinel?"

"Ronnie is just a clue. I'm looking for Kling."

"You are so full of *crap!*"

Putting force in the word cost him. He had to save up breath to finish. I didn't waste mine on a denial.

"You fucked me once before. *This* time you have to kiss me first."

"You know something?"

"I know what we both missed."

"What?" I was out of the chair.

"Foreplay, Pinel. Foreplay."

I sat back down. "Okay, Fred. What do you want?"

"You are so ready to put out."

"I'm your bitch. Use me. What do you want?"

"Something you alone will do."

His words yanked me back to Ronnie's hospital room and her gasped, *"End it."*

"Can't you just ... *wait*, Fred?"

He laughed, choking because laughing clearly hurt like hell. "You think I want you to kill me, don't you? And you're *weighing* it for Chrissakes." He caught what he could of his breath. "No ... dying I can still manage."

What then?"

He squinted at the window. "Is it day or night?"

"Night. Just after eight."

"Timing is all."

"What is it you want, Fred?"

"I want you to pick me up in your arms and carry me out of here."

"Christ, Fred, do I look like Make-a-Wish? It's too late to swim with dolphins or go to Disneyland."

"Take me to the *Banner*," he said.

Of course ... Of course.

Chapter Thirty-Eight

Hospice was a perfectly reasonable place to die and the reasons he should stay put so obvious I didn't bother. But as long as *will* remains, how and where it happens can be choices the heart makes for reasons reason doesn't know.

"Any impediments to you signing out?"

"I'm not talking about signing out. I'm talking about you carrying me through the door."

"Yeah, I got that part. But does this joint have court orders, commitments, that sort of thing?"

"Since when do you care?"

"It helps to know if I'll have to shoot your way out."

He spluttered a laugh.

"Better save your breath, Fred. Now?"

"I think it's now or never."

I stood and looked around. "What do you need?"

"Naked came I and naked go I hence."

"I'm not carrying you out of here naked, Fred. People will talk."

"I'm wearing pajamas, Pinel. It's a metaphor."

Certain syllables were hard for him – those that required breath. I put my keys in my hand so I could open the Blazer if we made it that far.

"Is metaphor the one with *like* or the other one," I said, bending to forklift him into my arms. He grimaced as if the bones poking through his pajamas were snapping and maybe they were, but panted grunts were his only protest. He laid his head against my chest and closed his eyes.

When I turned, I saw the Colonel staring at us, looking frightened.

"Our bus came," I said.

Sometimes any explanation is better than none. His face relaxed into a grin.

"About time," he said, glancing at his wrist for the long-gone watch. Missing it, he started tugging against his straps. "They got it! Every Goddamm thing a man has, they take!" He looked up. "Let me go with you. I ... I can walk. Really, I'm still strong. I could do it myself, but ..." His voice shuddered. "I ... I can't find my way anymore. I can bear most anything, but ... but *lost* is..."

"I can't do it, Colonel. I wish I could. Maybe your son will come."

"I ... I think maybe ... my boy's dead."

"I'm sorry."

"He died ..." He glanced at his empty wrist for the non-existent watch. "I know I should know, but time is so *fuzzy* anymore. Everything is either now or yesterday. I think he died yesterday. My boy, my wife. My Mom and Dad. My wife's Mom and Dad. Her brother. His wife. Their kids. Friends. Pets. Everything I ever loved or knew. All died *just yesterday.*"

A wave of emotion swelled and subsided in his face as if some leviathan thought, almost breaching, had returned to the deep, leaving the surface undisturbed.

"Say, mister, when you see my boy, tell him I just couldn't wait any more. Man's got to take care of his business, right? And listen, you tell him about me fighting those two cops who stole my watches. You tell him that now, hear? Tell him his old Papa got in a few good shots. You'll get a kick out of how he laughs. You can tell most everything about people by their laugh and, my boy, he always laughs big. You saw it, right? You can tell it. Tell him that part for me. Tell him that at least I got in a few good shots."

He started to laugh.

A *big* laugh.

"Colonel. I think your boy would make book on that."

Chapter Thirty-Nine

When the chipper nurse saw me carrying Fred toward the door, she jumped like a liquor store clerk spying a kid stealing a six-pack.

"He wants to leave," I said.

"He can't," she said.

I kept walking. She skipped along beside us.

"You can't just waltz away a patient no matter what he says he wants." Sensing the futility of talking to me, she appealed to Fred. "You won't survive out there, Mr. Barnes!"

The irony squeezed a laugh from Fred and a blush from the nurse. She darted to a phone to call for support. At street level, reinforcements blocked the door.

"5150 doesn't apply," I said authoritatively. "His problems are medical." Use a new concept five times and it's yours forever.

A plus-size orderly whose neck tattoos were presumably the tip of an ink iceberg beneath his shirt, drawled, "You know a lot about 5150's, do you?"

I'd have to deal with him first if it came to that, although with Fred in my arms, I didn't know how yet.

"A judge will decide that," said a gray-haired woman with the sour face of a nursing pooh-bah. "I can keep him here for three days."

"Only if you're God," Fred said. "Otherwise you get change."

Before the blockers stitched together a plan, I wormed my way between them. Fred absorbed every jolt with a clenched jaw. Cops were bound to show, but I hoped to be gone when they did. Luckily duty appeared to end at the exit and no hero followed me to the car. It gave me a moment to position Fred across the back seat, which I hoped would make the ride less agonizing. When I turned around, however, the plus-size orderly was approaching. Perhaps he took his job more seriously than the others, but I think he was just bored.

"Stay away from me," I warned.

He looked around, saw we were alone, and swung. I ducked and came up with a hard right to his solar plexus. Groaning, he clutched his gut, plopped onto his ass, and sat rocking.

"Away from me is healthier," I said.

I jumped in the car and sped south on Pacific Coast Highway to avoid Laguna traffic. Fred was out cold. I kept swiveling to catch signs of breathing and finally tilted the rear view mirror so I could watch him without ignoring the road. I called the Banner.

"Bernie? Pete Pinel. I'm bringing Fred for a visit."

I doubted his pause was reluctance, but rather the reporter in him imagining an untold story. "Great," he said. "When?"

"Thirty-five or forty minutes. I need to take the long way."

"I bet you do."

"I'll be carrying him. In pajamas."

"You or Fred?"

Editors!

I made it in thirty-five and parked out front, resigning myself to the ticket. The lobby guard saw me with Fred in my arms and buzzed us in. A wheelchair sat waiting. Fred's eyes were closed, but his nostrils flared like a tired horse smelling the barn. While the guard searched for a blanket to cover Fred's legs, I positioned him in the chair.

"He's not heavy; he's a *brother*," he said.

Since the *Banner* is a morning paper, the lobby was still. Long past deadline, reporters, advertising, and admin staff had left. Production and circulation crews came and went through the dock entrance. Upstairs the news staff would be skeletal – the night editor, a few copy desk people, a beat reporter with a late add. Possibly a divorced columnist on the wagon with nowhere to go or a starry-eyed copy boy with nowhere else he wanted to go. For a second I thought Fred was out again, but when he smiled, I realized that he was listening to some music of the spheres I couldn't hear – the pulse of a newspaper at night.

I rolled him onto the elevator and poked the button for the newsroom.

"I wonder who has the desk tonight?" he said.

"Bernie. I called to tell him you were coming by."

The elevator door opened on the kind of newsroom hubbub seen only at deadline or on election nights. Bernie had been busy.

"You're late, Fred," Bernie boomed. "Actually, you're *not*, are you? Good thing, too, since I need a quote for your obit." Bernie took the wheelchair handles and pushed Fred directly into the rowdy crowd. "Half these people almost begged off, thinking you'd die on the way over," he added.

Happiness was something I knew you could lose in a single heartbeat, so I held to the Greek maxim that said count no man happy until he's dead. They had an alternative formulation of the same theorem, however; a view that framed happiness as a final accounting, the bottom line of a life well-led. Fred was a demonstration of both notions. Well-lived, he smiled, completely happy in the moment, while his strained breathing was a whispered prophesy that likely he would remain so.

"Glad you didn't disappoint us, Fred," Bernie said. "These people have deadlines tomorrow."

"Don't we all," Fred said.

Chapter Forty

Feeling like a party crasher, I stepped off the elevator before the doors closed on me.

"Met by seventy virgins," I heard Fred say.

"You're not counting Monica, are you?" a voice chimed.

"My husband gripes I'm as close as it gets, sweetie."

A bottle of scotch appeared.

"Can you partake, Fred?"

"Pain medicine *ad libitem*," he said. "Who's holding?"

A grizzled copy editor I remembered from the old days offered a box of Marlboros. "With a prescription you can do grass in the first aid office," he grumbled. "Light a cig and the SWAT team shows up."

Fred fumbled at the box with shaky fingers. The copy editor removed a cigarette, planted it between Fred's lips, and flicked a Zippo. Fred began to cough violently. People waited.

"Outstanding," Fred spluttered finally. "*And* they are mild."

"Next he'll want sex," said a relieved voice.

"Monica!" shouted a chorus.

"Danny Tarver went to the *Times*," Bernie said to Fred over the laughter. "He's driving down from L.A. Christian has to bail from a fundraiser, but he'll show."

"This is a family affair, Fred," I said. "I'll blow and come back for you later. You were going to tell me something, though."

"Chiron wants his two coins."

"C'mon, Fred, I just meant—"

"I know what you meant. We need your computer, Bernie."

"This sounds interesting. What's up?"

"Give me a minute. What comes of it is a *Banner* exclusive. Right, Pinel?"

"Goes without saying."

"Say it anyway."

I said it.

Fred nodded toward his old desk. I rolled him over and kicked Bernie's chair aside to position him at the keyboard, but he stopped me.

"You type," he said. "I can't."

Deep furrows separated the bones of his hands where the muscles had wasted. I rolled Bernie's chair back and plopped down at the computer.

"Google Philosopher's stone," he said.

I clicked an icon and typed Philosopher's Stone in the search box. The screen blinked and filled with results.

"A few million entries," I said. "Start at the top?"

"Add cocaine."

I tapped keys.

"Whittled it down to fifty-thousand. So?"

"So smart people have compared cocaine to the Philosopher's Stone."

"I'm one of them."

"Erudite, ain't you? Now add Aragon."

I typed again. Fred squinted at the screen. I read aloud from the list.

"That one. Print it," he said. "It was on the wire and slated for the *Banner's* Business section. County bankruptcy news bumped it."

I scanned the pages as they rolled from a desktop printer. The article was a twelve year old *Wall Street Journal* interview with "Aragon's sponsored research scientist, Nobel Laureate, Walter Kling."

"Kling claims to have created a Philosopher's Stone," I said excitedly. "Some kind of catalyst that makes complex compounds from simple ones."

"By mimicking living cells. Read what he says about cocaine."

I skimmed the next few pages. "Calls cocaine one such complex compound. Compares it to a key that unlocks the brain's pleasure center – the ventral tegmental area."

"Remember that and keep going."

"He touts a designer version of cocaine. One that's non-addictive, works orally, and lasts all day. Sheez ... medicinal cocaine? I thought that went out with Coca Cola *classic* classic?"

Fred shook his head impatiently although the effort clearly hurt him. "Your madman is a Nobel winner, Pinel. Think he gives a rat's ass about another new drug?"

"So what's he after?"

"Answers."

"Like?"

"Who knows? He's a genius. We're not. But read the boxed quote."

"Supported generously by Aragon, I am perfecting my Philosopher's Stone – a golden key that will open *every* lock in the brain."

"A *master key* to the brain might be a genius's wet dream," Fred said.

I eyed the last page. "The writer calls it all a pipe dream."

"Clever, wasn't he?"

"Quotes experts who say no such catalyst is possible. Accuses Aragon of blowing hot air to float an IPO." I put down the pages. "Okay, Fred, but this never panned out. Aragon is belly-up. And what does it have to do with Ronnie?"

"Add Paul Malek."

I backpedaled to Google. Adding Malek winnowed the list to a few dozen entries.

"A year after the Journal piece a San Dismas nurse complained that patients were getting mislabeled medication. Open the *Banner* links."

I clicked the first one and scanned the lead.

"Kling was accused of under-the-counter testing of a new Aragon drug at San Dismas," I said.

"But the ward psychiatrist—"

"Paul Malek," I blurted.

"Insisted that he'd administered the drugs himself. Said the nurse had lied. The story died when the remaining meds checked out and it leaked that the nurse had a longstanding workman's comp beef against the Med Center. Open the second one. Six months later."

I clicked the mouse.

"A Christmas party at the Ritz?"

"Sponsored by Aragon. Burdick was there. Kling, too. A fund-raiser for—"

"Olivewood."

"Scan the list of honored volunteers."

"Malek! Then ... he was there when Ronnie was attacked. He left it off his resume."

"Maybe he's humble," Fred said. "Three names in two unrelated stories was coincidence, but I must've smelled *something*. I called Kling to ask if Malek was affiliated with Aragon. He denied it."

"But that call might have warranted a Fred Lynch folder. Particularly if he was lying."

"It's the only link I can think of, but it's one that ties together Burdick, Kling, Malek, Olivewood, and *probably* Ronnie." He had to take a moment to catch his breath. "Now ... recall that series of Formulas?"

"VTAFormula 1 through 27? ... Wait! Ventral tegmental area. The cocaine target."

"And one folder was 27Olivewood."

"Another Goddamm illicit experiment!"

My feet were tapping a time-to-go patter on the floor.

"You still don't have your money's worth yet, Pinel. During the inquest, I got a copy of *El Tigre's* autopsy."

"The body spent a week in the Pacific. What would it show?"

"Perjury. I was sure the D.A. would use it against you, but he didn't. Toxicology was negative for cocaine."

"He had bags of the stuff."

"Says you. The fire destroyed everything in that cistern and the flood washed it all to sea."

"I saw him snorting coke by the teaspoonful."

"Snorting *something*. Something the lab didn't detect."

I sprang from the chair. "Goddammit Fred, it fits! Kling finds his Stone. He uses it to make cocaine for Burdick along with his real interest – those brain keys. One of them is some designer drug crap Malek is testing on kids at Olivewood. *El Tigre* and his Fallen Angels go loco on it."

"But what else? You testified that Ronnie's death was more than random opportunity."

"You disagree? You read Kunstler's notes."

"Did *you*?" Stealing Kunstler's notes to get to *El Tigre* was my sin against the Fourth Estate that Fred couldn't forgive. "Think, Pinel. Kunstler was using the Angels to settle old scores against the world. He seized on what happened to Veronica as a tool. But nothing proved that he *targeted* her."

"No? Well I saw *El Tigre's* case file from Olivewood. He had a loony personal grudge against Ronnie. Kunstler fanned the flames."

"But what if someone else had a *business* grudge? Someone who did *more* than fan flames. Someone who might pay for action. Pay with designer drugs, let's say. Malek and Aragon had almost been caught once. If Ronnie had become a problem—"

I pounded a fist into my palm.

"*El Tigre* could have been the solution."

"Find what she had on them and we finally get the story right."

"Count on it, Fred." I clasped his shoulder. "And ... Thanks. For everything."

"Thank you." He looked around. "For this."

I called Bernie over. "When should I come back?"

"We'll take it from here, Pete," Bernie said. "Let me know if you draw heat. I'll make calls."

I shrugged. "I don't think we broke any big laws. I'll let you know."

Bernie grasped the handles of the chair, but I stopped the wheel with my hand.

"Are we square, Fred?" I said.

"Let's just say I stopped trying to make things right a long time ago. You should, too."

Bernie pivoted the chair and plunged Fred into a warm sea of people who loved him. On the elevator I held the door a moment. I heard tall tales and plain old bullshit passed off as memories. I heard shouts and hoopla, laughter – too much laughter – squelched tears, a smattering of silence, and detected a slight decrescendo, a regression *toward* silence. How ironic that a troop of gaily bedight word-knights, approaching the undiscovered country, would probably arrive at that forlorn heart of darkness where words pale.

I watched and listened, but felt distant, apart, a shadow, like I wasn't there.

So I let the door close.

Chapter Forty-One

Sharfstein's door was fashioned from massive planks of
dark, antique hardwood adorned with hand-carved panels –
a door befitting a fortress. The man who opened the door
looked regal enough for it, but a lot older than I
remembered from Ronnie's funeral. No doubt he thought
the same about me.

He wore an effete, silk kimono, but I recognized my
distaste for what it was – historical baggage. Actually, the
robe was expensive and plain – no cheesy, tiger embroidery.
Worse, he looked fit in it. He was scrawny for his height
and I could whip him easily enough, but he'd stayed strong
in his own way – runner strong, built for distance not heavy
lifting.

He squinted – ominous, I thought, in a heart surgeon –
but maybe it was the feeble porch light.

"Pinel?"

"Sharfstein."

Reluctantly he invited me in. A vaulted foyer led to a
soaring rotunda, a good investment in case he ever had to
lie in state while lines of grievers filed past. Gleaming white
marble floors mirrored a dazzling crystal chandelier and a
broad staircase.

"Miss Scarlett sold Tara after all," I said.

"It's home," he countered.

He ushered me through sliding double-doors into an adjacent library as if to isolate me from the living quarters. The room was lined with twenty foot high, floor to ceiling bookshelves served by a rolling ladder and spiral stairs rising to a wrought iron catwalk.

"Wow! Did you read all these books?"

"No, I didn't. What do you want, Pete?"

It bugged me that he could recall my first name so readily when I was hazy on his. I had always called him Doc or just Sharfstein. Stuart? … Stanley? Trying to recall, I noticed photos on his desk. A girl and boy – eight and six, maybe. And a woman.

"Your kids?" I said.

He followed my gaze. "And my wife. Simone."

"Good pictures," I said.

"Good family," he said.

I heard heels clicking across the marble floor and a woman's voice.

"Who was at the door, Steven?"

Steven. Yeah, that was his name. Steven.

She breezed into the library cinching the sash of a shimmery, red dressing gown. Startled to see a visitor, she said, "Oh, I'm sorry. Is everything alright, dear?"

"Simone, this is Pete Pinel. Veronica's first husband. He's lost his way."

The woman was a trim, Newport Beach blonde who looked younger than she was. She had a healthy, artificial tan and real boobs as far as I could tell. She glowed with the kind of daily, personal-trainer fitness that promised life eternal.

I saw her size me up and imagined a *don't-ask-to-use-the-bathroom* look in one arched eyebrow. I disliked myself for thinking that, however. After all, the woman was a stranger and I was no mind reader. Once again, it was just me … my anger keeping me stuck in an irrational rut. Veronica hadn't left me *because of* or *for* Sharfstein. And her death occurred on *both* our watches since I'd never considered mine over. I certainly had no brief against his family, except—

Except the fact that *Sharfstein* could have a Goddamm family.

"Would you like tea, Mr. Pinel?" She glanced uncertainly at her husband. "Or perhaps a drink?"

"He won't be here that long."

"Thank you, Mrs. Sharfstein, but your husband's right. I'm lost and I'll be going. I just need to ask him for a direction."

"Give us a few moments, Simone. I'll be up shortly."

"Good-evening, Mr. Pinel." She had a firm handshake. Like Ronnie's. "I hope you find your way."

The dressing gown swirled when she turned to go. I watched through the double doors as she ascended the staircase.

"Comparing people is a fools-errand, Pete. Too many variables. Now what do you want?"

"Aren't you going to chit-chat, Steve? Ask me what I've been doing for ten years?"

"I'm not interested."

I laughed. "Something about you always reminded me of me, Doc. It complicated the rest of what I felt."

He crossed his arms and waited.

"I have a new angle on Ronnie's murder."

"My God, man! Isn't there a statute of limitations?"

"Not with me."

His face was expressionless.

"The Fallen Angels were just a piece of it. A cover."

"I don't care."

I stared open-mouthed. If not stunned by his blasphemy, I might have decked him.

"Pinel! Look at yourself. You're still consumed by this ... this *disease*."

"Just let me see Ronnie's files. Her notes. Day-planner. Anything at all."

"I can't."

"You *have* to. I need to find—"

"I *can't*. I discarded everything, Pete. Ages ago."

"H..how *could* you?"

He gave me a few moments to let it sink in.

"Okay, Doc. Thanks for opening the door to a leper." I turned to leave.

"You know ... I'm not sure, but..."

I turned back.

"Oh, c'mon. We can look."

He led me down a hallway to a garage entrance, unlocked the door, and flipped a switch. Banks of recessed fixtures illuminated a black Bentley and a white Lotus SUV huddled together amid the emptiness of five bays. We stepped down onto a shiny, white floor that might have been a single slab of porcelain. Cherry-wood cabinetry lined three walls. Sharfstein opened and closed cabinet doors, pawed and pushed things aside.

"I was right," he said, rummaging through a third cabinet. He dragged forward a white cardboard box across which was printed in black ink *Veronica/Desk*.

"I had to clean out her desk at Olivewood. I put this in the garage because ..." He shrugged. "I forgot about it, I suppose."

He yanked the box from the shelf and dropped it on a workbench. Although the cardboard was neither stained nor yellowed, the box seemed ancient to me, like a relic that might crumble if exposed to light and air.

"Not much in it from the feel. Take it."

"Don't you want to see?"

"No."

"Okay. Thanks for the favor," I said.

"Hardly, Pinel. You're hell bound if you can't rid yourself of this."

"Stevenson," I said. "You read *some* of the books."

He pushed a wall switch. One of the sectional garage doors rolled up with a quiet hum rather than the usual tract-house clatter. I grabbed the box and shook it gently, wondering how much an imp weighed. When I stepped outside, Sharfstein allowed the door to fall shut as if it were a portcullis protecting his hearth from the curse I carried.

Chapter Forty-Two

I told myself my office was closer than home, which was true; but more importantly, home was too far from Xuân's. Zigzagging around drivers speeding slower than me, I checked my voicemail – way too many *old* messages and a new one.

"Two admissions, Pete. The first was to an open unit. I looked. It wasn't Walter. The second was to Aragon's research unit: Robert Kirk, an 80-year old male with end-stage dementia signed in by a private conservator for EEG mapping as part of an experimental drug protocol. He's off limits to everyone except Malek and the Aragon staff. Call me!"

I disconnected.

In my office I ripped the packing tape from the box with a single tug. Raising the lids, I peered inside. Ten years ago – because it was too painful to look at, yet too soon to let *anything* go – Sharfstein had upended drawers and boxed wholesale the contents of Ronnie's desk. Setting aside an answering machine, a flip-page desk calendar, and a small framed photograph of Sharfstein, I began to rummage through the detritus a desk gathers.

I glanced at receipts, an unopened Nordstrom's bill, a letter from a friend that had probably gone unanswered –the usual do-it-tomorrow things. I found a

small tin of Tylenol, a half-roll of Tums, a sample vial of
cologne, a box of cinnamon Tic-Tacs, an open package of
Beeman's gum. I squeezed my eyes shut imagining the
headache or upset stomach she might have felt the day she
didn't return. The cologne had long evaporated, but I
remembered how she smelled and it wasn't of cologne. I slid
a stick of Beeman's from the pack and flexed my thumb.
The stale gum broke like brittle glass. I shook the Tic-Tac
box over my mouth. The mints tasted like her kiss.

The bottom of the box was littered with dried up pens
and a thousand odds and ends. On the day my desk drawers
are dumped, the box will certainly include mementoes of
Ronnie. Was I nowhere in *her* reliquary?

Swirling the box as if panning for gold, I caught a glint
of yellow metal. The nugget was shiny – its shell-case
polished brass, its .45 caliber, copper-jacketed nose a
reddish mirror. The bullet certainly wasn't Ronnie's and I
doubted that Sharfstein had owned a gun back then; before
the nightmare fears that guns soothe became real to him.
No, the slug was mine. She must've found it in my pants
pocket, misplaced on a dresser, dropped behind a cabinet.
But why had it ended up in her desk? Had she *chosen* to
keep it at hand; a talisman, a totem, always there amid the
paper clips, spring clips, loose staples, prong fasteners,
push pins, a safety pin; unused rolls of scotch tape; white,
gummed, punched-hole reinforcements scattered like tiny
life rings – fasteners of every description?

I slipped it into my pocket.
Memento mori.

Retrieving the desk calendar, I rifled forward to a date I remembered now like my birthday: the hot, Indian summer day Ronnie went jogging and stopped to catch her breath beneath a stand of eucalyptus trees where the Fallen Angels sat unseen in the cool shade.

Only God can make a tree.

On the page before *that* day, I found a scribbled appointment.

Meet with Malek about mislabeled medicine.

And beneath that.

Call Pete????

I removed the calendar page, folded it carefully, and placed it securely in my breast pocket. The hospice nurse had nailed me after all. I *was* a debt-collector, a process server. And without knowing it, Ronnie had left me an important legal document to deliver.

A death warrant.

The answering machine remained. I unwound the cord and plugged it into an outlet. A glowing message counter read zero. When I pushed the *play* button, a robotic voice confirmed *no messages*. On impulse I pressed the *recorded greeting* button.

"Maybe I'm here. Maybe I'm not."

Ronnie!

"Maybe I'm listening right now, but just don't want to answer. You'll never know."

Another relic. My words and Ronnie's Sam Spade impression – our little joke on friends who couldn't believe she had married a private eye.

"And save your breath about how you've never been this route and don't know the ropes. Just do what you gotta do."

Beep!

She wouldn't have used the machine for her office phone, so why was it in her desk? Maybe for the same reason the box was in Sharfstein's garage. The message was part of her life, a part too fresh to throw away, yet nothing she wanted Sharfstein tripping over. It was just the kind of thing you store in a drawer or a cabinet or a cellar until what it represents is transformed into a heady memory you sip at your pleasure, while the bitter dregs of that memory, the physical thing, the remnant is discarded.

I pressed the button again.

"Maybe I'm here. Maybe I'm not. Maybe I'm listening right now, but just don't want to answer. You'll never know. And save your breath about how you've never been this route and don't know the ropes. Just do what you gotta do."

Again.

"Maybe I'm here. Maybe I'm not. Maybe I'm listening right now, but just don't want to answer. You'll never know. And save your breath about how you've never been this route and don't know the ropes—"

Sharfstein was right. The box contained a demon – a day of wrath whose evils would damn me. But was there also an angel of hope?

"Just do what you gotta do."

Slamming my fist against the erase button, I felt the mechanism shudder. The recorded tape reversed rapidly with a faint squeal like the garble on the *Sgt. Pepper* album that everyone knows says "Paul is dead." Beneath my fist the movement halted. I felt as if I had clenched my own heart in my hand and squeezed until it stopped.

I seemed to hear a fading echo.

Do what you gotta do.

"I am, Ronnie," I said aloud. "I am."

Chapter Forty-Three

Doors.

Things known; things unknown.

And in between? The doors.

Entrance doors. Exit doors.

Doors and choices.

Ladies.

Tigers.

Once again I stood before the thick, over-painted green door that in twilight had glowed like jade. Now, at midnight, it gleamed like obsidian, black and glassy. The lacquered surface mirrored orange streetlamps haloed by an autumn fog. The fog shrouded the ocean below and the hilltop above, as if *here* were all.

Despite dark windows, I rang the doorbell. I saw a flicker behind the peephole and heard the release of a deadbolt. The black door opened.

"I thought you weren't coming."

"Am I too late?"

"Of course not." She brushed at her hair. "If you'll forgive my appearance."

Baggy, flannel pajamas engulfed her. Bare toes peeked from beneath the bunched pajama legs. She turned to get the light.

"Leave it," I said, moving to the couch.

She locked the door and padded over to sit beside me.

"I thought you dislike dark rooms."

"I do."

She folded her legs beneath her. "So you *don't* forgive my appearance."

She expected banter. In meager light through the windows, I saw her frown at my silence.

"It's Walter, isn't it?"

"No. No, relax. I didn't mean to scare you. I got your message. That's Kling's at El Camino. I'm sure of it."

"So we ... we call the police?"

"Not yet. A judge won't grant a search warrant based on my hunch."

"What then?"

"I go get him. That's proof."

"Now?"

"He's safe for now," I said. "Burdick is behind all this and I have what he wants."

"That rock? I thought they took it."

"I think the rock was just a designer drug, probably one Burdick was using on Kling. What he wants are computer files. Kling created a catalyst that mimics the chemistry of living cells. He said it was a "master key to the brain." In an interview he called it the Philosopher's Stone.

"I never heard him use the term, but he was obsessed with that idea. Why ... this is extraordinary."

"Sure. If everything were above board, Kling would nab Nobel number two while our downstream Oppenheimer would reap ...?"

"A medical revolution comparable to ... to penicillin! Not to mention performance enhancement. Life extension. The possibilities are limitless."

"But not for Burdick. He got in too deep. Too many felonies behind this thing. He has to settle for limitless quantities of good old-fashioned and newly-fashioned street drugs."

Her sapphire eyes glimmered like tiny candles. "Walter *isn't* a criminal."

"Geniuses are hard to figure, Xuân. For people like me, anyway. But you're closer to his wattage and you know him. Was *anything* more important to him than his work?"

She looked down. The tiny candles vanished.

"Not ... for years," she whispered.

"He thought he was close to finding his one true answer to the only important question – that's what it sounded like in the interview. He hooked up with Aragon because Les Burdick *is* a criminal. He offered what other companies wouldn't – short cuts. Kling used his catalyst to make cocaine for Burdick and his gangster pals. We were flooded with the stuff for years. In return, Burdick fed Kling's science habit with more shortcuts. Secret research. Unwitting human subjects. Malek was in on it."

"Paul? ... Then perhaps Walter was duped."

"I wish it were true. For *your* sake. But it's not. How deeply Kling was involved, we'll see. Guilty knowledge? That's certain."

"He's a good man," she said, looking down.

"You know him. I don't. Regardless, whatever he had going with Burdick changed a few years ago."

"How?"

"The flow of cocaine stopped. I think Kling turned off the spigot."

"Why?"

"Conscience; fear that Burdick was close to going it alone; wanting time for his real work? Who knows? Regardless Kling must have kept the details of his Stone and its use to himself. That and his secret research files were encrypted and hidden. Burdick wants those files."

"But Walter became ill."

"More likely he was *made* ill with one of his own concoctions on a night Malek was on call."

"Pete! If they're *keeping* him ill, Walter could get well."

"Better anyway. I think Malek makes him better temporarily during those phony EEG sessions. He might be using other designer drugs to open those brain locks Kling talked about. They're trying to find his files and his password."

"And you have them?"

"Just the files. They were stored on his Kindle."

She glanced toward the desk. "That? I read Walter's books all the time. I haven't seen anything."

"Hidden in plain sight. Burdick would have scoured this place, but maybe you had it with you that day. Regardless, the clue was easy to miss."

"Is Walter ... protecting me?"

I tried to say it gently. "With enough time, the proper encouragement usually works. But you can't get blood from a turnip no matter how hard you squeeze. Kling doesn't *know* where he hid the Stone. He may not know the password either."

"I see ... *Partially* reversible."

"It fits. Whatever they gave him must've erased *some* things permanently. I think they're running out of patience or time. Aragon is about to collapse. They boosted his brain to the max with that rock he was carrying, and let him escape with it as an energy button to keep going. They probably bugged him to see where he went and what he did, just in case – how did you phrase it? – he knew but didn't know he knew.

"Why would he come to you?"

"Malek arranged Ronnie's murder. Most likely Burdick ordered it. Kling knew that. In return, he thought I'd help him."

"You have to let me see the files, Pete. I can treat him."

"The folder names are readable, but all the files are encrypted. Probably a C.I.A. connection. Without Kling's *open sesame* the files are irretrievable."

"Then ... it's hopeless."

I shrugged. "We have the Kindle. Burdick didn't. If we get Kling back to familiar surroundings; let him see you, talk to you; show him the Kindle, who knows? It may jog loose the password. Memory is strange. Some things just pop back, right?"

"We can hope," she said flatly. "When?"

I sighed.

"I need a night, Xuân. For a lot of reasons. I think I have to … reboot, I guess. Tomorrow I'll see straight again. Tomorrow I'll make a plan."

"Come upstairs," she said.

"I'm too tired to move."

"Then lie back."

She stood, tossed aside cushions, and disappeared. I stripped and stretched out on my back with an arm covering my eyes. I heard her return and felt the descending flutter of a soft blanket. She burrowed beneath the cover and wormed her way against me.

She had shed the pajamas – I felt bare skin against my skin along the length of our bodies. Her breath – tiny, warm puffs on my neck – began to move down my chest and stomach. I guided her face back to my face, kissed her gently, and lay without moving.

I wasn't *that* tired, so stopping her surprised me. It exposed a disowned need more primitive than sex, an animal drive that sex had often masked and excused; a need that her stillness suggested she understood and shared. We lay touching for the sake of touch alone until the separate rhythms of our breathing came together and we slept.

Chapter Forty-Four

I woke to the aroma of coffee and puttering sounds from the kitchen.

"That smells like good tea," I shouted.

Throwing on my clothes, I made for the breakfast bar. Dressed in blue jeans and a golden sweater, Xuân sat sipping tea.

"Starbuck's French Roast," she said as I poured a starter cup from the Mister Coffee decanter. "Cream is in the pitcher. No sugar, right?"

"Thanks, Xuân. For last night. For everything."

"Are you rebooted?"

"And updated. Seeing straighter than I have in a long time."

"So where do we start?"

"Burdick's research unit. Tell me about it."

"Are you familiar with Camino?"

"Only where it is. Acres of San Clemente palisade. Heirs of the founder have wrangled for years over selling it – more money in ocean view mansions than hospitals, I suppose."

"Aragon leased and rebuilt a third floor wing," she said. "Fifteen beds. All private. They use hospital services for food, laundry, pharmacy, but everything is handed off from hospital staff to Aragon staff at the door. No unescorted entry."

"Single door?"

"No. A two-door setup is common for locked units. Outer door, airlock, inner door. Only one door can be open at a time."

"Cameras?"

"On the ward, yes. I don't remember any at the entrance."

"Describe the doors."

"Heavy. Solid wood, I think. View panes at eye level."

"How about the locks?"

"Electronic. Password protected."

"Any place to hide a cam?"

"It's more complicated than that. Paul took me onto the ward once to see his EEG lab. He used an electronic key-fob to get in. I think he called it an RSA token."

"High tech. The token generates a new password every sixty seconds."

"I'll steal one."

"Why, Dr. Nguyen," I chuckled. "You changed."

"Convictions can be fatal *in extremis,*" she said without lightness. I remembered how effortlessly she had picked my pocket like Vietnamese urchins I had known. I remembered the brothel in Kling's photograph.

"Unfortunately, the token itself is useless," I said. "The token password is paired with a personal pin number. I'd need both. Could I break in?"

"You? Probably. But the unit windows all face the ocean and that side of the building hangs over the palisade. Plus psych hospital windows have to be secure."

I drummed my fingers.

"California is the land of regulations. What do they do in an earthquake? A fire? A zombie apocalypse?"

"Use emergency stairs at either end of the unit. And pass out wooden stakes, I suppose. But emergency doors are activated from inside."

I poured another cup of coffee.

"I'll need more Starbucks," Xuân said.

"And half-and-half."

"Any other requests?"

"A few for later," I said.

"So what do we do, Pete? The place sounds impregnable."

"As secure as a castle."

"That's discouraging."

"Not really. For security, castles were as big a flop as pyramids. They can't run; they can't hide. At best they buy time. The only impregnable one is in Fantasyland."

"... Okay ... but I'm thinking assault and siege are ruled out."

"I hate shooting up hospitals."

"That leaves ... subterfuge?"

"A-plus. I need an insider. It's a long shot, but I have an ally with friends in low places."

I used my cell to call the private number Mendez had given me. He answered but said nothing.

"I want to make a pickup at a certain hospital unit. You have a business relationship with its owner. Access could solve the problems we discussed."

"When."

"Now."

"This your number?"

"Yep."

"Wait for a call."

"*Dos vidanya*," I said.

Xuân looked puzzled. "That's Russian."

"When I spring Kling, I'll bring him here to tackle the password. Keep looking through his stuff. Use your psych tricks to dope out how he would pick a non-repeating, 48- character, alpha-numeric string he wouldn't forget."

"I'll just read his mind, Pete. I'm a shrink, right?"

"I *knew* you could do that."

We moved to the door.

"I'll call you when it's go-time," I said, scribbling on a business card. "If I haven't called back in, say, three hours, use this number. Talk to Manny Vasquez. He's Assistant Chief of Police for San Dismas and a friend of mine. He knows I'm working for you."

"What about that search warrant?"

"He won't need one for a felony in progress. Just tell him I broke in."

I opened the door on bright sunshine. The fog had lifted, the sky was clear. We stood for a moment at the threshold.

"I don't trust Russians, Pete. What's in this for your ally?"

"It's an unholy alliance. I'm figuring nothing."

"He may have similar thoughts."

I paused because I wanted nothing misunderstood.

"People may be hurt today, Xuân. Or killed."

"Make sure it's not Walter or you."

"But ... *otherwise?*"

She looked surprised. "I've known evil, Pete. I realize the cost of resistance. Besides, this is your work."

I kissed her in a way I hoped made up for last night. When I finally stepped back, I answered the question she had posed yesterday when I called from the plane.

"I'm alright with it, too," I said.

She smiled. "This subterfuge you're planning ... what?"

"Think Ulysses."

Her eyes narrowed. "Is there a *Siren* in this story?"

"Why, Xuân! I thought jealousy was an uncollectable debt."

"Philosophy is not an exact science," she retorted. "Well?"

I laughed. "In the beginning was desire. *Every* story has a Siren."

Chapter Forty-Five

As Iraq and subsequent escapades had
demonstrated, an invasion without Intelligence is likely
to sour. I needed the lay of the land, and thought I could
find a map of sorts nearby. Plans and permits for any
structural improvements to Burdick's leased unit would
have been recorded with San Clemente building code
enforcement. I turned North on Coast Highway and
immediately pulled up in front of City Hall, a two story,
red-tiled, white adobe. The building was old for Orange
County, a registered landmark. Someone had pilfered
the brass plaque, however, leaving a discolored
rectangle on the entrance arch. Inside, I glanced at the
lobby directory and tramped up the Spanish-tiled
stairway.

A rattling cough echoed down the vaulted hallway.
Its source was a white-haired clerk sitting alone in the
code office. Judging by the indelible, yellow-brown
stains on the first two fingers of his right hand, his
cough was more than a cold. Smoke-free workplace
rules had to chafe the old guy, but, confined to a solo
office, surrounded by blueprint file drawers, he probably

found a loophole – especially since his habit appeared to be worth dying for.

The clerk checked his computer index, determined that Aragon had indeed applied for permits, and pulled the files. While I inspected drawings, he excused himself and ducked between the cabinets. I heard the squelched creak of an opened window and more coughs. When the clerk reappeared – reeking of smoke and wearing a smile – I gave him back his files and left with the sketch I'd made in my notepad.

The unremitting coughing fit that followed me down the hallway and stairs made me wonder how much time the old man had left. Unless we choose the moment, none of us know, but I tacked three smoke-free days to my own aliquot and marveled that Kling's rock had accomplished something I had failed at for ten years.

Or was I simply ready?

Lacking word from Mendez, I pulled into a Starbuck's lot, climbed into the back seat, and changed into a tee-shirt, loose jeans, and sneakers from the bag I kept in the Blazer. I switched the Colt for a smaller Walther and pocketed the gun along with two full magazines.

Inside, the music volume was set to *stun*, a trend that started when CD's were added to the menu. I like Louis Armstrong, but not when he shouts in my ear, so I carried my French Roast back to the car. Maybe that was the point of the music. Drive off the Wi-Fi freeloaders who use the place as an office. Perusing the *Banner* I had purchased with the coffee, I found what I expected in an unexpected way.

Auctioneer Goes Home
by Fred Lynch, Banner Staff Writer

Seventy-eight years ago, Frankie Joe
Elliott, a self-made man who reveled in fast
ponies, hot dice, Cuban cigars, Canadian
whiskey, and seven-day work weeks, began
a journey that took him from Nashville,
Tennessee to Laguna Beach. Sunday night
he caught a bus for home.

Born in Nashville Jan. 9, 1929, Elliott
showed an early entrepreneurial streak
fostered by the depression. At the age of six
he excelled at collecting discarded bottles
and selling them back to bootleggers. At 12
he was smoking imported cigars and driving
his own gray La Salle convertible with a
license he obtained by adding four years to
his age. That gumption remains
memorialized: public records list Elliott as
83.

The La Salle helped land a job
delivering groceries. Elliott quit school at 14
and two years later bought a kosher deli,
reportedly the only one in Nashville at the
time.

"I think he liked bagels," joked a cousin,
Dotty Murphy, 79, speaking from Nashville.
"And sitting at a school desk all day? Not

Frankie. Too many ideas. Too much energy. Today they'd call him ADD and give him a pill. He read the paper every day, every *word*, especially the classifieds. His memory was amazing. He did arithmetic in his head like an adding machine. When people asked him where he went to college, he always said he went through Harvard, by which he meant "in the front door and out the back." I think my cousin was the smartest person I ever knew. And he failed seventh grade three times."

After World War II, Elliott and his 16 year old bride, Mary, moved to Detroit. Two full time jobs in auto plants were opportunities to sell watches and run break-time crap games. Recognizing TV as more than a fad, he used the money he put aside to found Empire Television Repair.

"Frankie loved to work," Dotty remembers. "And he was darned good at anything he did. Take that TV business. What did he know about electricity, much less electronics? But he hired people who did know, learned from them and even got himself a few patents along the way. Business was play to him, no matter the stakes. Sure, he had spills, but come-what-may, he knew he could get up and find his way. One thing for sure, Frankie was never lost."

For years he served as both president and late night TV pitchman for Empire. Branching out, he became Detroit's largest wholesaler of war surplus electronics.

In 1974 the Elliott's moved to Miami where his handicapped daughter, Millie, could attend a special day school. He called Millie his Princess and named the non-profit he established to help other handicapped children, The Princess Foundation.

Reinventing himself again as both a wholesale jeweler and commercial auctioneer, he earned an auctioneer's honorary title and became *Colonel* Frank. In later years The Colonel loved to hold court at his various businesses, friends aplenty, a long stogie in his mouth, a glass of V.O. in his hand.

Eight years ago, however, Elliott lost first his Princess and then Mary to cancer. Gradually he lost himself and – unable to find his way at times – he reluctantly moved to California to live with his son, John, a psychiatrist. Following his son's sudden death two years ago, Elliott resided at the Laguna Beach Memory Care Assisted Living facility.

"Every Goddamm thing a man has, they take!" he once told this reporter. Recently diagnosed with terminal brain cancer, his last weeks had been spent in the facility's hospice unit.

Elliott knew that Death would win by a knockout, but he wanted one thing remembered.

"I got in a few good shots," his hospice roommate remembers him saying. "You tell it. At least I got in a few good shots."

He also told his roommate that he was eager to catch a bus home and get on with his business. The hospice staff called him confused and tied him to his bed.

Sunday night, Elliott slipped out of restraints, removed a metal bar from his bed, and cold-cocked a security guard. Bolting onto Pacific Coast highway, he waved down a bus about to leave him behind. Responding to the driver's call, paramedics found the Colonel sitting unresponsive at a window seat and pronounced him dead.

Death remains undefeated, of course, and rarely yields a point. But in the last round of the Colonel's fight, one old writer's card had him scoring some pretty good shots, indeed. The Colonel died free, upright, moving, and on his way home.

This reporter likes to believe he went the distance.

Directly beneath Fred's last filing was a headline that read "Veteran Newsman Dies at Desk." A ten-year old half-column cut showed Fred looking healthy and happy. Bernie's obit was a good one – a story, really, a life story with a beginning, middle, end, and a meaning. I was saying my good-byes to Fred when my cell rang.

"Capistrano. Marie Callender's near the Mission. Now."

"Order me a pot pie," I said. Mendez disconnected.

San Juan Capistrano is a few miles north of San Clemente. It boasts an old Spanish Mission, the one the swallows allegedly return to each year on St. Joseph's day. Although the alleged swallows had flown the coop till March, flocks of tourists gathered all year long. Outside the Mission entrance I saw camera-toters pointing excitedly at crows.

Inside the packed restaurant milled a waiting lunchtime crowd. Mendez and a smallish man wearing coveralls sat nursing iced teas at a table for six. The waitress scowled as she passed, but was wise enough to do it behind Mendez' back.

"Rodrigo here works for Aragon at the hospital," said Mendez, when I dropped into a chair. "Tell him, Rod."

The little man worried the ends of a bushy, graying moustache. His eyes darted nervously and he talked in whispers.

"Two nights ago they brung in this old guy. Cuff marks. Fresh razor scrapes on his scalp. Yesterday Malek kept him in his lab for five hours. Guy didn't look so good coming out. Schedule shows him up to bat again at two this afternoon."

"Does he have to leave the unit?" I said eagerly.

"No. Malek's setup has an entry from the hallway for regular Joes, and another one from the ward for the guinea pigs."

I showed him my sketch. "Where?"

"Here," he said.

"What does Malek do in there?"

"Chokes his Chihuahua, maybe. How would I know, man? I look like Igor?"

"Are you working today?"

"Yeah. I'm missing lunch, too."

I pointed at the sketch. "Here. Just outside the ward door. A janitor's closet, right?"

"Yeah."

"Could you have something delivered that I can hide in?"

"You want a wooden horse?"

Smart ass.

"Something more discrete, Rod. A laundry hamper, supply cart, food cabinet."

He rubbed his palms over the top of his buzz-cut head as if polishing a bowling ball.

"You ain't aiming to smooth out the guy what brings it, right? I can't take no fall."

"Does he usually stick around?"

"Not long."

"Then take a minute. Fuss with the cart until he leaves. Any chance I'll be seen from inside sneaking from the closet?"

"Not much."

"So we're good. You push me inside."

He looked at Mendez. "You really need this, right, Sheik?"

"I need it."

"Okay, okay," Rod sighed. "I'll call for a hamper and stash you in the janitor closet on the ward. No one uses it but me."

"Including Malek?"

"What the hell would Malek want in a janitor's closet, man?"

"Let's sync up here, Rod. I need to be waiting for Malek in his lab."

"Ain't no cause for me taking a laundry hamper in there."

"Ooo..kay ... Do you take *anything* in there?

"Supplies, sometimes. I guess I could get a supply cart."

"Let's go with that. Now where can I hide in the lab?"

"There's a long counter with cabinets underneath. Can't say he won't need to get in them cabinets, though."

"A lot of life is luck, Rod."

"Sure. But you know what that penicillin dude said."

What was it with this guy?

"Yeah, I know. So let's prepare our minds for getting back out."

"*Your* mind, gringo. I *know* how I'm getting out."

"You say there's a door directly to the hall. Can I use that?"

"Not without a token."

"You can slip me yours along with your password after we get inside."

Rod whirled toward Mendez. "C'mon, Sheik! I got two strikes, man. He uses my code, it *makes* me."

"Chill out, Rod," said Mendez. "What's plan B, Pinel?"

I shrugged. "Malek, I guess. Will he have his token?"

"Sure he will," Rod said eagerly. "In and out all day."

"Then we're good."

"Uh … you're gonna need *his* password, you know?" Rod added reluctantly.

I flashed on Ronnie's calendar page and her scribbled 'Meet with Malek about medicine.'

"He'll give it to me," I said.

"God damn, Sheik!" Maybe it was my face. "This guy's not of the Friendly Persuasion. He's goin' down for mayhem at a *minimum,* and he'll *shop* me. Accessory, accomplice, abetting? Same as Murder One with two-strikes, man!"

Mendez gave me a stare-down glare. "Rod here is a citizen, Pinel. A working stiff who owes me a favor from his time inside."

"Rod, who?" I said, looking around. "I never met the man."

Mendez studied my face and said, "He's good, Rod."

Eying me like he would a strange snake, Rod said, "Lot to ask Sheik. You trust him?"

Mendez laughed. "Fucker'd shoot me while he's eating jellybeans, 'cause he knows I deserve it. But when he thinks his word is supposed to matter, it does. He's good."

"Okay, okay, he's good. But even if they don't prove nothing, I'm burned after this. I'll need a new job."

"You'll need a *better* job, Rod. Something with the county. Union steward, maybe. Some cash and a vacation, too. *No problemo.*"

Rod turned to me. "Okay, man-who-ain't-met-me ... once you're in, I go home with diarrhea. Like Sheik says, I'm a citizen, not muscle. Inside you're on your own."

"I *like* this plan, Rod. Gives me a warm glow. Make sure Malek's not in his lab and call for the cart about 1:25. I'll be in the closet." I rapped the table with knock codes. "One then two means you're waiting for the cart. Two then one means come on out. Should I write it down?"

"If you think you'll forget."

I glanced at my watch and stood. "Still time for lunch, Rod."

Mendez grabbed my arm.

"We'll need to trade afterwards, Pinel."

"Sure, Sheik. We're allies. My office as soon as I spring Kling. I'll call."

"You won't need to call, man."

Chapter Forty-Six

The janitor closet door was brown metal with a louvered vent at the bottom. Other than slats of light through the louvers, the room was dark. I hated dark rooms. After fifteen minutes straddling an overturned bucket, I especially hated dark, claustrophobic janitor closets that reeked of bleach and stale mops. I hoped that Rodrigo was a punctual sort.

I also hoped he could resist rooting out a competing offer. My faith in a two-strike *citizen* was zip and the thought of opening the door on Armstrong pointing a cannon was unpleasant. All I could bank on was Rod's fear of Mendez, but that was probably a good wager.

A one-two rap on the door told me that Rodrigo was waiting for the cart. I had called Xuân from the car just before I made my way to the closet. I glanced at my watch. A minute later I heard a conversation ending with *adios*. After another minute, I heard the two-one tap, ducked outside and crouched into the bottom of an opened, metal cart. Rod closed the door and we began to move, stopping and starting as he dealt with the lock, maneuvered through the two entry doors, and made his way into Malek's lab.

"*Vamos!*" Rodrigo hissed, swinging open the cart.

I scrambled out. The windowless room – a door on either side – consisted of an exam table, computers, screens, IV poles, and several wire-entangled, roll-paper recording devices that I imagined were EEG machines. Eager to *vamos* himself, Rodrigo slammed shut the cart.

"Which is the unit door?" I said.

"The one I'm opening right now, so get back."

"Wait. Give me your restraint key."

"Christ, man! You want *mole* on your meat, too?"

He fumbled in his pocket for the key and watched me wipe it clean of prints. Before I could ask for anything else, he skedaddled with the cart. In California, two-strikes keeps a guy stepping lively.

Opening cabinets, I found equipment Malek might need and settled on a cabinet beneath the sink that held mostly cleaning supplies. Palming the Walther, I nudged bottles to the rear and scrunched inside. The exam table was visible through a gap between the doors.

Fifteen minutes crept by until I heard the solenoid click of an electrical bolt. Kling – his head shaven – shuffled zombie-like into my field of view. Malek followed.

"Lend a hand," Malek grunted, struggling to maneuver Kling onto the table. Armstrong appeared.

So much for my sketchy plan.

They boosted Kling onto the exam table and cuffed his wrists to the frame. Kling sat open-mouthed, staring blankly. Malek dangled an IV bag from a pole, attached the tubing to a catheter in Kling's forearm, and opened the valve. Within a minute Kling's lifeless form exploded. Hurling curses, he bucked against the handcuffs, peeling skin from his wrists, almost snapping his pencil forearms.

"You mindless imposter!" he croaked, kicking his legs.

"Struggle helps neither of us, Doctor Kling," Malek said patiently.

Kling's spluttering and thrashing waned. Breathing deeply, he seemed to muster his thoughts.

"Do you still remember why we're here?" Malek said,

"I stopped making Burdick's cocaine."

"Wisely your files were hidden and encrypted. Burdick had to mark time. But his investors finally forced his hand and now time is up. Can you recall where we left off?"

"The detective," Kling said. "Pinel."

"Did you give him your password? Tell him where to find your files?"

"This is pointless, Malek. I don't remember! How could I, uh..." A cloud crossed his face. "Not be factual."

"Lie?"

"*That*. I couldn't, uh ... lie after all you've done to me."

"No, of course not. I ruled out lying months ago. All you remember is some device."

Unconsciously Kling's right index finger traced a rectangle. "That, uh ... *thing*."

"Which might be a smartphone? An external drive? An iPad?"

"Potter!"

"Potter what? Potter who? ... You don't remember."

"*You* did that to me."

"True, but irrelevant. Burdick won't accept that you *can't* remember. Tell me ... what year is it?"

"1985, of course. No ... no, that *can't* be right. Nine..teen ..."

Malek flicked at a tiny bubble in the IV tubing. "I'm running out of this, you know. *All* of your brain keys. And only your Philosopher's Stone can make them. Soon we'll have nothing left to reverse the dementia. You remember what that means, don't you?"

Kling seemed not to hear. "Did you tell me the year?"

"See? Your immediate and recent memory is progressively more flawed. Long term memory is punched with holes and failing, too. At this point, recall may truly be impossible, but the rub is, I have to *prove* it. Prove a negative. See our predicament? Oh, well! ... Let's try a different approach. You don't know *what* you told Pinel, but perhaps you recall why you saw him?"

Kling grimaced. "I ... I thought that if I told him what you and Burdick did to the woman, he'd protect me. Find my files. The evidence is all there. I kept it. My insurance."

Malek laughed. "Pinel would have killed you. His sense of justice is quite primitive."

"I'm not guilty of that hideous crime."

"Guilt is an outmoded construct for a mere chemical state. Your brain keys can transmute guilt into spotless conscience. Innocence into depravity. Or – as with Formula 27 – boys into beasts. You do remember *that*, don't you?"

"Psychopaths! Long before my experiments."

"So pejorative a term. They were neurochemically challenged. It made them useful."

"They brutalized that poor woman."

"One of their uses. Burdick decided that *she* had become un-useful. He's quite the pragmatist."

I squeezed the handle of the Walther.

"You're both monsters," Kling said.

"Another ugly word to describe a simple chemical state. But if we're going to use it, how monstrous was remaining silent to continue your work with fresh subjects?"

"What was done, was done. Samsara. I ... I rose above it. My work was above all that."

"Forgive my impertinence, *Doctor*. But if monsters do exist ... which of us is worse?"

Kling's head began to droop. "What ... what year is it? Did you tell me the year?

Malek told him again

"Is it Springtime?"

"November."

"I ... I remember Spring."

Malek increased the IV flow. Kling looked up.

"Which of us is worse? How dare you!" he spat. "I have devoted myself—"

"To *you*! ... Strutting. Preening. That constant tone of condescension. You're a narcissist, Kling. You wanted Pinel to find your files for *one* reason – credit for the Stone's discovery even if credit destroyed you and everything you've worked toward."

"How unimaginative you are," Kling said.

"You condescending—" Malek snarled, but he caught himself and took a few deep breaths. "Alright ... let's continue. You told the detective what?"

"The uh ... number box," Kling said, his attention caught by something I couldn't see. "How many, uh ..."

"Number box?" Malek turned his head. "The clock?"

"That! How many numbers. How much?"

"Still the scientist, I see. Yes, the antidote buys less and less time." Malek thumbed the IV valve to full flow. "So let's give you a good boost and then try a few more brain keys. First the key to the memory center. Then the neuropathic pain key."

Kling began to tremble.

"Keep him from trying to harm himself, Mr. Armstrong. I'll go prepare the solutions."

Reaching into his pocket, Malek withdrew an RSA token attached to his keychain. He punched his pin number into the hallway lock and added numbers from the token. When the deadbolt clunked, he pushed open the door, but halted and turned back to Kling.

"Ever jangle keys near lab rat cages, Doctor? It's quite a Buddha thing, actually. The jumbled frequencies trigger some unbearable terror. I imagine the mechanism is explained by your fear key. The rats cower, squeal, climb the cage walls, bite each other, kill each other. Hour after hour, day after day. No habituation. A reflex so primal, experience doesn't mute its expression. Delightful ... delightful to observe."

Watching Kling's face, Malek jangled his keys.

Chapter Forty-Seven

I waited for Malek to leave, carefully positioned my feet in front of the cabinet doors, and tapped on a sink pipe with the Walther. When I saw Armstrong stoop to investigate, I kicked open the doors and sent him tumbling. Piling from the cabinet, I sprang at him. Grunting and heaving, we punched and scratched across the floor. A flailing fist knocked the Walther under a counter.

Scrambling to our feet, we faced each other. I'd landed a good shot or two and Armstrong was cautious. He shuffled forward, moving warily. I appreciated the compliment and let him come. Slipping his left, I took a jarring roundhouse on my shoulder to step inside. One, two, three jabs opened him up just enough to land a solid hook to his ear. Staggering backward to shake it off, he planted both forearms in front of his face, and stomped forward. I suppose he expected me to break my knuckles on the bones of his arms attempting to score points on his chin. But someone once said if you ain't cheatin', you ain't tryin'. I kicked him in the balls.

Armstrong oofed and doubled over. I spun him around and kicked him again from behind. Grabbing the back of his shirt, I rammed him head first into a corner of the exam table and imagined the thin temporal bone of his skull crunching. He stiffened, dropped to the floor and – save for a rapid, shallow panting – lay still.

"You … you were inside!" Kling said, staring at the cabinet as if it were a prop in a magic trick.

"I'm here to rescue you," I said, although, after what I'd just heard, I was lying. "I have your Philosopher's Stone."

"How can I be sure? I … I can't remember?"

"You'll have to use the password."

"Password …" he said, mouthing the sound.

"Everything is encrypted."

"Yes. That, uh … that Agency." He shook his head with frustration. "Many projects. You know who I mean."

"The C.I.A. Do *they* know the password?"

"I … I don't *think* so. I access a program to encrypt the work I do for them. I chose a new key and used it for my own files."

"What was it?"

"What was what?"

"The key. The *password*."

"I've told Malek all this. I don't know." He started tugging at the handcuffs. "I want to go!"

"Malek has the cuff key."

"NO! No, no, no. Now! I can't see Malek again. I can't!"

"Shh! You'll get us caught."

He continued to squirm. I retrieved my gun from under the counter and waited beside the door.

Chapter Forty-Eight

When he opened the hallway door, Malek spotted Armstrong on the floor and dropped a tray of supplies trying to bolt. I yanked him inside by his coat. The automatic door slammed shut.

"Any excuse," I said, jamming the Walther into Malek's gaping mouth. Spitting blood and tooth fragments, he started to wobble, so I sent him sprawling. He propped himself spraddle-legged against Armstrong and moaned.

Armstrong moaned, too. I'd taken a .38 from his belt, but – assuming he was seeing angels – I hadn't patted him down. Birdies seemed more likely now. He opened his eyes and reached for an ankle holster.

"Gun!" I shouted, as he yanked free a .25.

Instinctively he looked for a second threat, buying me an instant to kick the bloody side of his head and finish whatever damage had been done by the exam table. He hit the floor and stiffened, arms at his sides. Two spasms arched his back off the floor before he went limp.

I flexed my toes, worried I might have broken some on Armstrong's head. In sneakers, a kick wasn't the smartest play, so I guess I still had issues. I made sure he was dead, frisked him for any other weaponry, and pocketed the .25 before Malek got ideas. Resistance from that quarter was unlikely, however. Malek's eyes were rolling. Tears spilled down his cheeks and blood oozed between the fingers of hands clamped over his mouth. I retrieved his key ring and freed Kling. The old man leaped up, bounded over Armstrong, and slapped Malek hard – two, three, four times. He had issues, too.

"Here's the skinny, Malek," I said as he rocked back and forth, sobbing. "Pay attention! This is on the test. I don't favor torture as a way to mine info. It rarely works. But what I want, I know you know." I dangled his RSA token. "I'll know right here, right now, if you lie, and we'll just keep at it. So – unlucky for you – torture is the perfect tool for this job."

When Malek opened his mouth to scream, I poked the gun barrel back inside as a muffler.

"What's your RSA pin?"

He mumbled around the barrel. I ripped it out again. The front sight took meat and another tooth.

"0821!" he spluttered through his hands. "Mother's birthday. 0821."

I turned toward the hallway door. Kling had yanked out his IV. He was holding an open, brown vial from Malek's spilled tray and eagerly licking a crystal. If it was the rock he'd shown me in my office, it was smaller.

"What are you doing?" I said.

"Dosing myself. The IV ran out." His speech was already clearer, more rapid. "I'll need these, too," he said, grabbing up the small IV bags from the floor.

"Find a box or something. Hurry. We're leaving."

Kling rummaged through cabinets, emptied a cardboard box and began to throw things inside. I punched Malek's 0821 pin into the lock followed by the six digits on the fob.

"Get to the elevator and hold it for me," I said, easing open the door.

"What about Malek?"

"Just hold the elevator." I peeked into the hallway.

With a super-nova flash and the roar of worlds colliding, the universe exploded. My nose splatted against the latch jamb. I slumped to my knees, trailing a streak of blood down the casing.

You have to hit a man hard to cold-cock him from behind; hard enough to spill his brains because, if he's still conscious, he's pissed, and I was both. I hadn't considered Malek so hands-on, but intended to correct my mistake ASAP. Rolling onto a hip, I raised the Walther to put a long-overdue bullet through his forehead. The world I saw reappearing through the nebula left by the big bang made no sense, however. Malek was still curled on the floor, whimpering through his palms, and, beside him, Armstrong was clearly halfway to hell.

Something cracked across my shoulder, jarring the gun from my grip.

"You're going to kill me!" I heard Kling screech. "They said you'd kill me!"

I looked back. Kling stood brandishing the IV hangar from the exam table like Excalibur. I lunged for his legs, but face-planted, empty-handed, when he hopped backwards. Excalibur fell in a swift, silver arc, and I was good-nighted.

Chapter Forty-Nine

Something existed.

Then awareness existed.

Next came awareness of awareness, of something being aware. Awareness of me.

Then came a terror that thundered past all its false names and shadow images to spring full-blown from Spiritus Mundi.

Fear without object.

Intrinsic fear. Original fear.

Fear of everything. Fear of nothing.

Fear of not being.

Fear of *being*.

I begged for the lucid dream moment that would offer a choice between consciousness and oblivion. As always it came as a voice, but not as a voice that promised salvation this time. The voice was Kling's — loud, pressured, maniacal. I knew that if I chose consciousness, my fear would explode. My only hope was to abandon hope, to embrace *not* being. I opened my eyes anyway because ... because *fuck Kling*!

The fear surged, but, strangely, its *grip* weakened. And not because my eyes were open; what I saw made me cringe. Fear had morphed Kling into a hideous apparition, some nightmare archetype. Recoiling like a mouse engulfed in the exploding shadow of a swooping falcon, I strained against leather straps binding me to the exam table. But – in the defiant equivalent of an upraised middle finger – I willed myself to face him. And once again a moment of willed rebellion trumped, if not the fear, the fear's *control*. When Kling frowned, I sensed an inkling of hope.

He adjusted the thumbwheel valve of an IV poked into my arm. Within seconds I was wracked with fear shakes and would have whimpered if the words *fuck you, fuck you, fuck you* weren't stuck in my throat. Nevertheless, I *refused* to close my eyes or look away. Kling seemed perplexed.

My mind was clattering like an old IBM punch-card sorter, sifting thousands of cards and spitting out the few relevant ones. Batch one: Kling was dosing me. The fear I felt was from the drug; just a trick like water-boarding – you *feel* as if you're drowning but you're not.

Remember that!

*No matter **what** you feel.*

I forced myself to look around, reconnoiter. Armstrong was still dead. Malek sat gagged and motionless, handcuffed to a chair. He, too, was hooked to an IV bag. Having only Kling to worry about was a positive, but – trick or not – the fear flooding my veins made it hard to hold the thought.

I made myself look at Kling again.

"Kiss my ass!" I shouted, finding my voice. The words weren't part of a plan, just part of me, but Kling's expression made them a plan. Words aren't sticks and stones, but they can hurt *almost* as much. The *right* words, anyway.

"You gawky nerd. Egghead. Bookworm. I'll dunk your head in the crapper. I'll eat your Goddamm lunch."

Kling sprang at me. Swinging too close for leverage, he landed a baby blow on my chin that almost broke his thumb. Squealing, he jumped back, wagging his hand as if he'd caught it in a car door. My mind spit out more punch cards. The first said that such words – obviously heard before – were a weapon. The second warned that, if he kept hitting me, he'd get better at it. Most importantly, however, was one noting that pain and rage *both* blunted my fear. Perhaps emotions were contained like potatoes in a sack – only so many fit before some started to spill.

I had another tool.

Kling massaged his hand.

"Silly ... silly of me to play *your* game. Emotion so distracts a scientist."

A free tip. Thanks, pal.

"Actually, your response to my fear key is rather intriguing. Fear is basic. Paleocortical. Reptilian, really. Malek was quite correct about rats and keys." He studied my face for a moment. "Micro-expressions are reflexive. They can't be suppressed. You *are* terrified. And yet, you don't *act* terrified. You act angry."

Sure, I'm terrified. And yes! I'm angry. I'm angry because I know you're deliberately terrifying me, you fucker. A man is not a rat.

"I wish we had more time. Up to a point, personality traits can override a chemical state."

"Damn right, Kling. We get to *choose*," I growled.

"A formulation more philosophical than scientific, but I agree. We choose ... up to a point. We'll explore that point in a moment. First I want you to see another Kling Key in action."

The eponym was new. Maybe the rock was giving his narcissism a nitro-boost that I could also use against him.

"Cool alliteration. Or better! Cuckoo Kling Key."

"You're trying to annoy me."

"Your grasp of the obvious is astounding. I bet the King of Sweden was enthralled with you. Of course, those royals are inbred, aren't they?"

His bitter expression – good for me or bad – was at least a reaction. When he closed the pinch-wheel valve on my IV line, my tubful of fear drained to a *fear of being restrained by a lunatic* level, which, given the situation, seemed appropriate.

"That, uh ... agency has been delighted with my tools."

The sorter dropped another punch card. Overdosing was keeping him sharp and making him grandiose, but he still had trouble finding words.

"That, *uh, uh, agency* is the C.I.A," I snickered. "How many times do I have to tell you that?"

He almost hit me again, but checked himself and quickly licked the crystal. Another card fell. Kling *needed* my information. Whatever gauntlet he ran me through left me alive and lucid until what I told him proved correct. Torture really *is* a lousy tool. I could say anything and buy time.

I was prepping myself for Round 2 when Kling surprised me by switching his attention to Malek. A large

IV with a smaller piggyback bag ran to a catheter in Malek's neck. Kling ripped a bloody gag from Malek's mouth, but the man remained motionless, staring dumbly.

"Cat have your tongue?" Kling cackled.

Nothing.

"Malek and his deceased associate attacked me in my lab," Kling said. "The compound in the large bag is what they used to make me ill; what they used to *keep* me ill. It's the *antithesis* of a skeleton key; it *locks* most of the brain's locks. One is aware, but helpless, a mind imprisoned in a body over which it wields no influence. The smaller bag contains a solution of the crystal in my hand – a temporary antidote they used to make me lucid for their *torture* sessions. I showed it to you in your office." He snickered. "Lacking tolerance, I imagine you had quite an experience with what you licked off your finger. Intravenously, the initial activating effects will be immediate for Malek. Watch."

Kling thumbed shut the larger bag and opened the valve of the piggyback. Responsiveness flooded Malek's face.

"Dr. Kling! Don't do this to me! Please. I ... I ... can help you! You need my help."

Kling placed his thumb on the closed valve. "Soon you'll be of no help to anyone. *Ever.*"

Malek started to scream. Kling laughed, poked the gag back in place, and turned to me.

"Observe the expected response to jiggled keys. Of course, Malek *is* a rat."

Kling picked up a small syringe that might have been a scorpion or tarantula by the willies it gave me.

"Fear was merely to prepare your brain chemically for this key: the key to memory. Do you know what memory is?"

Combat is all about balance. Getting an opponent off balance is a winning strategy.

"A paradise from which one cannot be driven, a hell from which one cannot escape," I said, trying to sound smug.

"How erudite."

"Bet you don't know who said it."

"I have no time for nonsense," he snapped.

Score!

He removed a plastic covering from the glinting needle and held the syringe to the light. He flicked at an air bubble and pressed the plunger until a single drop oozed from the needle like venom from the fang of a milked cobra. I saw Malek lean in to watch. I doubted it was from scientific curiosity. He was pissed about his teeth and eager to see me dance.

"The medium upon which we record experience is of limited capacity. Almost immediately overwritten," Kling began pedantically.

I hoped for a *long* lecture.

"A mere sliver can be saved – prioritized bits, all highly processed and tightly compressed. Memory is *not* recorded experience; it is Photoshopped experience. We extract and delete details; we burn in certain areas, dodge and blur others; we alter the image using filters of personality, intelligence, prejudice, mood. Drugs can enhance, dull or even eliminate the *formation* of memories."

Kling poked the syringe into a port on my IV. The stillness was so complete, I heard the soft squeegee sound the needle made penetrating the rubber gasket.

"*Recall* of our creations is a different matter. Memories are *made* in specific brain locales that can be targeted. Once made, however, memories are broadcast across the cerebrum. They exist everywhere simultaneously as an interconnected web. That's why massive brain injury leaves long term memory relatively unimpaired. Normally a memory is lost only with a general decline in cortical processing or when the neurochemical pathways to *all* of its links fade through disuse. Such pathways can be precipitously erased, however. *Chemically.* By bunglers!" Whirling, he slapped Malek again. "That's why this key failed with me!"

He glared for a moment and then turned back. I nodded eagerly as if to say … *Please, go on!*

"If a memory is *not* erased … merely dormant from disuse or suppressed, it can be recovered by activating one of its significant links. I verbally or visually trigger a *probe* memory. A conflicted and irreconcilable, *partially*-repressed memory works best. It acts like a lock pick inserted into all of its activated links. The compound in this syringe then "jiggles" the picks until the links locked by repression or recalcitrance open. So exposed, those memories can be enhanced and recalled. Or alternatively, destroyed."

Keep him talking. Stall!

"You're blowing smoke up my ass, Kling."

"Such a colorful idiom to cloak your stupidity. I first tested the concept during shock treatments. At the moment of shock, I triggered a conflicted memory that I suspected was linked to repressed *pathological* memories. The seizure induced by the shock was insufficient to *erase* the linked memories – I later created a chemical that could – but it discharged the emotional valence that kept them repressed. They could be processed and integrated."

"Aren't patients put to sleep when you zap their brains?"

"I could hardly trigger a probe memory during sleep."

"They consented to being awake?"

"Oh, I doubt they would have," he laughed.

I hoped for more, but school was out. He craned forward. I was ready to bop him with my forehead if he got close enough, but he was smarter than Malek.

"After Burdick and Malek had that woman murdered, I kept track of you. I have an entire file. I know just the conflicted memory to rattle your cortex and bypass every defense. You'll tell me where my Philosopher's Stone is."

"You don't have to do this," I said lamely.

"Of course not," Kling replied. "We agreed on that. It's a choice."

He poised his thumb over the plunger of the syringe. His face was that of a kid at a circus who expects a good show.

"Wh..what conflicted memory?" I said.

I felt a hot jet in my arm and, simultaneously, his cold, wet lips against my ear.

"Veronica Sharfstein," he whispered. "Veronica Sharfstein. Veronica … Veronica … Veronica…"

Chapter Fifty

Remembering?

Since when had *forgetting* been an option?

Kling was throwing me right into my Briar patch.

The persistence of bad memories was something I'd known since childhood. Even then Dali's painting of melting watches was a favorite image because a world of melting watches felt *so* familiar.

This turn I could do standing on one foot, I thought.

Until it hit me.

* * * * *

"I told you not to come here, Pete."

I see Veronica blocking the threshold of our home in Laguna Beach, a place her father left her, the house she grew up in.

But wait. This isn't happening; it already happened, so you're remembering it. And it's not a repressed memory, a conflicted memory. If anything, it's always there. Stay alert. Maybe it'll morph into something else, something nightmarish. Keep talking to yourself. Tell yourself whatever happens is just a bad trip. Talk yourself down.

"Veronica ...?"

"How much clearer could I be?"

"Veronica! You're acting like — "

"I told you I didn't want to see you again. Ever. It hurts too much."

*It **does** hurt this time. Like going under the knife with only a bullet to bite on. Why? What's different? What have you always missed? Is it because you're seeing it with such a peculiar focus? Look at Ronnie's face; the emotion in her face is so crystalline. But ...? No, wait. Don't look directly. See. See! The rest is blurry. Her clothes? Just clothes. Not what she was really wearing. You don't remember what she was wearing. The room behind her? You remember a room, but not **the** room. It's just a vague backdrop, like a painted scrim. And flickers. Like seams. Like that occasional slight mismatch between edited cuts in a film. You've edited this experience with a laser focus on Ronnie's emotions. But what you **don't** see is usually the key. What did you ignore?*

"Veronica! Let me —"

"No! No more talk. No visits. No phone calls. No quick coffees for old times' sake."

"Ronnie ...?"

"Please, Pete, just leave."

Okay. You remember what comes next. You say the words – the alpha and omega words, the make-it-right-again, make-it-good-again words.

"I *love* you."

"Don't say it. Don't say ANYTHING! I won't play this scene over and over like we did at the hospital."

How ... how can she say that? How can she take it back now?

"I can barely walk yet, Ronnie. Don't make me stand out here. Inside we can—"

"NO!"

There! You've not seen that before. You've never felt it. You're flinching at her sudden, violent shrug of your hand from her arm. You're tucking your chin, raising a shoulder. Instinctively protecting yourself. As if ... as if you're in a fight.

"You're nuts! I live here."

"Community property? I'll buy you out."

"Christ ... you *are* nuts!"

How the hell could she say that? Did she ever know you at all?

"Look at me, Veronica."

"I'm through looking at you. Night after night I looked at you. I watched. A month sitting beside your bed in that hospital room. Watching! ... Would this be the night you died? Would this one?"

"You think it was roses for me?"

"You chose it. I didn't."

"Right! I chose to get SHOT!?"

Lower your voice, Goddammit!

"You chose to go to that bar knowing it was likely. For what? For Jesus Ramirez."

"He's my friend."

"A friend? ... A high school buddy you let claim the life of your *wife*. Did you even think about me? Did you?"

"He was in over his head."

"And you saved him."

"Veronica, I told you—"

"ALWAYS THERE!"

"No one is always there, Ronnie. I couldn't be."

"Is … is *that* what you thought I—?"

"What?"

"It doesn't matter."

You didn't understand then; you figured it out later. But remembering this now, you **do** *understand. And that's different, too. If memory is Photoshopped experience – Where did you hear that? Who told you that? – then maybe its re-experience is edited, too, using a filter of who you are now.*

"Be reasonable. You have a life. I do, too."

"Of course you do. And I wasn't in it. I don't even want to be now. People died."

"Who gives a rat's ass?"

"Stop it. They weren't animals."

"No, they were men. And they were shooting me!"

There it is again! So obvious this time, and yet you've never seen it, never felt it. Your weight is shifting. Feel that? Your shoulders are starting to turn. See? You're about to walk away. You're walking away! And there. A choice. Shoulders sagging; weight shifting back to both feet.

"Look, Ronnie, I understand the bleeding heart. You're a doctor, you save people. But these weren't good guys, okay? Not patients. Not kids from Olivewood. They were—"

"Stop it. STOP IT! I won't hear all this again."

Oh, God! Her emotions so crystalline! She's choking back sobs. Her chest is shuddering. Tears, mascara streaking her cheeks. I don't want to bring this pain and fear and guilt on her. She's above that, beyond it, free.

WHERE IS THE PHILOSOPHER'S STONE?

Who cares? You can't think about that while she's hurting. You can't bear to see her hurting.

"What was I supposed to do, Veronica? What?"

"Think of me, that's all. Just think of me. You had your … your friend. Your duty. You had your job. But where was I, Pete? Was I even there? You had your life. Where was I?"

"Veronica …?"

"We've played this out, Pete."

"Veronica, I love you."

It's like you're under the knife, but awake. A terrible lucid dream. Choose oblivion. Don't feel this part. Erase it as you always have. Erase the pain of that awful, awful hesitation.

"… I … *thought* I loved you, too."

She doesn't mean it. She can't! Erase that feeling. She's just in pain. She just needs time. Distance. Distance from your work, that's all. She wasn't meant for your work. You knew that all along. You can't have, uh … feelings or whatever about that. You knew. You knew that you … that you weren't—

*But … but not **bad** enough either. Not bad enough to find out from a Goddamm newspaper. Not bad enough to have your Goddamm phone calls ignored!*

"Maybe I'm here. Maybe I'm not. Maybe I'm listening right now, but just don't want to answer. You'll never know."

Leave it alone. So many good memories. So many sunshine memories. Why this one when you were ... when you were ... so ... Goddammed—

WHERE IS THE PHILOSOPHER'S STONE?

Who cares about that when she's still using your message? It's yours, damn it. Her Sam Spade impression, but your Goddamm words.

"And save your breath about how you've never been this route and don't know the ropes. Just do what you gotta do. *Beep.*"

"Ronnie? ... Ronnie, pick up. C'mon, sweetie. Please! I know you're there, so pick up ... Just talk to me. I need to talk. I want to see you, Ronnie, please. I'm hurting here!"

That echo. How empty and hollow the receiver feels against your ear.

"You know I love you. I know you love me."

*You know she **thought** she did. You're remembering that this time.*

"Dammit, Ronnie, let's fix this! ... Ronnie? Pick up. Pick up!"

Nothing. Nothing but a recording tape hissing softly like a burning fuse.

"Change your message. It's mine!"

You're seeing yourself bang down the phone and kick a pile of Banner pages to retrieve a crumpled People page. You're re-reading the society squib you'd missed that morning. "John Sharfstein, MD, Newport Beach heart surgeon, seen at a South Coast Repertory fundraiser squiring Veronica Lamb."

Her maiden name. As if nothing ever happened! No, it wasn't final yet. It wasn't over.

"Maybe I'm here. Maybe I'm not ..."

"Squired? Is that what they call it in the family papers? IS IT! Well, how about I go kick this guy's squiring ass! ... No. For..*get* it! I've tried, Ronnie, but I'm done. Don't bother to call, 'cause I'm not answering either! Adios."

Go ahead. Smash down the phone. Wad the People page. Throw it at the wall. But listen, too. Words in your head. Words you wouldn't hear then, words you erased.

I won't play the sap. I won't play the sap!

Grab the beer and get back to the couch. And watch your damn step before you fall and break your neck. You're half-drunk – half of you half-drunk. The other half won't answer the phone. Dial again. Try again. But talk to yourself, listen to yourself. Feel what you're feeling that you didn't feel?

If I feel, it's over.

"Maybe I'm here. Maybe I'm not. Maybe I'm listening right now, but just don't want to answer. You'll never know."

So choose. **Don't** *feel. You need her. You need her now. Later is later. Deal with the inevitable later. Wear the gold hat. Play the sap. Don't feel. Keep the connection alive. Choose.*

"Oh, Christ, Ronnie. It's the beer talking again. Sorry. Honest, I'm sorry! Go back to sleep and forget this crap. But, call me, okay? At least call me."

Anger toward the hated? That comes naturally to you, doesn't it? It's righteous anger. Just anger. And Justice is black and white. Scorched earth. Nothing transmutes that elemental fact.

*But anger toward the loved? Anger at Ronnie for trying to love only a **part** of you?*

You disowned it.

Anger at a sap for trying to love completely with missing pieces?

You disowned that, too.

You chose oblivion. You closed your eyes and were borne back, ever back.

Poor Ronnie.

Poor Pete.

It's a crying shame. You both tried, didn't you? Tried to be who you were and who you weren't at the same time.

*And **that's** the crying shame.*

So cry! ... And let it go.

Wh..what's happening to you? Almost a physical sensation. Like a breath of fresh air through an opened door; like stale air escaping a sealed room. Why? What door did you open?

WHERE IS THE PHILOSOPHER'S STONE?

That voice again? What is ...? Wait. I get it! It's Kling. I remember now. A conflicted, irreconcilable memory used as a lock pick. I think it worked, Kling. But not as you expected.

Listen!

Listen!

From a doorway at the end of a hall spills laughter unencumbered by pain or fear or guilt. It's magnetic!

You're drawn through the door. You're seeing her for the first time again; you're seeing her again for the first time – a memory that seems somehow rain washed and rainbow new. Her brilliant eyes make a catch in your breath; her radiant smile, her cockiness, her wit, and all her sweet etceteras capture you. You're falling like a potzer checkmated in three moves.

"So ... until we meet again?" she says.

In another time or place, you might have turned somersaults for her, or walked a fence or balanced a straw on your nose, and you're loving how you would have gloried in her face when her heart beamed at your silly conceits. But clever is good, too, and you do clever well.

"No one knows what was written before we were born," you say.

Would you have chosen a different path had you known? Possibly, but probably not, at least you hope not, although you would have known to take more photographs along the way for that day when memory fails.

"Dee..p," she drawls. "You've watched every Charlie Chan movie, haven't you?"

Listen to how you laugh together; how your own laugh – saddled with that foolish weight you accord sorrow – lacks Ronnie's joyous lilt. But once again, you're right. If you take her example, you'll come closer ... close enough to sustain a dry man in a bad land.

WHERE IS THE PHILOSOPHER'S STONE?

"All the debts are forgiven, Kling," I hear myself say aloud. "Try a locked door. This one's wide open."

Chapter Fifty-One

"Fascinating, Mr. Pinel. I wish I had time to study you thoroughly."

Kling's voice, far away, drew closer with every word. Briefly I was living in *two* worlds, but gradually the world of the exam table supplanted the one in my head. I saw Kling toying with the valve on Malek's IV bag. Still gagged, Malek was squirming again. I glanced at my own IV.

"You turned it off," I blurted.

Kling looked back.

"To let it clear your system. That one won't take long." He returned his attention to Malek. "Each key is different. This one, for example, the one my erstwhile colleague used on me. It *poisons* vital enzymes. The proper dose leaves the mind – sensation, perception, cognition – unaffected. Response, however – except for brainstem reflex – is lost. A self-conscious mind unable to make itself known. Will remains, but willed action is impossible. A mind without choice. You can't imagine that horror."

Kling glowered at Malek.

"This fool used the *wrong* dose. It was only partially reversible. And he overlooked the effect of repeated exposure. Existing enzymes are poisoned and the cells that manufacture them are *destroyed*. Since those cells don't regenerate, the effect is relentlessly progressive. And *permanent*. It's a strange metamorphosis. Rather like a butterfly returning to its chrysalis never to emerge. That end for me has been written."

He wiggled Malek's IV line and began to chortle.

"Of course, a single, massive overdose has the same effect. Within minutes."

Malek grunted pleas through his gag.

"Come, come, Malek! It's not an execution. You have a long, long life ahead of you."

Kling licked the antidote crystal and cracked open the IV valve. Malek squirmed. His face was twisted in terror.

"I'll remove your gag when you can no longer scream. I know the room is soundproof – you demonstrated that often enough – but superior minds detest loud noises. On the other hand ..." Kling looked at me. "Our aggrieved observer might savor the sound."

Kling wanted me to watch and – despite the gut-churning knowledge that I was next – I wanted to see. I recalled the bored disinterest Malek had shown when he said *she had become un-useful.*

"Malek *stole* from me. He stole my mind!" Kling's voice was pressured and brittle. Clipped words tumbled together. His eyes were wide and electric. "A mind for a mind. Wouldn't you agree, Mr. Pinel? Justice!"

So much for eternal cycles and philosophy trumping hate.

"You're preaching to the choir, Kling, but, frankly, I think your antidote has pushed you over the edge, man."

"... I see ..." he said with a sudden, unnatural calm. His hand clutched the pinch-wheel valve. A simple flick of his thumb, up or down, spared Malek or condemned him. "Then I'll leave the choice to your *unimpaired* enlightenment."

The drug coursing through Malek's brain was jamming locks one by one. His squirming had ceased. He made no sounds. The sun was setting in his eyes.

"Ask him, Malek," Kling cooed, removing the gag. "Ask him to save you."

He could barely budge his head to look at me. He was so silent, I figured that words had left him. Trembling with effort, however, he dragged two back.

"He..lp ... m..me ..."

That enlightened I'd never be.

"Sorry, man, but ..." I tugged at my restraints. "My hands are tied."

Yelping savagely, Kling thumbed open the IV valve and pranced around the chair while the light in Malek's eyes – dwindling like a dying pyre – flickered out forever. I shuddered. Not for Malek, he could rust in Hell! I shuddered for what I knew was coming.

Survive enough tough spots and you master a skill that can save your life – not to scratch an itch and reveal something critical at a key juncture. So far I had steeled myself against a reflex that I'd feared would ultimately become irresistible. With that shudder, it did.

I looked at the clock.

"Time is not in your favor, Mr. Pinel," Kling said, noticing my furtive glance. "Malek always left orders not to disturb him. He often kept me here an entire day."

"That's good. We don't want to feel rushed."

"What are you up to?" he said, checking the restraint straps.

"Dumas said to wait and hope."

"Who's Dumas?"

"You really should read more, Kling. How will you ever get on Jeopardy?"

"Silly trivia," he snorted.

"Yeah, I couldn't get on it either."

Stamping to the counter, he pawed through Malek's supplies.

"Most of my brain keys, like piano keys, play a single note, so to speak. Combining them, however, I create chords – every nuance of cognitive function just as it occurs in the brain." He brandished two IV bags. "I can wrack you with inconsolable grief. Unforgiveable guilt." He held up a syringe. "Adding this? Intractable remorse. You might bite off your tongue attempting suicide. I saw that response once. I can make you feel lost, alone, unloved and unlovable."

I wanted to say *been there, done that*, but my mouth was too dry. Cursing my lack of control, I looked at the clock again.

"DOCTOR MALEK!" boomed a ceiling loudspeaker. "Policemen!"

Fists thudded against the inside door of the lab. Muffled voices shouted, "Open up! Police! Open up."

"It's over, Kling. Where can you go?"

He glanced at Malek.

"Not back *there*. Not yet!"

A barricade ram banged against the ward door. Using Malek's fob and the pin number he had given me, Kling opened the hallway door and darted outside. The automatic door clunked shut behind him. The ward door crashed open.

"Kling ran," I shouted. "Hallway stairs."

A walkie-talkie squealed. "Six and Seven. Subject on foot."

A face peeked cautiously into the room.

"Sheez, Manny," I said. "What took you so long? Xuân must've called 20 minutes ago."

"Traffic was murder," he said.

Chapter Fifty-Two

"Cut me loose!"

Eyeing Malek and Armstrong, Manny stepped inside. Rick Wagner and Tim Mulligan followed. I spied a couple of beat cops through the doorway.

"Quit stalling, Manny. I've had a hard day."

"Cool your jets," he said. "You're part of a crime scene."

While Rick tried the hallway door, Tim squatted beside Armstrong.

"I'm looking at a body here, Manny, and a ... a *something*." He waved a hand in front of Malek's staring eyes and got nothing. Squeezing two fingers with a pen between them was equally fruitless. "Hey, pal. Can you hear me? Can you talk?" He looked my way. "What's his problem, Pinel?"

"He's off the grid, Tim. Permanently."

"No joke?" He flicked at the empty IV bag. "Probably doesn't need this then."

"No. It's done its work," I said.

He yanked out Malek's IV line.

"Mine, too. C'mon! Take it out!"

"What's your rush," Rick said, moseying back from the hallway door.

I glanced at the nearly full IV bag dangling above me. "Sword of Damocles, okay! Heard of it?"

"Sure," he drawled. "Kid pulled it out of a stone and became king."

"Goddamm it, Manny. Cut me the fuck loose!"

Removing a strip of tape, Manny pulled out my IV line. When I started to bleed, he pressed his shirt sleeve against my arm.

"Screw that, man! I got six pints! Loose, hear me! Cut me loose. What if there's an earthquake or you fuckers all have heart attacks. I need to be out of these straps. Now!" I was squirming on the table, tugging at the restraints. "There's a key in my pocket."

Rick laughed. "Why didn't you free yourself then? That's why you get the big bucks, right?"

"I'm not Houdini, Rick. You gonna get me the fuck out of these, or what?"

"Shut your trap before I Miranda you," Manny snapped. "Given the situation, I'm struck by the perfection of your alibi."

Tim stood and joined the other two. "You nailed it, Manny." He tugged at my straps. "Locked room. In restraints. Drugged. It's perfect."

Manny shrugged. "Yeah … *too* perfect."

"How's that?" said Rick.

"Because he's *not* Houdini. Let him up."

Tim rummaged in my pocket.

"That's not the key, Tim."

With the click of the last lock, I popped from the table. I was rattling off a rundown for Manny when his walkie-talkie squealed.

"Officer down! Officer down!"

"Go!" Manny barked to Rick and Tim. "Grab a Doc."

A static-garbled exchange with dispatch told the story. The cop and his partner were chasing Kling across the parking lot when three males, two black, one white, jumped from a blue Ford Escort. Dealer plates. They started shooting, snatched Kling, and escaped down PCH.

The shooters didn't sound like Sheik's crew and Burdick was the only other player on my scorecard. A firefight with cops and a daylight kidnapping seemed out of character for a billionaire, but maybe he had been sampling Kling's wares, too.

Rick buzzed in on the intercom.

"We're here, Manny. Dragged a psychiatrist along."

"Poor wounded bastard is lost for sure."

"He'll be okay. Ambulance is on the way. Tim is coordinating with C.H.P."

"Tell the Sheriff we're trespassing in his yard. Have him bring a coroner and lab crew."

Keeping the Kindle part to myself, I finished my rundown. Manny shook his head.

"Better living through chemistry," he sighed. "Just what we need. Synthetic cocaine."

"One golden egg among many," I said.

"And Kling's the goose. Explains the desperation."

"How's that?"

"An SEC-DEA task force padlocked Burdick's whole operation this afternoon. Typical Federal cluster fuck. Six dead at Pelican Hill. Burdick wasn't even there. Raids were probably posted on Wiki-leaks."

"Why didn't they hit this place?"

"A hospital? That's a whole roll of red tape. Are these patient's endangered?"

"Probably not. Not *overtly* anyway. I think it's largely a legit research unit. Better cover that way."

"Good. That'll buy the Feds time. God knows they'll need it."

"Where do you think Burdick will come to roost?"

"Most of his money – meaning the money of his investors – has left the country. He'd probably like to join it."

"Can he?"

"No trouble getting drugs in. I imagine he can get himself out. Probably made one last grab for the brass ring on his way."

"Whatever brainwashing they've done on Kling has shrunk it, and his physician-heal-thyself plan isn't working. I don't think he has much time left for Burdick's experiments."

"Experiments?" Manny scoffed. "Burdick is no scientist, Pete. He's a hammer who sees everything as a nail. I don't think Kling has much time either."

Chapter Fifty-Three

The grilling I got left me well done, but I wasn't strapped to a table for it and, in the end, I walked. Entering without breaking was only a misdemeanor and my license bought me some leeway since various capital crimes had been in progress, including the kidnapping of my client. I had to gloss over Malek's missing teeth and Armstrong's head, but since neither of them was talking, self-defense covered it.

Inside the Blazer I found missed calls on my cell – several from Xuân and one from an unidentified caller whose message was merely a number. I recognized the voice and dialed. The pick-up was silent.

"My package has gone missing again," I said. "Did you take it?"

"I followed who did. I was outside waiting for you."

"You still don't trust me, do you?"

"Not a bit. Your package is at an old airfield in the desert. Avoids those ugly customs inspections."

"Private jet. It's the only way to fly."

"Jets can't use short, dirt fields."

"So our friend opts for practicality. He still there?"

"Waiting for the plane, I suppose."

"Three guys?"

"C'mon! We'd be having a different conversation, man. He bunks half his army here; the rest at the mansion. I have ten guns coming – all I could muster this fast. It's probably about even unless his security boss shows."

"From Hell? Unlikely."

"*Nice work!* I would have given odds against."

"On any given Sunday, you know?"

"How about his troops?"

"Scratched. So, where are you?"

"Riverside County near Aguanca."

"Never heard of it."

"Who has? Through Temecula. 79 to Sage. North to Wilson Valley. Go east 5 miles. It's a ridge road over an empty, desert flat. No runway, but you won't miss the place. Two rows of old wooden buildings. Looks like a ghost town."

"Okay. I'm an hour away, but if they try to sky, you'll have to shoot the tires on the plane or something. The Stone is worthless without the package."

"Great to have a strategic wizard on the team. You should jot down some of your other ideas and mail them to me."

"Just *wait* for me."

"Better think this through, Pinel."

"Who are you, my mother? Think what?"

"If this is your kind of action. You won't be fighting your way *out* of anything; you'll be fighting your way *in*."

"I was a Marine. That's what we do."

"Forty years ago," Mendez snorted. "You could probably screw six times a night back then, too. But age isn't what I'm talking about."

"What the hell *are* you talking about?"

"*You*. How you roll, man ... Your personal problem is a blood feud. *Hot* blood. Impulse. Target. Nothing in between. Nothing to stop you. But this? ... Right and wrong might start to get muddy for you midway. Doubts could cost me."

I saw his point.

"This airfield ... completely dirty, right? No innocent bystanders?"

"C'mon, man. No one is innocent."

"Put it this way. Anyone there on a higher moral plane than you?"

He laughed. "Just you, *cabron*. *Maybe* you."

I took a deep breath and blew it out like cigarette smoke.

"I intend to resolve my personal problem *personally*."

"Watch what you wish for, *amigo*."

I called Xuân and filled her in.

"So Walter doesn't have the Stone?" she said.

"No. Still with me. If things fall my way, I'll be bringing him home in about three hours."

"Was he ... still ..."

"Holes in his memory and word finding problems, but ... overall his matrix was pretty damn functional. He was licking that rock every few minutes. I imagine they'll let him keep at it, but he called it a short term fix and, well ... if he wasn't insane already, he is now, Xuân."

"I see. Try to bring whatever he's using. I'll fetch some supplies."

She was holding on to hope, so I didn't say anything, because hope is all we really have. But, either way, Kling

was finished. If Xuân unlocked the files and found a
cure, he was spending the time he had left in San
Quentin. And if she didn't? A tougher prison.

"Should I call Chief Vasquez again?"

I considered what was about to go down.

"No. Don't," I said.

"But ... he's your friend."

Manny could see shades of gray – maybe not as
many as I was burdened with, but he saw them. All the
gray in the world, however, can't whitewash black and
white.

"Well ... that's just it, Xuân. We *are* friends. *Best*
friends, which, in case you don't know, is closer than
brothers. But Manny won't help me this time," I said.
"He might even have to kill me. And that's something
I'd hate for him to suffer."

Chapter Fifty-Four

I found the airstrip easily enough because three sidelined Chevys marked the spot. They sat idling in plain sight along an overlooking ridge. If Mendez was counting on surprise, he'd lost it. Pulling up at the rear of the column, I donned the shoulder rig again. Manny had confiscated my Walther. Pocketing several loaded magazines, I got out, hoofed it past two cholo-packed cars, and joined Mendez, sitting alone at the front.

Below us, wooden buildings flanked a dirt street. Mendez was right. Sagging overhangs, weathered paint and boarded windows made for a ghost town appearance. Gusts of wind kicked up dust and rolled tumbleweeds.

"Am I too late?" I said, sliding into the passenger seat beside Mendez.

"You cut it close." He pointed at the approaching dot of a plane.

"So where's Burdick and company?"

"They're here. Plenty of them, trust me. Cars are stashed in the hangar. That's why I'm waiting for the rest of my crew."

"What's the plan?"

"Charge. Shoot. Repeat."

"You're a regular Westmoreland."

"He was a General, right?"

"Some said so." Staring warily at the cluster of ramshackle buildings, I added, "Forget the Martians, Sheik. This looks more like Earps against the Clantons."

"You old guys love your westerns," he guffawed. "Are you saying I'm finally one of the good guys? Saying we're like bros?"

I couldn't help but chuckle.

"Too much to get my head around. Let's say you're Doc Holliday."

"TB or not TB," he said with an enormous grin.

"I wouldn't have figured you for a sense of humor, Sheik."

"No," he said, locking the grin away. "No, you wouldn't have figured."

Three men in a ten year old Ford – they must've missed the memo to steal a Chevy – skidded to a stop beside us. They rolled down their windows and Mendez barked orders. The Ford roared forward followed by the Chevys. Sheik punched the gas and fell in behind.

"Okay, old man. This is how we do it on *my* side of San Dismas."

He said it with an air of ... *pride*? What the hell? He was showing off for me!

Bumping and careening, we swooped single file down a looping, rutted road toward the hangar. Crashing through two gates, the lead Ford took the second gate over its hood into the windshield and end-over-ended, smashing half-way through one of the hangar's tall, sliding doors. The caravan of Chevys slewed sideways. Sheik's crew spilled out firing. Burdick's guns blazed through windows. Bullets pocked the cars and pinged off dirt. Two of Sheik's boys fell charging for the breach in the door made by the Ford.

"Manuel!" Sheik barked, waving a hand.

A kid, all of sixteen – Sheik's age when I schooled him in the park – darted toward the Ford, tossed a grenade through the gap, and took his wages … a burst of machine gun fire that ripped open his chest.

The grenade exploded with a *whoom*, showering glass from a row of vent windows at the top of the sliding doors. Sheik and his boys ran forward. I followed with covering fire. An adrenaline-charged high stamped the moment in my memory. Whatever else we were in real time, in that prolonged, removed instant, we were a team taking fire; we *were* brothers.

Two more of Sheik's crew caught slugs squeezing through the buckled door past the protruding Ford. Others scrambled over them, guns booming. Our so-called plan, however, left both flanks exposed. I saw two guys spring from behind the left corner of the hangar with leveled shotguns.

"Mendez!"

He dove in a head-first slide. The blast, barely missing him, punched a choked pattern in the Ford's rear quarter-panel. I took out the shooter and sent his pal ducking.

"I'll get him," I shouted, scrambling left. "Cover right!"

Already on his feet, Sheik collared two of his men, waved them toward the right side, and squeezed past the Ford into the hangar. His two conscripts rounded the corner without looking, pulled up short, and started shooting. Braced against the hangar wall, I waited a moment for the shotgun to peek out. When it did, I grabbed the barrel and yanked the gunman into the open.

Scuffling – neither of us about to let go the gun – we dragged each other down. Rolling in the dirt, I drove a knee into the guy's groin one, two, three times, felt his grip failing, and added a head butt. I wrenched away the shotgun, jumped up, and cracked his skull with the stock as he tried to scurry crab-like away from me. Sprinting to the rear of the hangar, I looked around the corner, spied an open door, and beyond that, out of sure-shot range, two of Burdick's men covering the other side. I missed twice with the .45, but goosed them around the corner. A dozen shots were followed by silence.

Manny was right. Way too old for all this grabass, I was wheezing, but had no time for a breather. Inside the hangar, gunfire was slowing, becoming sporadic like popcorn in a microwave. For what I thought was coming next, I considered the shotgun, but I hadn't checked the load. I dropped it on the ground, jammed a fresh magazine into the Colt and aimed. Four guys, Burdick's from their looks, exploded through the door like flushed quail. Fanning out, they made straight for the desert, showing no inclination to circle back.

Convincing myself the deserters' next stop was Palm Springs and seeing no one manning the opposite corner, I ran for the door, but almost pissed myself when landing gear screeched down behind me. Trailing a huge cloud of dust, a Twin Beech shot past and disappeared around the last building.

I inched the .45 into the doorway chest high, withdrew it slowly, and then crouched to peek inside. Anyone awaiting a reconnoitering head to appear would aim high.

Unless he had read the same book.

The inky blackness inside was broken only by a square of sunlight on the floor. Not getting shot in the head, however, filled me with optimism. I dived through the doorway and rolled.

Chapter Fifty-Five

If nothing happens, you feel silly doing that stunt. But in the moment, your heart is galloping, visibility is usually zip, and you're waiting for a yellow blossom in the dark to punch your ticket or – much preferred – reveal a target.

Face down with the .45 thrust straight out, I was still in phase one. As my eyes adapted to meager light filtering from outside, however, I saw nowhere to hide in the low-ceilinged room. I jumped up and scrambled to a closed door set in the far wall.

I had no reason to believe a fire was raging in the next room, but from habit, I pressed my hand against the door. I'd fought my way out of a few building fires – one set by a woman who wanted to destroy evidence, namely me – so I knew the drill. I'd nurtured the habit, however, more as a precaution against impulsiveness with regard to *any* closed door. Finding this one cold, as expected, I put my ear to it.

Gunshots jerked me back, but since none went through my ear, I eased the door open. Across the hangar a lone gunman was taking aim over the upside-down front-end of the Ford that had crashed halfway through one of the sliders. Leading with the .45, I squeezed inside, but not as quietly as I planned. The gunman whirled. With less light it might have gone another way, but the hangar's overhead fluorescents added choice to impulse.

"Nice you could join us, Pinel."

"Wouldn't have missed it, Sheik."

"I think you pretty much did," he said, returning to his position behind the Ford.

Hustling across the floor, I took stock. The hangar housed about ten haphazardly parked cars. Scattered among the cars lay at least a dozen bodies.

"How many left?" I said.

Sheik's gaze was riveted outside.

"Mine? One unhurt. Up there."

He flicked his head toward the tilting vent windows blown out by the grenade. Lying prone on the service catwalk was one of the goons who had tailed me earlier. Under different circumstances, missing him would have been a career limiting move. His partner, like a dropped shield, was lying next to Mendez, facing away toward whatever advancing threat had put several rounds in his chest.

"I piled four wounded into the Lincoln there," Sheik added. "Some might make it if we finish this fast."

"And Burdick?"

Sheik kicked the leg of a corpse. "Most of these are his. One bunch ran."

"Out the back. Four of them."

"Good shooting, old man!"

"No need. They weren't coming back."

He shook his head. "Stake in the heart, Pinel! You never saw a monster movie, man?"

"Where's Burdick and Kling?"

"The building beside the gate on the right. Burdick uses it as a lab. No back door." Sheik kicked the body again. "This one gave him up. Said Burdick was shocking the old man's nuts or something. Four guys to help."

I peered across the Ford chassis at a squat, windowless building.

"When the shooting stopped here, they made a break for the plane. Jorge and I drove them back."

"Down any?"

"Winged one."

"Plane still here?"

"Out of pistol range at the end of the street. Jorge has a view. It's idling into the wind, ready to go, but no one has budged. Probably just the pilot."

"Think Burdick knows we're outgunned?"

"Easy enough to count two shooters over here. I would have."

"We can use that, man! I was still out back so he's not counting me. As long as he sees you and Jorge, Burdick thinks he has a lock. I'm your case ace."

"Sheik! Door's opening," shouted the lookout.

Sheik crouched lower over the chassis and took aim. I squeezed in beside him, but stayed out of sight.

"Mendez! Mendez! You still alive," shouted a voice through a crack in the lab door.

"I'm here, Burdick."

"We can make this a win-win."

"Fucking CEO's and their buzzwords," Sheik snorted.

"Plane is ours; Kling is yours," Burdick said. "Maybe you can get something more than Harry Potter out of him. I'm through trying."

"Why not just wait you out?"

"The Professor is spoiling fast. Any window you have is closing. Besides, I suspect we'll soon have guests we'd rather not talk to."

"You didn't call the cops."

"Neither did you. But you can't wage a full-scale shooting war without someone noticing."

"Out here you can."

"That's a big bet, Mendez. Count on cops, if not the Army."

"He *might* deal ..." Sheik whispered. "What do you think?"

"Make any deal you want, Sheik, but Burdick isn't leaving here. *Ever.*"

"Figured as much."

"Try this," I said. "Agree to swap. Five against two, Burdick will take a chance."

"He won't hand Kling over until he's on the plane. Probably leave a guy to cover his takeoff."

"That's how I see it, too."

"Then you also see Jorge and me outgunned in that empty street, Pinel."

"Attrition won't win this one, Sheik. Burdick's calling the shots and at the end, *he* has be standing, not one of his gunmen. With everyone in the open, he won't trust to luck.

I'll go out the rear and wait between the buildings – get the drop on them while they're backing toward the plane."

"Get the *drop* on them? You mean like, reach for the sky? Christ! You old farts *overdosed* on westerns."

"You have a better idea?"

"Damn straight. Even the odds while they're watching me. Get two easily, maybe three."

"Shoot them in the back?"

"It's the practical thing to do, man."

"Yeah. I'll give you that. But ..."

"Goddammit! I knew your conscience would—"

"Look, I'll take *Burdick* out with a drone, if it's the only way to do it. But I can't feel good shooting guys I don't know in the back."

"Burdick's crew? They're evil sons of bitches, Pinel. Trust me. *I* know them."

"Then *you* shoot them in the back! If you're going to kill a man, it better be righteously personal or self-defense. Otherwise you're a stone killer yourself. If you can live with *that*, man, lie down, you're dead."

"What crap! You just want to see Burdick's face when you do it."

I shrugged. "Maybe there's that, too."

He waved his hand dismissively. "This plan isn't working for me. I'm standing in the open facing five *desperados*. Mortal fucking stakes, Pinel. What do you do when the shooting *does* start? Go for their hands?"

"I won't be aiming for hands."

"Oh, suddenly it's righteously personal."

"People make choices. Choosing to kill me is as righteously personal as it gets."

"Maybe there's hope for us, yet" Sheik muttered. "Look, you want justice and Burdick dead is your justice, right? So shoot *him* in the back *first*. The others will definitely be trying to kill you then. If we make it, I'll describe Burdick's face for you."

"You wasted yourself on accounting, Sheik. Should have been a lawyer."

"You're going to listen to me?" He was smiling.

"If there's no other way. Yes."

"Mendez!" Burdick shouted from the lab. "Kling's time is running out."

"You're carrying more of the risk," I said. "Has to be your call."

"You think you're clever, don't you, *Wyatt*? Fishing for me to say the word."

"What word, *Doc*?"

"O.K."

Chapter Fifty-Six

While Sheik cut a deal, I scrambled out the back, ran toward the plane and ducked between two small buildings to the street. The idling engines sounded nearby, but when I peeked around the corner, the plane was still too far for a clean shot. In the other direction, I saw the door to the lab open and Burdick's men exit one by one. All were in shirtsleeves. One had a dark bloodstain spreading under his arm. Guns drawn –one fully automatic – they fanned out across the street in front of the hangar. Last came Burdick gripping Kling by the collar. Although the old man shuffled leadenly, his mouth moved with what looked like words. Sense or nonsense, I couldn't tell.

Stopping suddenly, they raised guns. I heard the rumble of one of the hangar's large sliders grinding open.

"What are you doing, Mendez?" Burdick shouted, shielding himself with Kling. "This is going south fast."

"You can see I'm standing right here."

"Don't dick with me! Where's your man, I want to see him standing there, too."

"I've given Jorge a job to do."

Burdick and crew glanced about nervously, ready to storm the hangar for cover."

"Easy. He's here. Blow the horn, Jorge."

I heard an auto horn blare from inside.

"I have four dying soldiers in this car who might still make it at a hospital. You want to come sort through yours, you're welcome. Jorge can take them, too."

"I have a plane to catch."

"Jorge is going to drive out of here. Nice and slow, both hands on the wheel. Hospital is twenty minutes away. I'll finish up our business here myself."

Burdick nodded, playing with the angles like a G.P.S. recalculating a route, only it was Mendez who had made a wrong turn.

"Mighty white of you, Sheik. Probably win Orange County's Top Place to Work Award next year. Just make sure your driver knows not to stop or turn around. We have a good line of sight down that ridgeline." He stepped back and waved his arm. "Give him some room, guys."

I saw a black Lincoln nose out onto the street. It continued slowly through the broken gate and then accelerated up the hill.

Everyone except Burdick kept glancing nervously at the car as if it were important. Burdick knew it wasn't. He stared straight ahead, undoubtedly at Mendez. He saw the opportunity and, without moving his hand, fired BANG-BANG ... BANG.

His men flinched. One squeezed off a round and almost shot himself in the foot. I knew it was over, however, because no one took cover. Shaking off the surprise, they watched Sheik fall, face forward, through the hangar door. One of Burdick's men strode over and shot him again.

In the back.

Chapter Fifty-Seven

I took that one first – head, chest – but missed the others as they scattered. Dragging Kling like a seabag, Burdick scrambled into the hangar. One crony snapped off a few shots my way and followed. The other two ran for the lab building. The bleeder was slow and I got him. The quicker one made it.

My lousy marksmanship had me in trouble. The lab offered clear fields of fire on the street as well as the facing sides of the hangar; an assault was suicide. Sitting still was no better, though, since Burdick could circle out the rear door and come up behind me.

Snap life-or-death choices are made with the gut, however, and I doubted that he would. Burdick was a weight lifter. Men who spend that much time moving ever more massive hunks of iron a yard or two at a time are Hercules, not Odysseus. With his back to the wall, Burdick would choose power over guile. I pictured him blasting out the hangar door in the heaviest car.

I still had him covered, though, and the plane was past me, so he had another choice to make. If his gut told him I was a rope-a-dope fighter, he would send his man to pin me down while he escaped. If he took me as more Mike Tyson, he would station the guy at the back door.

My gut said attack. I emptied my magazine at the lab to mark my position, slammed in a fresh load, and sprinted to the rear of the hangar.

Once again I found myself in a blind dive-and-roll – one made infinitely worse by the stuttering thunder of a machine pistol and a swarm of rounds punching holes in the wall a few inches above me. Rolling again, I snapped off shots at the blooming muzzle. Sweeping upward, the yellow flashes strobelighted the ceiling and stopped. Hearing the gun clatter to the deck, I sprang to the door and added a head shot to the gasping gunman's woes.

Already behind the wheel of an idling black Escalade, Burdick had probably been waiting for the gunfire to stop as his signal to bolt. In the passenger seat, however, Kling chose that moment to sink his teeth into the driver's right arm. I aimed, but Burdick elbowed the shifter into drive as he shook the old man lose.

The squealing Escalade roared toward blue sky. Putting three slugs through the rear hatch to no effect, I heard two shots that *weren't* mine. The Caddy veered sharply. Heeling over as if about to roll, it careened into the Ford protruding through the closed hangar door. In the tall rectangle of the open door, I saw Mendez propped on his side, a gun in his hand. The gun slipped from his fingers and he slumped, face in the dirt.

Burdick grabbed Kling's shirt and dragged him through the driver-side door. Firing over the roof of the car, he pinned me behind a cabinet. Squeezing past the Ford, he tossed Kling over his shoulder and ran. I galloped outside,

but shots from the lab pushed me back. Burdick
charged through the open door.

I gripped Sheik's feet and pulled him inside,
smearing a swath of blood across the cement floor.
Rattling moans and gurgling coughs told me he
wouldn't make it.

"Mendez ..." I said. "*Sheik*."

"What?" he spluttered.

"I thought they killed you, man."

"You fucking never saw a monster movie, Pinel?"

Chapter Fifty-Eight

Keeping an eye on the closed door of the lab, I ripped a shirt and belt from the nearest body, wadded the shirt over Sheik's bloodiest wounds and cinched it with the belt.

"Anyone win?" he groaned.

"Last reel. Earps are in trouble." I put a round in the lab door to let them know I was alive. "Burdick and a goon have Kling."

"Mexican standoff."

"That's ironic, Sheik."

"I'm Nicaraguan, Pinel. You assume a *lot*, man."

Maybe he was right. I'd assumed his two shots from the grave were mere reflex. I'd assumed he'd leave his wounded behind before he faced five men alone.

"I want to say something," he rasped, eyes squinched shut, teeth clenched. "About that night in the park."

"Is this the time?"

"Won't get another. That night ... me and Frankie? Worms! ... Threatened your lady. Frankie even tried to back-shoot you. For a stinking buck! But you? Like Goddamm Mike Hammer, man."

"You're embarrassing me, Sheik."

"Would you fucking listen? ... No good guys in my world, man. No heroes. *None*. I remade myself because of *you*."

"Scared straight?"

"Scared of *nothing*! But I *chose* ... call it *straighter*. Easier for you?"

"I don't recall you helping old ladies cross the street."

He paused. Not to gather his thoughts, but his breaths, and his basket was empty.

"I stopped robbing them," he gasped. "I didn't rape them to get at their old men. I didn't *keep* them from crossing the street just because I could."

"You merely killed people."

"I never murdered any."

"I tell myself that, too."

"C'mon! Those Earps, that Holliday – they took short cuts for what they *had to have*. I had to have the *world*. Like *breath*! Earning it was out. But *taking* it I could do. Yeah ... *that* I could do." His gasps were wetter, faster, shallower. "Take or get taken, Pinel. That was my world and I wouldn't play the sap!"

"Listen Sheik, I ..."

"Door!"

I whirled and snapped two more shots at the lab. The door slammed.

"You expect me to say you're a good guy?"

"Achilles? Earp? *Pinel*? ... Good *enough* guys. Heroes."

"Save your breath, Sheik."

"For what?" He gripped my arm with all his remaining strength. "For what? I want you to get it right."

He was dangling over the abyss and looking down. Some guys would fill those seconds cursing their bad luck. Mendez was trying to set some record straight, which was a better way to spend the time, since what else do we leave behind, if anything, except a record.

"In your cowboy movies ... what'd they say? No room in ... this town ... for both of us."

He laughed, but the laugh became a coughing fit that sprayed blood over me. Sweet and decorous death is not.

"But all ... those years ... *we* ... never crossed." Every breath he took was a struggle to fill the little bit of lung he had left. "You *assumed* ... I was scared."

I shrugged.

"Get it right! Not *scared* of God, man! I steered clear of corners where the only out was over you because—" The last part was gargled. Another coughing fit seized him. "Because I *respected* you."

"Last call, Sheik. If you have a point, make it."

"Born to die young, man, but ... but ..."

His voice trailed off. I knew the quote. Achilles. But he probably wanted to say it, so I shook his arm.

"But what?"

"I'm owed *some* honor for it."

His eyes closed. I thought that was it, but I didn't want to assume. I shook him once more.

"What now, man?" His eyes remained shut.

"Your name. Your *real* name. Tell me again."

"You don't have the sounds." His voice was very far away. "It's all in the sounds, like music."

"Shee-o ..."

He opened his eyes. "Damned *yanqui* accent. Xiuhcoatl," he sighed with his last breath and lay staring.

"Shee-wha-koa-tl," I said, as best I could, repeating it a few times. The ears are the last to go, so maybe he heard.

Chapter Fifty-Nine

"Burdick!" I shouted through the door. "If you want out of there, you better talk. I'll set you on fire, hear me? I'll go out the back and shoot up your plane."

The lab door cracked open.

"You don't sound like Sheik's crew."

"Pete Pinel."

Silence. He was probably recalculating his odds of escape, and arriving at the one answer. With me breathing, his odds were zero.

"You can still have Kling, Pinel."

"Good. That's what I'm here for."

"So let's do this thing. You call it."

"We all walk outside. Mosey toward the plane. Trade there."

Silence.

"Burdick?"

"I don't like it. I'm thinking."

He was doing more than thinking. I heard a muffled pounding coming from the rear of the lab. If they chewed a hole in the back wall, my advantage was lost.

"Take your time," I lied, looking around for inspiration. Cars. Bodies. Fuel cans. Guns. Tool boxes. Keeping watch on the lab door and staying in the shadows, I fired a red Oldsmobile and jockeyed it into position – a straight shot through the slider to the lab. I dragged over a body and propped it in the passenger seat.

"*Tempus fugit*, Burdick," I shouted, shooting once at his door. "I'm getting antsy."

"Okay. Deal. Let me figure out what to do with Kling. He can't walk anymore."

"Make like he's a barbell," I yelled, lashing the body to the steering wheel and securing the wheel with cords. "Carry him."

Emptying a couple of jerry cans of gasoline over the interior of the Olds, I tossed several open ones in the front seat, found the button that controlled the intact hangar door and opened it wider.

"What are you up to, Pinel?"

"Giving you a good view in here. Ease your mind."

The pounding stopped. I glimpsed a figure dart from behind the lab toward the rear of the hangar. I grabbed a heavy tool box and leaned it against the seat just behind the accelerator.

"Okay. Here we come," Burdick bellowed.

"Kling first. Then you. Then me. Then your man." I hoped the last part would throw him off. "Show me Kling."

Gripping Kling's collar, Burdick inched him outside – milking it, giving his man time to get in position.

"Your turn, Burdick," I said, flicking Jesus' Zippo.

When Burdick minced outside, hunched behind Kling, I tipped the tool box onto the accelerator, knocked the shifter into drive, and tossed the lighter. Roaring through the hangar door, the Olds erupted.

Burdick jerked two reflex rounds through the windshield into the corpse, but lost his grip on a terrified Kling and had to scramble back inside empty-handed. The fireball Olds, ripped by two more explosions, hurtled past Kling and slammed into the lab door.

"Kling. It's Pinel!" I shouted, running to grab him. He froze with fear.

"*Xuân* sent me!"

He stumbled into my arms.

Although Burdick could probably out-lift me, I followed his example and slung the gaunt old man over my shoulders. Hoping the henchman was waiting for Burdick at the hangar, I ran toward the plane, which still sat idling with its nose into the wind. Buffeted by prop-wash, I took cover behind the fuselage and shrugged Kling onto the dirt.

"Stay down," I ordered over the drone of the dual Pratt-Whitney's.

"The crystal. Burdick. I have to—"

I dropped a foot on his back to keep him from bolting. My last round was chambered. I dumped the empty magazine and jammed in my remaining clip.

At the other end of the street, the wooden lab – engulfed in flames – exploded, showering planks and embers through a black, mushrooming cloud.

"Let's make this work, Pinel," Burdick shouted from the gap between the last two buildings. "Tell me what you want."

"I'm good," I shouted back.

I saw the henchman peep around the end building. He had a bead on me over the tail section. I backed toward better cover at the front. The henchman inched around the corner.

"Call him off, Burdick?" I yelled, raising the .45 toward the cockpit.

"Wait!"

Burdick stepped forward, his gun leveled at my head. The plane wouldn't stop them for long. With me dead, they could always drive away.

"Kling says you have his Stone," Burdick bellowed over the engine noise. "Now you have him. I'll be stuck in some stinkhole. Probably catch Ebola. Isn't that enough?"

Burdick and his goon advanced by inches, improving their positions with every inch, but careful to make no single inch definitive.

"I don't give a damn about Kling and his Stone. You know why I'm here. Veronica Sharfstein."

"Okay, what can I say, Pinel, you got me. But jeez, man! It getting so gonzo – all those guys butt-fucking her and everything? That wasn't *my* call."

I held it in. I'd seen how Burdick operated. He was goading me and I knew he'd try again. Keeping the goon in the corner of my eye, I focused on Burdick's face. He fixed on mine. Another explosion ripped the lab. Neither of us flinched.

Air Marshalls. Secret Service. All professionals who work a hostage-taking are trained on a simple fact. The brain bogs down running simultaneous programs, and the talking program – a million years in development – is a RAM hog. When the mouth is moving, programs like choosing to fire get hind tit. If you're prepared, as Burdick had been with Sheik, it's just enough time.

I was hoping Burdick thought he knew a trick no one else did, but narcissists usually do, and guys who pump iron in front of a mirror all day are narcissists. I watched for his lips to part, the intake of breath, listened for the first sound.

"She—"

I hit him twice, low in the gut. You're supposed to go for the head, but I wasn't through with him. The goon fired. I whirled. BAM BAM BAM BAM BAM BAM. Three guns exploded in a wild, puckered-asshole dance of instinct, experience, panic, and luck. All of us ended up in the dirt, and while I didn't *think* I was hit, sometimes you don't know. The goon lay facing me. His forehead sported a dime sized hole. Burdick was alive, if not well. Stumbling blood-soaked toward the plane, he had fallen face down beneath the tail section, still clutching his gun.

"Drop it, Burdick. DROP IT or I'll empty the magazine in places that won't kill you right away."

He let it go.

"Push it aside."

He did.

"The crystal!" Kling cried.

"Now the rock. SLOWLY. Let me see your hands."

He pawed in a pocket, withdrew a brown vial, and tossed it. Kling polled to his feet, scooped up the vial and shuffled toward the hangar.

I stood. Burdick looked at me, which was fine, because Sheik was right. I wanted to see his face. I wanted to watch his eyes search frantically for an out. I wanted to see every spark of hope fizzle in the drenching realization that the end had already been written.

He made no excuses, offered no bargains. I think he was wise enough to know that pleas would backfire. I wanted silence. I would have gagged him if he spoke. All I wanted to hear now was an echo in my head of Veronica's laughter and the sounding-block *bang* of a gavel when I squeezed the trigger.

Everything I wanted to see in Burdick's face, I saw when I leveled the gun. The pilot, however, panicked and punched the throttles. Knocked off balance by the prop wash, I dived to avoid the split tail boom. Burdick – seizing his only chance – grabbed the tail wheel as it bumped over his outstretched arm. The plane accelerated across the flat, dragging him behind.

Lying prone, bracing the .45 in two hands with a supporting elbow, I took aim. For the first few seconds, I might've made the shot, but this new turn was chock-full of promise. I clambered to my feet to watch, ready to hightail after him if necessary.

A Twin Beech is called the smuggler's plane because all it needs is a short, dirt field. It's airborne at 70 knots, or sooner with a light load. Probably hoping to put as much distance between us as possible, Burdick didn't know when to let go. The plane lifted off and climbed steeply with Burdick dangling.

How long would he hold on? It was an appealing question. He was gut shot and bleeding, of course, but weight lifters thrive on pain and limits. I recalled the rippling muscles beneath his suit – great upper body strength, and I hadn't hit him there. I was upbeat, confident that he'd make a good showing.

The plane banked left and left again, angling back toward the field. At first I thought the pilot – knowing who was encumbering his tail wheel – was returning. But as he continued to climb, I realized that he was merely breaking from the take-off pattern and setting a course. Why should he worry? The tail wheel would free up long before he needed it to land.

The plane passed almost directly overhead with Burdick, a speck, still clinging. I imagined the unquenchable lactic burn that was searing the muscles of his arms and shoulders: a burn as relentlessly contagious as a firestorm; a burn that would engulf and scorch his soul with the horrific inevitability of letting go.

The plane rose steadily, as gracefully as a swan. Burdick suddenly plummeted like droppings. I pictured him hurling invective through a falling angel arc whose terminus was described by a plume of dust that rose from the dry earth. A capricious gust of wind scattered the plume, leaving no marker at the spot where, bursting unseen, he had wasted his vitriol on the desert air.

Chapter Sixty

Kling had screwed me once already and I had no idea what he was up to, so I entered the hangar cautiously, braced for a hurtling car or a shotgun blast. Instead I saw him hunched over a workbench. It looked as if he'd pulverized his rock on a sheet of paper and was rolling a length of pipe back and forth over the powder. Oblivious to me, he trailed his finger through the powder, snorted a dab, and rolled the pipe some more. Finally satisfied, he raked out a thick line – maybe a third of the total – and craned his head over it. Loudly snorting the line up his nose, he reared upright. His eyes were gleaming again. Words spilled out.

"Hydrophilic. Poorly absorbed, very poor, need it fine," he blabbered. "Very fine. This is good, extremely fine. It's good, quite good, right to the bloodstream, best for now. It's working."

He tipped the creased sheet of paper and dumped the remainder of the crushed rock into the brown vial. He tucked the vial into the shirt pocket of his hospital pajamas.

"You *do* have my Stone? You found it, right? You must have. You did. You said you did, didn't you?"

"I found it."

"Where? I couldn't remember. They tried, but … nothing!"

"On your desk. A Kindle."

He grimaced as if straining to remember and shook his head.

"A ... a *what* did you call it?"

"A Kindle."

Unconsciously he made a rectangle with his finger. "Those things ... with, uh ... words. Books!" he shouted as if playing Pictionary.

"E-books."

He looked baffled again.

"Electronic books. A Kindle is a hand-held computer that stores and displays them. Yours had a Harry Potter novel on it."

"Potter. I remember something about Potter."

"Harry Potter and the Sorcerer's Stone. Does that help you with the password?"

"Password ... password ..." he muttered to himself. "Maybe if I see this ... what did you call it?" He traced a rectangle again.

"Kindle."

"Perhaps if I see it."

"Okay. Let's go see it."

I found a car with keys and pushed him into the front seat. I drove up to the mesa road, wiped the car down, and transferred him to my Blazer. Heading for San Clemente, I gave him the Kindle from the lockbox. He turned it over in his hands, eying it from various angles.

"If you enter your password, your files will open. It's a long string of letters and numbers, probably linked to something familiar, something always there so you don't forget."

"I don't remember what's always there. Maybe if I see ... My house! *That's* familiar."

"That's where we're going. Xuân will be there."

"I ... I remember Xuân," he whispered.

We drove a long time in silence. I began to wonder if he had flamed out for good.

"Still with us, Kling?" I said.

"I remember," he said. "648936. That's it. That's the password."

"No cigar, Doc."

"It's—"

"The password for your garage and your email. It didn't work."

"But ... I always use it. It's always there. And I ... I remember saying it."

I handed him my phone.

"See the keypad? Just like the garage door opener. Remember?"

Struggling with the idea, he hovered a shaky finger over the keys. Abruptly I seized the phone and stared at the number pad.

Something always there.

Scrolling through my contact list, I called the throw-away cell number Ricky had slipped me before I left so I could bypass the human firewall. He answered after five rings.

"I hope you're ready to start work, Pete. I left the ringer on and Jeri was in here. She'll have this thing disconnected for sure. I don't know how, but she will."

"Can't have you frittering time away on Angry Birds, can she? Listen, about that password I'm looking for – some systems use a pass*phrase*, right? A word generates the random hexdex symbols. Could that be the case with the Kindle?"

"Not as secure, but … it *could*. The program would be encrypted behind the logon."

"648936 … the one we tried. That's a name on a keypad. Nguyen. Could the passphrase be *Nguyen* or *Xuân Nguyen*?" I saw Kling's lips move when I said it.

"Too short."

"How about a *spoken* password. Like you used for Amazon."

"It's possible, Pete. Your Kindle has a microphone. A few digitized words would be plenty."

"That name?"

"A little short, but … maybe. Have to try it."

"So if I'm right and I say it at the logon screen, I'm good?"

"How secure would that be? Remember me telling you the janitor can't order dirty books on mine? The password is generated by a *voiceprint* of the phrase. It has to be spoken by the one who recorded it."

"So if the voice goes …?"

"Everything behind that logon screen goes with it."

I looked at Kling. "Like a dead brain."

"Close enough. Nothing on *earth* will revive it."

"But wouldn't he have a fail-safe? Some backup plan? Why would a guy lock his life's work with a key that dies with him?"

As soon as I said it, however, I recalled Ricky's finger circling *delete*.

"Maybe your Potter fan is *also* a sole proprietorship," he said.

Chapter Sixty-One

Kling said nothing for another half-hour, but I doubted that he'd passed through the door to wherever he was going, because his lips were moving. I took that as thinking. Geniuses probably do a lot of silent, solitary thinking. Perhaps he was building new molecules in his head, new keys to yet undiscovered locks ... or imagining that he was, anyway. It turned out, though, that he was simply talking to himself. Whatever brain he had left was occupied at *my* level. With remembering.

"Only twelve!" he suddenly blurted. "A *prostitute*."

"Children aren't prostitutes; they're *slaves*," I growled, sorry I'd been right and ready to slug him. He certainly proved how fucked up a genius could be. "Your kind of action, was it?"

"That's disgusting!" he said.

His head was slow to turn, but his eyes were still alight, although the glow was somehow more fathomable.

"Trying to relate to people taxed me. I felt too sorry for them. They seemed so limited, so handicapped. Prostitutes – *adult women!* – were ... practical. I never felt as if I were harming anyone until I saw what I saw in Saigon."

His face was pained. He took a slow, deep breath.

"Xuân was a *child*. Just a child! Filthy. Starving. The Mamasan dragged her from a back room by her hair and shoved her at three men who began to paw her. They called her *Bu...* – a *horrible* name. They objected to the Mamasan's price. One man spit on the girl, slapped her, knocked her to the floor. Another unzipped his pants and started to urinate on her. Xuân looked up at me. The look was ... not a *plea*. She had no hope of deliverance. No hope of compassion. She *recognized* me. Can you understand that?"

"Sure. Her father was American. You were probably the only one she had seen in ten years and we all look alike."

"Except ... *I* felt it, too. Recognition. I took her away from those vile men."

"Oh, really? How?"

"I was younger once. With my fists. My feet. A chair. A broken bottle." He didn't say it boastfully. "The Mamasan grabbed her back, began to beat her with a cane. I yanked it from her hand and thrashed the witch."

"Goddamm!"

"She couldn't help who she was, of course. But ... neither could I. Not then."

"That's a bucketful of balls, Doc. You'd have been lucky to leave alive *during* the war. *After?* An *American?* How'd you swing it?"

"My host for the evening had influence."

"Who was that? Ho Chi Minh? Damn! ... So what did you do?"

"I bought her."

"Oh, swell! You read her fairy tales for an hour. Did she ever tell you what happened after you left?"

"We left together. I *bought* her. From the Mamasan. Xuân was—" The words stuck in his throat, but he forced them out. "She was ... *bui doi. Anything* was permitted. I could have killed her with my hands for a few dollars more. We left immediately and flew home the next day. I, too, had influence."

"C.I.A.?"

"What's that?"

"Influence."

"I couldn't *raise* her," he said. "Nonetheless, while neither of us use the words, she *is* my daughter; I *am* her father."

"A lifetime from a single look," I mused.

"Is it so unbelievable?"

I remembered my first moments with Veronica – her cathedral window eyes; her look of joyous wonderment.

"Not unbelievable at all," I said.

"Souls are separated across time and space. Stories are written before we were born. In *some* of those stories, we find each other again. Do you understand that?"

"I understand the *wish*."

We drove farther in more silence. This time, however, he *was* fading. I shook his arm. When he looked up, his eyes were almost as vacant as Malek's. The end he had described – that reverse metamorphosis, butterfly to pupa – was close to complete. The visible Kling would soon be erased.

"You need another toot, Doc."

He didn't understand.

"Your rock. In the bottle."

He looked at the vial in his hand. I put a palm to my nose and sniffed. Trembling, he fumbled with the lid of the vial, poured powder in his palm and snorted. He seemed to respond, but that time I couldn't say how. He was alert, but quiet ... until we passed the Angel 'A.'

"That poor woman," he whispered, looking away. "Forgive me."

Grabbing his shirtfront, I careened onto the shoulder and back, almost flipping the car.

"No chance!" I snarled. "What if had been Xuân?"

"I ... I don't know," he said, trying to pull away.

I shoved him back into his seat. "No, you *don't* know. No one knows what he'll do when everything, *everything* is lost."

"I still ... hope," he said.

"Hope for what?"

"That I would *try*. Try to break the cycle."

His head fell. His shoulders shook. He was sobbing. *Was it ... empathy?!*

What the hell was happening to him?

Chapter Sixty-Two

Doors.

Things known; things unknown.

And in between? The doors.

Entrance doors. Exit doors.

Doors and choices.

Ladies.

Tigers.

Once more I stood before Xuân's door. In twilight the green lacquer had glowed like dark jade. In moonlight it had gleamed black and glassy like obsidian. Kindled now by the red-orange rage of a dying sun, the door smoldered like an emerald in firelight.

You can't go through the same door twice.

The words in my head, or at least the idea, I remembered from the *Weeping Philosopher*, Heraclitus, who had said it about rivers. Buddha might easily have said it, too. Perhaps they had corresponded.

Because I'd confiscated Kling's vial for Xuân, he was board-like and mute by the time we arrived. I had to carry him up the stairs. His face was a mask. He showed no recognition of his house, but merely stood staring into the lacquered front door as if transfixed by some augury.

Xuân opened the door gowned in her ceremonial Ao Dai. The sunset rays imbued the white silk with the shimmering radiance of an ember. Kling's head rose leadenly, but I read a slight quiver in his lips as a catch in his breath and all he had left of a smile.

"Wed..ding ... day," he forced out. "I ... re..mem..ber ... Springtime."

"I'm hoping the Ao Dai spurs his memory," she said.

"It has. That's more than I've seen from him in twenty minutes." I shouldered Kling inside and handed her the vial. "That was the rock he was licking earlier. I think it lost its kick, so he powdered it."

"Insufflation?"

"If that means snorting it, yeah. It worked wonders the first time; not as much the next."

"Sit him at the table," she said, opening the vial. "How much did he use?"

"About a third of what he had left. That's the last third."

"So he needed it twice over the last ... hour?"

"Close enough."

Rummaging through supplies she'd laid out on the breakfast bar – glassware, IV bags, syringes, bandages, chemical bottles – she emptied the vial into a test tube and added a few drops of various liquids. She lit the gas stove and swirled the tube high over a burner, touching the bottom to her wrist occasionally. While she worked, I switched on the Kindle and brought up the password prompt Ricky had steered me to. I wasn't *sure* what to do, but enter and submit buttons looked familiar.

"Kling? Kling, listen! You remember Xuân?"

Stupid question. His ashen eyes strained to follow her every move.

"Say her name. Just her name. She's always there, remember? She's the password."

I touched the enter button and held the Kindle to his mouth.

"Xuân Nguyen," he said flatly. A row of asterisks filled a password box. The sound had registered. I hit submit.

Unrecognized.

"The password is what?" Xuân said. "A voiceprint?"

"A voiceprint codes the password. The password keys the encryption."

"That's not how he says my name."

"In Vietnamese, Kling. Tonally. *Xuân Nguyen.*"

He tried again.

Unrecognized.

"That *has* to be it," I said.

"This may help."

Xuân stepped behind Kling and drew the few cc's of serum she had prepared into a small syringe.

"That's the last of it," I warned.

"I know. Bend his head forward."

"What are you doing?"

"Intrathecal injection. Directly into the fluid surrounding his brain."

"Christ, Xuân! A fingernail scraping of that stuff lit me up like Times Square."

"Exposure builds tolerance. Besides it's a last hope. I want to fully activate whatever is left of his brain. Pull his head down. Chin to chest. He should be in a halo for this. Don't let him move *at all.*"

Straddling his lap, squeezing his legs between my knees, I leaned my elbows on his shoulders and pulled his head forward with my hands. Xuân positioned the syringe at the nape of his neck, in the hollow just beneath his skull. Inserting the needle a millimeter at a time through the opening in the base of the skull, she drew back on the plunger with her thumb until clear fluid rushed into the syringe. Depressing the plunger all the way, she withdrew the needle.

"That *can't* be healthy," I said, grimacing.

"No. No, it's not. Was the effect rapid nasally?"

"About fifteen seconds."

"Then this should—"

Kling almost sprang from the chair.

"Xuân! Xuân, you've done it," he spluttered, struggling. "Everything is clear again."

The brain shot had worked!

"Can he move now?" I said.

She nodded. When I stepped back, Kling stood and turned. Xuân wrapped her arms around him and buried her face in his chest."I've missed you," she said.

He placed his hands on her shoulders and bowed to kiss the top of her head. For a few moments they were completely alone since touch was their sole experience.

Pulling away, Kling picked up the Kindle. "This ... this, uh ... *object*," he said.

So much for Panacea.

"It's supposed to be my Philosopher's Stone, Xuân. You have to—" He glanced at me and hesitated.

"I know," she said.

"Have to what?" I said.

She took the Kindle.

"He called me from the hospital, Pete. While you were drugged. I tried to calm him, but there was nothing more I could do. Your friend was already on the way."

"Why didn't you tell me that?"

"I'll explain, but let me open the files first. I don't think we have much time. Walter ... you spoke into this microphone. Remember?"

"I ... *think* so," he said.

"What did you say?"

"I ... don't remember."

"Your name is the best guess, Xuân," I said. "His regular password spells Nguyen on a keypad. Plus he's been muttering *I remember Spring* like he did when he saw you at the door. Maybe he ... how did you put it? ... knows but doesn't know he knows. Nothing else to go on."

"I want you to remember something, Walter."

She guided him to the small photograph, holding his hand as he had probably held her hand leading her through the dark doorway in the picture.

"Remember this day? Charging those men? Caning that evil woman?"

The expression on his face was the one in the photograph.

"You asked my name. I couldn't remember it at first. When I did, when you repeated it, I heard my name for the first time since my mother died. I was Xuân! I was *Springtime*, Walter. My *real* name. Springtime. I *wasn't* dust of the earth, not night soil. I was Springtime." She tapped the photograph. "Say my name as you said it this day."

She lifted the Kindle to his mouth. He said her name, adding the traditional female middle name *Thi* and using the proper family, middle, given name order.

Nguyen Thi Xuân.

The sound was more than tonal, more than musical. If ever there were something eternal, something always there, something *forever* Spring in the way a man spoke a woman's name, that *Open Sesame* voiced it.

Xuân glanced at the Kindle and touched a button. The screen flickered. Even from across the room, I could see that the files had opened. She studied the contents.

"This is it, Walter." She held the Kindle for Kling to see. "Your Philosopher's Stone and ... everything *else*. Just as you described."

He studied the screen for a moment, and then looked at me. The vigilance, the arrogance, the angry glare had disappeared from his face. All I saw was relief.

"When he called from Malek's lab, he was convinced you would tell him where to find what you had. Without the password, however, how would he *know* it was the Stone? He feared the real one would be found; that the files were unsecure. He asked me to protect his work."

"Okay. You have. Can you fix him with it?"

"Walter ... Walter!" He was fading rapidly, losing touch with the reality around him, becoming lost in the photograph. Xuân took his chin and turned his head. "Is there anything in these files that will save you? Anything?"

Words were a struggle. "Uh … long times." He circled a finger. "Sun rings. You know, uh…"

"Years," she said gently.

His eyes drifted back to the photograph.

"Can your computer friend copy this, Pete?" Xuân said. *I intended to ask him to.*

"As long as it's unlocked. Otherwise the encryption is foolproof and Ricky wrote it."

"What should we do until then? For safekeeping."

"Just don't lose it. It'll stay unlocked until Kling reenters the password."

"Which soon will be impossible." She touched Kling's cheek. He turned like a baby toward the touch. "Remember what you said when you phoned, Walter? About the value of your work? Preserving your work?"

His leaden motion seemed to be a nod. Xuân pressed a button on the screen and held the Kindle to Kling's mouth.

"Say my name."

He spoke. Before I could react, Xuân hit *submit*. The screen flickered back to the logon prompt.

"Wh..what did you do?"

"I locked it."

"It has to be *his* voice, Xuân. And he's losing his words. Today is the day memory fails. He'll forget. Even *you*. He *will* forget."

Kling stared at the photograph.

"But *you* wouldn't, Pete. You'd have destroyed him with those files."

"What about saving his work?" I said.

"The Philosopher's Stone? For some downstream
Oppenheimer? No ... he realized the consequences of
that two years ago. He wanted his *other* work saved, his
good work. Let the *evil* be interred this time. Leave him
his *name*."

"That's not justice!"

"You mean it's not *retribution*." She sighed. "Would
it matter to you, Pete, that Walter was experimenting
on himself even before Burdick? Or that the work itself
changed him – his obsession with it? That happens with
men. Has it happened with *you*?"

"I'm who I am."

"Are you who you *were*?" Even as she said it, she
winced. "That wasn't fair, Pete. All I mean to say is that
people change. *Walter* changed. Whatever he did – he
was ... he *is* ... *more* than that. If only in what he is to
me."

"You ignore the rest?"

"No. Not ignore."

"You *massage* the rest."

"That wasn't fair either, Pete. I *weigh* the rest." She
glanced at Kling who was engrossed in the photograph.
"Did Walter use unwitting subjects in his research?"
She shrugged. "*Informed consent* is quite elastic; a
reason I left the field. Were subjects harmed? Perhaps.
Experiment is perilous. Did Walter knowingly take that
chance? Probably. From some misguided sense of a
greater good. But harm was not his *intent*."

"Ronnie died because of him!"

"Bad men did that, not Walter. He covered it up, yes. After the fact. As much after the fact as what I'm doing now. We're both guilty. But neither of us is a murderer."

I saw her staring at my clenched fists.

"You still can't let go, Pete. I know what you're about to do."

She knew me better than I knew myself, then, because, *I* didn't know what I was about to do. All *I* knew was rage-fired impulse. The .45 was suddenly in my hand, the safety off, the hammer cocked. Xuân pivoted to shield Kling.

"Move!" I shouted.

In a single, fluid motion, she wheeled and fired a small, flat automatic extracted from her tunic with a pickpocket's finesse. A slug slammed into my forearm, knocking the gun from my hand. I stumbled backwards, squeezing the wound with my other hand.

"Forgive me," she said.

"All things are Buddha things," I groaned through clenched teeth. "Even Tigers, right?"

"Even Tigers," she said, her leveled gun dead steady.

She was fierce *in extremis* – probably from experience. Convictions then can be fatal. Killing me point blank was a sure bet, however, while hitting my arm was a crap shoot. Once again I saw her as estrogen fierce. Fiercely *protective*. Of someone she loved, and in a way, protective of me, too. I had no beef.

"Look through the supplies on the counter," she said. "There's an Ace bandage."

I wrapped the elastic band tightly over the wound and secured the tail under one of the loops. The blood was oozing not pumping and I could still wiggle my fingers. The arm would be fine, although losing it would have served me right. Impulsively drawing down on the two of them standing together had been boneheaded. The rage I felt was solely at Kling and pointing a gun when you're unwilling to shoot is stupid. You might be facing a hero.

I felt the grip of another impulse. A sordid impulse. From what muck inside do such things spring? Mendez saw it as *hot blood*. Xuân called it the id. Either way – impulse, target; nothing in between; nothing to stop it.

But Xuân also said where id was, there ego shall be. And I'd insisted to Kling that *choice* stands between; that *choice* is a catalyst that can slow or stop impulse. So, in truth, I chose. I chose to reject mercy and consider justice served. I Goddamm chose to make a base impulse real.

"Bui doi!" I spat.

The words were like a flashbang. In the moment of Xuân's stunned shock, I snatched my gun from the floor with my left hand while Kling shook himself free.

"BAD MAN! BAD MAN!" he shrieked, blocking Xuân's aim as he charged straight into my .45.

I had what I'd chosen: a clean target. But Xuân's betrayed grimace and Kling's gallantry had muddied the crystalline right and wrong of the impulse. Recognizing you're on the wrong side of a fight can hamstring you. I couldn't act. Kling simply ripped the Colt from my hand, slapped it across my face, and stood glowering.

"Walter! Walter!" Xuân pleaded. "We accept his nature. Allow him to rise above it and forgive himself."

Kling dropped the gun, turned his back, and shuffled to Xuân. Gently smoothing her hair, he tipped her face upward – looking for tears to dry, I imagined. Whatever else I felt about the man, at that moment admiration tipped the scale.

With her automatic still trained on me, Xuân put an arm around Kling's waist.

"Your eyebrow is bleeding, Pete," she said. I blotted it with my sleeve. "Please ... don't go for your gun again. We were friends, I think. Briefly, but ... close. I believe it would burden you to kill me. And you would have to."

What I'd just done to her felt worse, but I wasn't about to kill her because ... well, she was right. That, *too*, would burden me.

"I cannot ... pay ... my debts in ... this lifetime," Kling said to me. His gaze fell, as if from shame.

Was he a good man once? Xuân thought so. But being a good man is like sobriety – a day-at-a-time accomplishment. Perhaps his genius, his drive, his work had ultimately painted-over that man with opaque layers – the Kling I had seen. Likely his antidote had intensified and fixed those layers; look what the merest speck had done to me. If my understanding was correct, however, the "master lock" Malek had misused was inexorably securing every door in Kling's brain and erasing all outward traces of him. Perhaps, working backwards, it was also expunging those dark overlays to expose briefly, through some closing window of opportunity, the pentimento beneath. Apart from intellect, was Kling becoming the man he had once been?

"You'll have Justice soon enough, Pete. A *just* Justice. A *merciful* justice."

Goddammed koans!

Could Justice *not* be Just?

And *merciful* Justice? Justice was black-and-white. Mercy was black-and-white. Either-or. They were *opposites.*

Obviously not to her. Or to Manny who loved both. And my lack of mercy for Xuân didn't feel Just at all. So maybe, if you weigh things, Justice and Mercy are a yin and yang that belong together in some proper balance. I'd have to think about that. In the meantime, I looked at Xuân and shrugged. She bowed her head in acknowledgement and turned Kling back to the photograph.

His shoulders began to shake. Soon, I knew, sobbing would be impossible for him, except in that life-long solitary confinement deep within where no one would see or hear.

"... I am ... des..ending ... into..."

He was slipping away before her eyes. His jaw was locking. Soon all words would be gone.

"No, Walter. *Ascending*. See the picture? This moment is part of everything we are. It's a master key that opens every lock and frees us from the cycle. Seize this moment, Walter. The photograph is a doorway."

I saw the photo clearly now, read the story it told of a tiny girl rescued from Hell. Kling couldn't know the ending of the story then, of course, so naturally his expression bore traces of anxiety, burden, and pain. But the soaring feeling I had noted in his face from the first no longer puzzled me at all. I'd worn the look myself a time or two. He felt like a *good guy.*

His shoulders relaxed; he seemed to shrink as if preparing to disappear into the photograph. I imagined all his madman fire, all his madman remorse quenched in the engulfing tranquility of that perfect, freeze-framed eternity.

Kling chose his final words. "I ... re..member ... Xuân," he said.

I knew what was coming. I could have intervened. But ... people choose. I saw now how important it was to both of them that it be done and how *right* it was that *she* do it. So I let go. That was the aliquot of mercy for the justice at hand — as close as I could get to forgiving the son-of-a-bitch. But that's what forgiveness really is, isn't it? Letting go. And knowing when? That may be the smartest thing anyone can learn.

Placing the barrel of her automatic at the base of his skull, in the tiny hollow where she had injected a last, brief springtime, she fired. Catching him in her arms, she sank with him gently to the floor, knelt, and blotted his wound with the sleeve of her Ao Dai. The blood diffused through the white silk like a burgeoning, red Lotus blossom.

"Spoiled," she whispered, pondering the stain. "But then, a wedding gown was never written, Walter."

Brushing at his face, she licked her thumb to wipe away some smudge I couldn't see. Despite the gun in her hand, I felt no threat. She wore the peaceful smile that had been so alluring while she slept, one that seemed to encompass all things in a forgiving embrace.

And yet ... Her eyes were *open* now.

Death lay at her lap.

How could she possibly smile?

"What are we going to do, Xuân?"

"*We?*" She bowed her head and looked up again. "Such a kindness. Especially after ..." She nodded toward my arm.

"I hope you can let go, too," I said.

"After Thành Vì? How could I not? Your parents chose your *real* name, Pete. Bedrock."

She blushed. Her face seemed to glow as if touched by some errant ray from the sunset. Her sapphire eyes flared.

"I've known few men, Pete. Many forced themselves on me as a child, but, well ... I wasn't there at those times; I went somewhere *real*, somewhere *permanent*. And later? Men seemed to vanish in Walter's sunlight. Like stars. You were ... an evening star, I suppose. Something I recognized in you *mirrored* bright light."

She hesitated, glancing at Kling as if he might hear her.

"What I said about lust was really far too simple. Our feelings always reflect the past because that's where our stories were written. My *biological* father was also a *Second Louie*." The words seemed to tickle her tongue. "My mother showed me a picture of him when I was small. It was far too dangerous a thing to keep, so I'm sure the face I recall is imagined."

She closed her eyes, summoning the memory.

"But that *gleaming sword!* I could never forget his sword. He looked so *heroic*. I used to have dreams of him defending me with it. Perhaps he had in some *other* story."

She opened her eyes and looked away as if embarrassed at some failure.

"As you can see, I struggle with samsara. In my head I know that *everything* is too dangerous to keep, because we can't. Desire will merely bind us in grief. Still ..." Her smile never faltered. "I would have liked to see *you* with *your* sword."

"NO!"

I lunged before her hand rose, but the gun was instantly in her mouth and fired. The muffled pop was that of a champagne bottle spilling effervescence like wasted stars. She arched backwards, banged off the wall, and collapsed onto Kling. They lay unmoving, one tall, one tiny. She might have been an exhausted child who had sneaked into father's bed to snuggle.

I stared for a long time as if peering through an opened door into a dark room. Xuân had *accepted* death – not only her own, but that of her greatest love lying at her lap – as if *life* were an aberration; as if something permanent beyond life rendered this brief span a foolish illusion; as if by relinquishing illusion, she could exist with no past, no pain, no fear, no guilt; dwell forever in Peace surpassing understanding; inhabit a frozen eternity where *this – all* of this – didn't matter. I felt the tug of a vague impulse, an obscure siren call from that farther room.

Touch the door before you go through that one, Pal.

I wasn't asleep, but I seemed to hear that demanding voice of my lucid dreams.

C'mon! Wake the fuck up! You've been through this perfect snapshot crap, now let it go. No past? That's where our stories were written. No past means no present, no future. Nothing! That's your peace surpassing understanding. Oblivion to the first fruit of the first tree: knowledge that life is good; that its loss is evil and Goddammed inevitable.

The voice was strident, proclaiming his one true answer to the only important question.

*All things are Buddha things only to a stone or to a corpse. To the living, things are good or evil. And we **know** it. They matter to us. We care. That's the sweet and sour savor of that first fruit. In the beginning was desire.*

So choose, you woebegone son-of-a-bitch, I seemed to hear. *Life or oblivion. Life or death. Life or nothing. Get your shit in one bag. Either-or. That apple Adam ate made you human, but it wasn't free. Pay your debts. Choose!*

The bill tolls for me, I reiterated in acknowledgment of a madman who had *always* been there, although I had muted that part of myself for a long time.

The bittersweet thought seemed to be an antidote of sorts. Able to act again despite what I felt, I called Manny and told him what had happened: Kling – a dupe and then a victim of Burdick and Malek; Xuân – a mercy-killer and suicide. I omitted Ronnie and all the rest. Kling could keep his name. Xuân had paid enough for it.

"Are you alright, Pete?" Manny said uneasily.

"Sure."

"Then say you'll be okay until I get there?"

"I liked her, Manny. I liked her a lot. I understand about Kling, but ... she shouldn't have killed herself. She shouldn't have done that. I'm mad."

"You don't sound mad. Can you tell me you'll be okay?"

"I'll be okay. I'll let it go. But I'll always be mad. And hurt, too, because ... life is Good, it's loss is Evil. I *can't not know that*. I can't. Some debts we incur before we're born."

"Okay, that's it. I'm sending paramedics. Sit down. Don't move. Don't do anything."

"I *said* I'll be okay, Manny. I'm just ... full of weariness. All things toil to weariness, you know?"

"No, I don't know. What does that mean? Tell me."

"Sensitivity training, right?"

"Mexicans are born sensitive. What the hell are you saying, Pete?"

"I'm saying I'm on my feet. I'll answer the bell. I'll go the distance. Because I *choose* to. Because it matters. To *me*. But it's ... It's, uh..." I sighed. "No words for the feeling, man."

"Yeah ... I know. We'll figure it out."

I had a while to wait. Death, when it's certain, is no rush. No lights or sirens. Strictly Code 1.

Waiting, I reexamined the little photograph, an illustration from a story written long ago, one endlessly repeated from time out of mind.

Good guys and love – a *human* story, one that mattered each time it was told. So I pocketed the picture as something worth saving.

For that day when memory fails.

-30-

www.ingramcontent.com/pod-product-compliance
Lightning Source LLC
Chambersburg PA
CBHW061313170626
46817CB00001B/161